BORN
TO
HANG

Center Point
Large Print

Also by Terrence McCauley and available from Center Point Large Print:

Dark Territory
Get Out of Town
The Dark Sunrise
Blood on the Trail
Disturbing the Peace
The Revengers

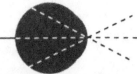

**This Large Print Book carries the
Seal of Approval of N.A.V.H.**

BORN
TO
HANG

A JEREMIAH HALSTEAD WESTERN

TERRENCE
McCAULEY

CENTER POINT LARGE PRINT
THORNDIKE, MAINE

This Center Point Large Print edition
is published in the year 2023 by arrangement with
Kensington Publishing Corp.

The text of this Large Print edition is unabridged.
In other aspects, this book may vary
from the original edition.
Printed in the United States of America
on permanent paper sourced using
environmentally responsible foresting methods.
Set in 16-point Times New Roman type.

ISBN: 978-1-63808-968-1

The Library of Congress has cataloged this record
under Library of Congress Control Number: 2023944420

Chapter 1

Aaron Mackey balled up the wanted poster and threw it across his office. "Seeing Jeremiah Halstead's face on one of those turns my stomach." The United States Marshal for the State of Montana was furious. "And Judge Owen added that five-thousand-dollar reward on his head just to spite me."

Deputy Marshal Billy Sunday allowed cigarette smoke to drift from his nostrils. "He surely did."

Mackey remained angry. "He knows Jeremiah shot those men while he was arresting Zimmerman. It was legal and they weren't real deputies. They were just hired guns, and everyone knows it."

"Knowing it and proving it are two different things," Billy said. "And getting angry and tossing paper around won't change much. You held up sending out those posters for as long as you could. Now Judge Owen is threatening to hold you in contempt. If you delay it any longer, he might just throw you in jail for your trouble. Jeremiah wouldn't want that, not on his account."

"Judge Owen." Mackey said the name as if it was a curse. "That crook isn't fit to shine Halstead's boots, much less accuse him of murder."

Billy flicked his ash in the tray on Mackey's

desk. The black man had heard his old friend make the same argument many times in the several weeks since they had let Halstead flee Helena. And it always came down to the same fact. "You can't control what a judge does, only what you do. And you gave Jeremiah several weeks to get clear of here. That's more than anyone else would've done for him."

Mackey did not think it was much. "It was either that or have him rot in jail all this time." He got up from his chair and looked out the window. The sky had been a dark gray for days as snow moved in. A thin blanket of white covered the ground, boardwalks, and roofs of the city.

And he knew that if it had snowed here in Helena, it would have snowed even more up in the Flathead Mountains. That was the direction Halstead was last seen heading with supplies Mackey and Billy had arranged for him.

But Mackey had not heard from Halstead since the day he had left town. He had no idea of where Halstead was or if he was still alive. Several small settlements were scattered around the base of the mountains. They were used by trappers and miners looking to ride out the winter, but no one had reported seeing him there. Mackey knew Halstead was tough and resourceful, but no man was tougher than the elements or the terrain. Especially when they were riding alone in unfamiliar country.

Mackey looked up at the framed map of Montana on his wall as if it could find Halstead for him. "Where is he, Billy?"

The black man tucked his cigarette in his mouth as he stood and went to the map. "I've been giving that some thought." He tapped on the dot representing Helena. "We know he set off from here several weeks ago in the direction of the Flatheads. He doesn't know this land as good as we do and since he's not much of an outdoorsman, I figured he'd look to play it safe. He'd stick to the last place he'd think anyone might look for him or find him. That means he's probably gotten himself to the high ground and hopes to find an old mine or cave where he could hole up and ride out the winter."

That was what Mackey had thought, too. And feared. "The supplies we gave him won't last that long. I should've told him to just ride straight west into Idaho."

"He'd know people would be expecting him to do that, which was why I think he stayed up in the Flatheads instead." Billy frowned up at the map. "I'd wager the weather's been mighty bad up there this past week or so and he's probably down to the last of the supplies we gave him. If his horses are still alive, I think he'll be riding down to the lowlands."

That made sense to Mackey. "Go on."

"Since he'll be looking to stay away from the

7

larger towns like Missoula and I don't think he's made it as far south as Butte, there's a good chance he'll be coming out somewhere in between them." Billy's finger come to rest on a sparsely populated part of the state near the Flatheads. "I'd say that'll put him somewhere right around here."

Mackey could not find any fault with his friend's logic, but it was far from good news for Halstead. "That's an area as big as some states back east." The map painted an ugly picture for his deputy. His friend was out there somewhere alone, half starved, and desperate.

Billy tried to take some of the sting out of his idea. "Jeremiah's a good-enough shot to hunt for food but he's probably running low on bullets by now. He doesn't know the area, and that Texas mustang he rides isn't meant for this kind of weather."

Mackey sat back in his chair. "I never should've sent him out there alone, Billy. I should've kept him here while we fought this thing head-on with Judge Owen."

"And then what?" Billy asked. "Let him rot in a cell for a crime he didn't commit? Riker or Mannes would've paid a man to stick a knife in him before the trial got started and you know it."

Mackey had known Halstead's enemies would stop at nothing to end his life. It was why Mackey had broken the law by helping Halstead flee

8

before the charges became official. "We could've made sure he was protected. Locked away where no one could get to him."

"That wouldn't have done any good," Billy reminded him. "Jail's still jail, Aaron."

"He could've taken it. Weaker men have survived prison and thrived after it, too."

"But Jeremiah's already spent three years in an El Paso prison paying a debt he didn't owe. Another stint inside would've either killed him or killed his spirit. You couldn't do that to him and you were right to spare him from it."

Mackey knew Billy was right. They had made the best decision at the time and there was no point in regretting it now. "All I know is that he's somewhere out there in the wilderness. He's alone and more scared than he wants to admit." He tapped his finger on the large pile of wanted flyers on his desk. "And now that these have been sent all over the state, every nitwit with a rifle and a dream of getting rich will be looking to collect that reward Judge Owen put out on him. The poor kid just beat Zimmerman's bounty only to have a judge pin another target on his back."

"Sounds to me like you ought to think about sending someone after him."

Mackey and Billy looked around to see Deputy Joshua Sandborne, Halstead's friend and partner, leaning against the doorway of the office.

"Didn't anyone ever teach you to knock?" Mackey scolded him.

"I grew up around cowboys and ranchers, remember?" Sandborne smiled. "I never got around to learning the ways of polite society."

Mackey had been glad when the young man had fully recovered from the bullet wound that he had received in Battle Brook. Mackey noted the experience had robbed him of some of his boyishness, but at twenty-four, he was still the youngest deputy on his payroll. Halstead was only older by a few months.

Billy stepped away from the map. "How long have you been standing there?"

"Long enough to know it sounds like Jeremiah needs some help." Sandborne stepped farther into the office. "Help from someone who knows him and the country he's found himself in."

"You volunteering for the job?" Mackey asked.

"I've worked with him for almost a year, and although he'd be too stubborn to admit it, I know how he thinks. I can't think of anyone who could find him faster than me."

Mackey had never known Sandborne to be so assertive before. His wound had made him grow up some. The marshal knew pain had a way of changing a man. "What do you think about what Billy has been saying just now?"

Sandborne looked up at the map. "I'd say you're right about him sticking to the Flatheads for as long as he could before the snow forces him down to the lowlands. He wouldn't have gone to Idaho because he'll be counting on you to fix his problems with Judge Owen for him. He'd want to stay close. All the more reason why you should send me out there to look for him."

As much as he wished otherwise, Mackey knew that was a bad idea. "You're still getting over being shot. You're in no shape to go riding around out there by yourself in this weather. I'd be liable to be down two deputies instead of just one."

"Except I wouldn't need to ride much," Sandborne said. "At least not all the way." He took Billy's place at the map. "I could get the train here in Helena and take it to Missoula. From there, I'll head out to those trapper settlements you were talking about. Even if someone saw Jeremiah, we wouldn't know about it here. The telegraph lines haven't reached those towns yet and they don't get regular mail in winter. There's a chance they might not even know Jeremiah's a wanted man until the thaw in the spring."

"And if they know he's wanted?" Billy asked.

"Then, when I find him, I'll take him into custody and keep him from being strung up at the nearest tree for the reward money."

Mackey could tell by Billy's expression that he thought Sandborne's idea might be a good one. The marshal was beginning to agree. "Taking the train *would* save you a lot of time. But as soon as you reached Missoula, you'd be right in the thick of the elements. You'd have a good day's ride ahead of you before you reached one of the settlements. You sure that hole in your side is up to the trip?"

"It's not just about what I want to do, boss. It's about what needs to be done. It's about what Jeremiah needs. Judge Owen was none too happy that you took your time sending out those wanted flyers. Sending me out after Jeremiah will prove you're doing your job, even though you're Jeremiah's friend."

Billy said, "The boy's got a point, Aaron. The timing could work out in our favor, too."

"Timing?" Mackey asked. "What timing?"

"One of our friends at the railroad tells me Mark Mannes is on the next train to Helena. He ought to be here in a couple of days."

Mackey soured at the mention of the attorney who had started this mess. The man who had helped Zimmerman gain control of Valhalla and turn it into his own private estate. "He's probably coming to deliver another payoff to his cousin Judge Owen."

"Probably," Billy agreed. "He also might be looking to raise a stink about you dragging your feet in the hunt for Jeremiah. Being able to say you've already got a man looking for him would take some of the starch out of him. It could buy us some time to find some other way to get these charges dropped."

Mackey could see Billy was clearly working on something. Experience had taught him it would be a good idea to let it play out.

The marshal said to Sandborne, "You sure you're up to it? There's no shame in it if you're not. I need Billy here with me, but I can send Lynch or one of the others instead."

Sandborne said, "I wouldn't volunteer for it if I didn't know I could do it."

He admired the younger man's courage. At thirty-four, Mackey was far from an old man, but he was no longer young. A year ago, he would not have thought about sending Sandborne out alone, but a year was a long time. What the young deputy lacked in experience, he more than made up for in bravery and determination. His time with Halstead in Battle Brook had proved as much.

"Get yourself down to the stable and pick out the two strongest horses we've got. Then head over to the general store and load up all the supplies you can carry. Keep in mind that it's not just for you, but for Jeremiah, too. I'll want you on the next train steaming west. Send us a telegram to let us know when you've got him and wait for my orders. That last part is just as important as finding Jeremiah. You have to tell us when you find him. Do you understand me, deputy?"

"I understand, boss," Sandborne said as he almost ran out the door. "I'll get right on it."

Mackey sat back in his chair as he watched Sandborne run to carry out his orders. "We were never that young, were we, Billy?"

"Younger," his deputy reminded him, "and just as foolish. But we got the job done, didn't we?"

"Yes, we did." Mackey remembered what his old friend had said earlier. "What do you have in mind for Mannes once he gets here?"

Billy took paper from his shirt pocket and began to build himself another cigarette. "I don't know yet, but I'll think of something."

Mackey was sure he would.

Chapter 2

Cold.

Jeremiah Halstead used to think he understood the meaning of the word, but he had never experienced anything like this.

He had known the unrelenting heat of the furnace that was the west Texas desert. He had known what it was to be on a half-dead horse without a drop of water or a hint of shade in sight. Even now, as cold gripped him, he remembered how the heat could boil all the strength out of a man and make him beg for death.

But the ice and cold that had battered him on the Montana mountainside for a week was every bit as harsh as the Texas desert had been. Here, the water he needed to survive was all around him in the form of snow, but it was unfit to drink unless it was boiled first. With kindling for a fire in short supply, the mountain was worse than the desert. It was as if nature itself was mocking his plight.

After Mackey and Billy had allowed him to escape Helena before the murder warrant became official, Halstead had decided to hide among the nearby Flathead Mountains. He was unfamiliar with the terrain but had heard stories about how it offered many caves and mines where he and his horses could find shelter. He had been counting on the rapid approach of winter to have forced the miners and trappers off the mountain and down into the relatively warmer lowland areas.

Halstead had thought the lack of civilization would be perfect for a man on the run from the law. He had planned to stick to the high ground, to scrounge whatever he could among the abandoned mining camps he expected to find on the mountainside.

But Halstead learned too late that he had been wrong. There were no mining camps—abandoned or otherwise—among the Flatheads. The few structures he had found had long since been splintered by crushing snow and ice. He and his horses had no choice but to sleep in whatever caverns they found.

The constant cold dampness had made it impossible to get warm. The ceaseless howling wind made it difficult to sleep or keep a fire lit. Then the snow came in force.

Despite careful rationing, his supplies quickly dwindled, and hunting became a necessity. Despite being an excellent shot with a rifle, he had never been much of a hunter. He had accidentally fouled the meat of his early kills by cutting into the wrong organs with his Bowie knife. The deer and elk meat he had butchered proved difficult to cook over the weak fires he had managed to build with damp wood. Even his mustang Col and his pack horse had been hungry enough to eat meat, which he knew was bad for them, but reluctantly gave them. He had lost track of how many times he had vowed to give himself up in the next town he found in exchange for a warm bed and some hay for his weary, starving horses.

He had cursed himself for fleeing to the mountains instead of seeking refuge in Silver Cloud. He had friends there who were still grateful to him for saving the town. They would have gladly harbored him if he had asked.

But he cared too much for his friends to put them in such danger. Someone would eventually try to collect the reward he undoubtedly had on his head by now. He would never be able to live with himself if he was responsible for one of his friends getting hurt because he was a fugitive.

After waking one morning to find his pack horse had frozen to death, Halstead knew he had no choice but to come down from the mountains in search of better shelter and food. His stubborn mustang had to bear the weight of his few supplies as they trekked to the lowlands. Fortunately for the mare, the burden was light.

The constant wind on the open range grated his skin and cut into his bones with every gust. The glare from endless stretches of snow and ice made it difficult to see.

Every step was fraught with danger. Col

struggled to find her footing as Halstead led her through the waist-deep snow and thick ice beneath it. He had draped his bedroll and every blanket he had across the mare's back to keep her warm on their journey, but he knew it was not enough to protect her from the unforgiving cold. Horses were susceptible to pneumonia, and Halstead was concerned for her life, not to mention his own.

Halstead felt the ground begin to level out and thought he might be seeing things when he spotted the outline of a crooked roof in a clearing just ahead. The pines in this part of the lowlands were thicker, and the snow beneath them was only knee-deep.

Branches of bare bushes poked up from the field of white, giving Halstead hope that dead grass might still lie beneath the snow for Col. Even dead grass was better than nothing. If he could just get some food for her and some warmth for himself, they might have a chance of surviving.

Halstead pulled Col behind him as he trudged closer to the clearing. The small shack was built out of odd sizes of misshapen planks of wood. A small barn stood next to it, and the roof was in good condition. Col quickened her pace at the sight of shelter.

He pulled the mustang inside, then lifted the small sack of supplies from her back, followed by his Winchester and saddle. She had carried her burden too long and had earned a good rest. Despite the cold, he pulled off his coat and piled it on top of the blankets and bedroll on her back. He hoped the layers would help her own body heat keep her warm.

"There you are, old girl," he whispered to her. "We'll get ourselves fixed up in no time."

He spotted a pile of damp hay piled in the far corner of the structure. He led her over to it and wrapped her reins around her foreleg to keep her from wandering off. The horse lowered its head to the hay and began to eat. He was glad at least one of them had found food.

He looked back at the shack and noticed the snow had drifted high against the door. The lack of smoke rising from the stovepipe told him the place was likely abandoned, but likely didn't make it so.

Halstead pulled the Colt Thunderer from the belly rig slung on his left side and slowly approached the door. He reared back and gave it a kick, but it didn't budge. He had to put his shoulder against it three more times before it finally opened.

He swept the shack with his pistol, looking for any movement. He had endured too much cold and hunger to be careless now.

A single window on the left wall allowed just enough gray light for him to see that no one had lived here in quite a while. Iron-jawed traps hung from nails on the walls, confirming this place had once belonged to a trapper. Dust and cobwebs coated the canned goods on the shelves and the stove in the corner beneath it. A lanky white spider scurried into the small cord of wood stacked beside it.

Halstead fought the urge to rush to the stove and start a fire as he continued to sweep his pistol to the right.

He spotted the corpse of a man on a straw mat on the floor against the far wall. He was beneath a thick pile of blankets and pelts. His long gray beard and hair reminded him of Warren Riker, but he knew this man was not him. He had left the older Riker boy dead back in Battle Brook months ago.

This man he took for an old trapper had clearly died peacefully in his sleep. The freezing winter had turned his skin gray but kept his body preserved.

Halstead slid the pistol back in its holster and slowly approached the remains. Even in death, he saw the man had a thick, sturdy frame that had undoubtedly served him well for many harsh seasons in the wild.

Halstead regretted what he had to do next. "Sorry about this, old timer, but I don't have a choice. Life is meant for the living, and I need this place more than you do."

He grabbed hold of the corpse by the shoulders and began to pull it free. Three large rats scurried out from beneath the blankets and pelts before running outside.

His strength sapped by unending cold and a lack of food caused Halstead to struggle as he dragged the body out into the snow to the far side of the shack. He had hoped Col would not be frightened by the sight of the dead man, and she continued to chew at the hay without notice.

Halstead grabbed his rifle, saddle, and bag of supplies. He carried them into the shack and heeled the door shut before dumping his belongings on the floor. He quickly began to load wood into the stove, found a dry match in his pocket, and thumbed it alive. His hands shook as he tried to get the fire started.

It was almost as cold inside the shack as it was outside, so he took the dead man's pelts and pulled them tight around his shoulders. The stench of death and rat droppings did not bother him. He sat on the floor in front of the stove and welcomed the growing warmth of the fire.

Halstead knew he should have counted himself lucky for having found this place, for managing to remain free despite the warrant out for his arrest. But the struggle to survive the harsh Montana winter had dulled any sense of gratitude. *Not dulled it. Frozen it in place.*

He was certain that word of the warrant must have reached most of the state by now. Mannes had probably talked his cousin, Judge Owen, into sweetening the pot by offering a reward for his arrest. Every lawman, bounty hunter. and fortune seeker was probably looking for him now. Halstead had survived those who had tried to collect the ten-thousand-dollar bounty that Ed Zimmerman had placed on his head, but this was different. This reward would be backed by the government. And unlike Zimmerman, they would gladly pay on delivery.

Halstead would have no choice but to treat everyone he met like a potential enemy.

Fortune had helped him find this trapper's shack, but he knew his luck would run out eventually. He would soon have to risk going into a town, but he would worry about that later. For now—today—he had a roof over his head and hay for his horse.

He rubbed his hands in front of the stove to get warm. At least Abby was not enduring this hardship with him. She was safe back in Helena in the home they had once dreamed of enjoying together.

The thought of her warmed him now. Abigail Newman, the dark beauty who had captured his soul on the train to Battle Brook. The woman he had rescued from the clutches of a no-account gambler. The woman who had managed to save

Halstead from himself when his fight against Zimmerman had almost destroyed him.

He had been forced to leave Helena without so much as a goodbye. He hoped Mackey or Billy had made her understood why. He hoped she had not grown to hate him. Such hope had sustained him through the many long and lonely nights on the mountain.

Halstead began to feel better as the fire in the stove grew warmer. He nodded off but snapped awake and pulled the blankets and pelts tighter around himself. He could not sleep yet. He had to stay awake and eat something.

But he needed warmth more than food. His mind drifted back to a recent time when he thought life would get simpler once Ed Zimmerman was dead. He had never taken joy in seeing a man hang, but the outlaw had been an exception. He had chased Zimmerman across Montana for more than a year and had begun to doubt he would ever bring him to justice. He had allowed that pursuit to consume him and drive him close to madness. But Mackey, Billy, and Joshua Sandborne had pulled him back from the brink, and he had finally seen Zimmerman dance at the end of a rope.

Halstead had never believed much in ideas like goodness and evil before but he believed in such things now. If a man could ever embody true wickedness, it had been Ed Zimmerman. There was no way to kill true evil for it always found a way to survive the grave to continue its dark work. Zimmerman had proven that when, even after his death, his attorney Mark Mannes had gotten his cousin Judge Owen to sign a murder warrant against Halstead for killing Zimmerman's men at a train station in Wellspring.

Halstead knew he had been well within his rights. He'd had a warrant for Zimmerman's arrest when Zimmerman's men had tried to stop him. The killings were as legal as the law itself. But Halstead had learned the law was whatever a man in a black robe decided it was. The deputy star he had once pinned to his chest only meant what a judge allowed it to mean.

He had spent almost three years in an El Paso prison for a crime he had not committed. Now, he had been forced to become a fugitive from his own system. To become the kind of man he had once hunted. An outlaw. The sword of justice was at his throat. Mackey had allowed him to keep his deputy star when he fled Helena. Halstead hoped he would be able to wear it again one day, but for now, it was just a hunk of metal in his pocket.

If he had ever possessed a sense of humor, Halstead might have found some humor in his fate. But there was nothing funny about being away from his duty, his friends, or the woman he loved.

In fact, there was nothing at all except for the

warm sleep that rose within him and enveloped him in its darkness.

Halstead had not realized he had fallen asleep—much less fallen over—until he woke with a start. He had not slept so soundly in weeks. On the mountain, even the slightest noise had been enough to wake him, just as he was sure one had awakened him just now.

Instinct caused him to reach for the Colt holstered on his left side.

The icy feel of cold steel against his neck caused him to stop.

"Your next move will be your last." The man's voice was rough, but even. "Slip your hands out from under them blankets nice and slow."

Halstead thought about flipping over on his back as he drew, but the rifle against his neck convinced him otherwise. He had been foolish enough to allow himself to fall asleep. Now he was paying the price.

As soon as he slid his hands out from beneath the blankets and pelts, another man yanked the covers free before tossing them aside.

He cut loose with a high-pitched cackle of delight. "Look at them fancy guns he's totin', Luke! And here I was thinking Christmas would never come."

"That was last week, you idiot." Luke pressed the barrel hard against Halstead's neck. "Now, stranger, my friend Duro here is gonna reach down and take those pistols off you. If you so much as blink while he's doing it, you're dead. You understand me, boy?"

Luke and Duro. That meant two of them but there might be more. Tough odds that only grew worse if he was unarmed. "Yeah, I understand."

Halstead retched from the musky stench off Duro as he snatched the Colts from both holsters. The man smelled worse than a full stable in summertime.

"Good boy," Luke said. "Now sit up nice and slow and slide yourself over there so your back is against the wall."

Halstead did as Luke had told him. He pulled himself against the wall, glad they had not noticed the Bowie knife tucked in a scabbard at the back of his belt.

The floorboards creaked as Duro danced across the shack. He held up the pistols for a third man in the doorway to see. "I got 'em, Singe! Pulled 'em off him without hardly any trouble at all."

Singe stepped inside. "Shut your fool mouth before I take 'em from you."

Halstead watched Duro tumble down onto the same straw mat where he had found the dead man. The smell of death did not seem to bother him, either.

Halstead saw Luke's and Singe's faces were caked in dirt and grime. It was difficult to tell where their matted beards ended and the brown hides they wore as coats began. All three men wore shapeless hats that might have been fashioned from beaver pelts, though it could have been raccoon or some other animal. Halstead had never been much of an outdoorsman.

He pegged them all to be about thirty, but it was difficult to tell such things in the weak light that filtered into the shack.

Luke offered a yellow gap-toothed grin as he kept the long rifle aimed down at Halstead's chest. A single shot Springfield favored by trappers. Halstead took that as a good sign. *One and done.*

"Keep doing like we tell you," Luke said, "and you may live through this, mister."

As Duro babbled to himself on the mat while examining the Colts, Singe took a knee as he examined Halstead closer. He had sharper features than the other two, something they probably took as a sign of intelligence. "What's your name, boy?"

Halstead locked eyes with him. "Why? You plan on being friends?"

Singe backhanded him. Halstead rocked to the side as strong bursts of light filled his vision. The trapper was faster than he looked.

"Around here, we call that sass," Singe told him. "I don't take sass from anyone, especially from a lousy claim jumper such as yourself."

"I didn't jump anyone's claim." Halstead touched his mouth and examined his fingers for blood. He was not bleeding, but his ears still rang from the blow. "This place was empty when I found it this morning."

Luke kept the Springfield aimed down at him. "The dead feller out in the snow says otherwise."

Halstead pushed himself back up into a sitting position against the wall. The feel of the knife handle at his back offered some comfort. "That man was long dead and frozen stiff when I got here. The rats were gnawing on him when I found this place a few hours ago. Look him over for yourself. He was dead long before I got here."

"Could be," Singe allowed. "Could be that you jumped Old Carl a while ago. Murdered him in cold blood, then dragged his body out there while you helped yourself to his food and fire. Such things happen all the time in these parts."

"But not here and not with me," Halstead said. "The only time I touched him was to bring him outside. I would've buried him if the ground wasn't frozen solid."

Singe looked up at Luke. "What do you make of him? You believe we've got a Christian gentleman on our hands here?"

Luke kept the rifle steady. "Looks more like one of them heathen Blackfoot savages if you ask me."

"He does look a might dark at that," Singe said. "You a savage, Mister Sassy Man?"

Halstead did not bother responding.

Singe asked Luke, "What do you think we ought to do with him?"

Luke's response was immediate. "Shoot him. Take his clothes and horse and sell them. Those pistols alone will fetch a fair price."

Halstead was not sure he would survive this, but if he did, he would make Luke pay for what he had said.

Singe looked back at the simpleton on the mat. "You get a vote, too, Duro. What do you think we should do with him?"

"I don't care." Duro was closely examining one of the Colts he had taken from Halstead. "Kill him or let him go as long as I get to keep these two beauties."

Luke looked back at Duro. "That doddering simpleton doesn't even know what a vote is."

Halstead used the distraction to flatten his right hand flat on the floor and slide it toward his back. He was that much closer to the blade, and neither man had noticed.

Singe frowned down at Halstead. "Well, that leaves me in quite a mess, stranger. Here I was, hoping we could get some sort of agreement on what I ought to do with you. Luke here wants to shoot you, and Duro back there doesn't care either way. Guess that leaves it up to me. You got anything to say for yourself while I think it over?"

Halstead knew Singe had already made up his

mind. He was hoping Halstead would beg for his life. Plead to be allowed to go. He wouldn't give him the satisfaction. "I do, but I don't want Luke to hear it. Come closer, and I'll tell you."

Singe's frown turned into a grin. "I know I don't look like much to a fancy man such as yourself, but I know I don't look that stupid."

Halstead shrugged, inching his hand backward on the floor toward his knife.

Singe's grin held as he said to his partner. "Something tells me you're wrong about this one. I've been lookin' him over some and he's no heathen. In fact, I'm pretty sure his mama was a Mexican gal and his daddy's people came from one of those far away countries with a fancy name."

Halstead's stomach tightened as he watched Singe take a piece of paper from his shirt pocket and unfold it. A wanted flyer with a pretty good likeness of himself drawn on it. And a five-thousand-dollar reward printed in big letters below his face.

Singe looked down at the paper, then at Halstead. "You can see the resemblance, can't you, mister? I think we're looking at Jeremiah Halstead himself."

Luke looked down at the paper, giving Halstead a chance to inch his right hand closer to his back. "Never got around to learn how to read, but I'd say that looks an awful lot like—"

Halstead knocked the barrel of Luke's rifle with his left hand as he got to his feet. The rifle boomed, striking Singe in the chest, knocking him flat.

Halstead pulled his Bowie knife with his right and plunged the sharp blade through the hide and deep into Luke's neck.

The dying man stiffened as Duro fumbled with the Colts. Halstead pushed Luke backward as he yanked the rifle from his grip.

Luke landed on Duro just as Duro was about to fire one of the pistols. Luke's bulk absorbed the bullet and pinned Duro flat on the straw mat.

Duro struggled to get his hands free as Halstead gripped the empty rifle by the barrel and swung the stock down like a club, striking Duro on the temple. The first blow knocked him out. The second killed him.

Halstead turned as he brought the rifle up to swing again, ready to hit Singe. But the man was still lying on the floor in front of the stove, clutching at a large hole in the lower part of his belly.

The dying trapper looked up at him. "Guess I was right about you being Halstead."

Halstead rested the rifle on his shoulder like a club. "Yeah. For all the good it did you."

Singe's hands shook as he lifted them. They were covered in his own blood. "I've never been shot before."

"There's a first time for everything." Halstead lowered the rifle. Singe was no longer a threat. "You boys bounty hunters or trappers?"

Singe placed his hands back over his leaking wound. "What difference does it make now?"

"None for you," Halstead said, "but knowing might help me. Might make me inclined to help you now."

Singe winced in pain. "Ain't no one who can help me now except Jesus."

"You'll be shaking hands with him soon enough. How soon depends on what you say next. Answer my questions, and I'll end this quick."

"And if I don't?"

"I drag you outside and let nature take its course. You might die before the wolves or a badger finds you. Maybe one of those rats that were gnawing on your friend outside. Belly wounds can be tricky. You could last longer than you think. Your choice."

Singe coughed. "You're a real bastard, Halstead."

"You don't have enough time for insults. Are you boys bounty hunters or trappers?"

He watched Singe's breathing become more labored. His body was already beginning to quit on him. "Trappers. The three of us were wintering down at Barren Pines, about five miles south of here. The sheriff posted that flyer on you and it got us to thinking. He told us you might be coming this way now that the weather had turned ugly. Our money was already getting thin, so we decided to come looking for you. That reward money would've gone a long way with us. Guess it didn't turn out like we'd hoped."

"Guess not." Halstead remembered seeing Barren Pines on a map somewhere but knew nothing about the place. "This sheriff in Barren Pines got a name?"

"Fremont. Jason Fremont. A dangerous man. Almost as dangerous as you're supposed to be."

Halstead looked down at the hole in Singe's belly. "I'd say you learned how dangerous I am."

"I reckon I did." Singe tried to laugh but coughed up blood. He looked up at Halstead. "Anything else you want to know? You'd best ask while I can still tell you."

"Anyone in town know you were coming to look for me?"

Singe weakly shook his head. "The three of us kept to ourselves. We didn't want anyone trying to collect on you. There's a lot of lean and hungry men wintering in town. You'd do well to steer clear of that place if you can."

Halstead set the empty rifle against the wall well out of Singe's reach. "I'll remember that."

He placed his boot on Luke's chest and pulled his knife free. He wiped it clean on Luke's coat before sliding it back into its sheath.

Singe coughed again. "Didn't see that knife when we pulled the blankets off you."

"You weren't supposed to." He grabbed the dead man's hide and hauled him off Duro's corpse. He found one of his Colts on the straw mat beside him. The other was still in his hand. Halstead took both pistols and slid one in the holster slung to the left of his belly.

Singe was weakening fast and barely spoke above a whisper. "You going to make good on your promise?"

He moved the pistol to his right hand. "I always do." He aimed the Colt down at Singe's head. "Any last words?"

Singe looked away from the gun. "See you in Hell, Jeremiah Halstead."

"Give Zimmerman my regards."

Halstead fulfilled his promise and squeezed the trigger.

Chapter 3

Halstead searched the dead men carefully before depositing their remains outside the shack.

After searching their saddlebags, Halstead removed their tack and draped the ruined hides from the dead men across the three horses to keep them warm. The animals did not fuss at the scent of blood from their previous owners, but they helped Col eat some of the hay in the back of the barn. It was going on dark by the time he brought the saddlebags into the shack to make a full inventory of what Singe, Luke, and Duro had left behind.

It was not much.

Half a box of cartridges for the Springfields and a dozen rounds for his Winchester. The trappers in Barren Pines might take the rifles, but the horses, saddles, and bridles would certainly bring much more. The knives each man had possessed in life were still sharp and were worth good money.

That was as good as the news got for Halstead. The only pistol he had found among the dead men's belongings was a Walker Colt with a poor hammer and a loose cylinder. It was a piece of junk. There was no ammunition for his Colts, either. He had fewer than twenty rounds left for both pistols.

Singe and his friends had obviously not planned on being away from Barren Pines for long. They had not even brought bedrolls. Only biscuits, a bit of jerky, and about half a pot's worth of coffee grinds. It was hardly a feast, but it was more than he had.

In one of their saddlebags, he had found a tintype of a woman with long, light hair in a flowing gown. She carried a parasol over her left shoulder. The parasol had more material than the gown, which was sheer and revealed the subject had a healthy bosom. He turned the picture over and read what had been written on the back.

"Glamorous Glenda, with love."

Neither the name nor the woman's image meant anything to Halstead. He imagined she must be a showgirl who Singe or one of the others had seen during their travels. He tossed the picture in the stove.

As he watched the tintype burn, he knew he was in a bad way. Singe and the others would not be the last looking to cash in on Judge Owen's reward. Halstead knew he could not stay in the shack. He had been found once, and the tracks of the three miners would lead others from Barren Pines to him. He could not go back up into the mountains. It had snowed for most of the day, and the passes were bound to be even more treacherous than they had been that morning.

He did not like the idea of going into town,

but he did not have a choice. His supplies were exhausted, and he needed food. Shelter. So did Col. Trading what little the dead men had left behind was his best chance for survival. It was too dark to travel now, but if he left at first light, he might be able to make it in and out of Barren Pines before drawing too much attention.

He picked up the wanted flyer from the floor and looked at it closely. It was a good portrait, right down to his narrow eyes and the break in the brim of his hat.

The description next to his picture was accurate, as well:

"Age, 25. Height, 6 ft even. Weight, 180 lbs. Dark hair, eyes, and complexion. Can be mistaken for a Mexican or Indian. Known to carry two Colt Thunderer pistols. He is wanted for the murder of two deputy sheriffs in Wellspring. The above reward will be paid for his capture or positive proof of his death."

He had a full beard now, and his clothes hung loose on him. He might be able to blend in for a little while, but not for long. Towns in this part of Montana did not get many travelers in winter. Three men had ridden out of Barren Pines looking for him. He would be looking to trade in three horses for money only a day after they left. It would not take long for people to figure out how he had gotten them.

He fed the flyer into the fire and watched

the flames consume it. Going to Barren Pines was a bad idea. It was practically suicide, but he would be dead anyway if he did not go. He needed ammunition and supplies. He would not last another week, much less until the spring otherwise.

Halstead shoved more wood in the stove. He dumped the coffee grinds into an old pot he had found, packed it with snow, and set it on the stove. He gnawed at some of the jerky while he waited for the water to boil. It would not be as good as the coffee Billy Sunday usually made, but it would see him through the night. Sometimes, lousy coffee was the best a man could hope for.

Just after first light the next morning, Halstead got Col and the three other horses ready to travel and rode toward Barren Pines.

Halstead kept his eyes moving among the trees as they went. He looked for tracks in the snow to see if any other riders had come through the area. All he saw was evidence of small game like rabbits and squirrels.

He heard a bird scream high above him and saw a vulture beginning to make a lazy circle in the sky over the shack. Singe and his friends were about to become popular with the scavengers of the woods. The birds would also attract attention of anyone who happened to be looking for him. He urged Col to move a bit faster through the snow as he pulled the three horses behind him.

Halstead was forced to lean to the left to avoid some branches sagging beneath the weight of heavy snow. He had just reached a clearing when a gunshot echoed through the forest. A bullet struck a nearby tree.

Halstead pulled his Winchester from its scabbard as he dropped over the side to the ground. The impact was lessened by the thick snow. The horses he had been leading followed Col's lead and remained where they were. The mustang was long accustomed to the sound of gunfire.

Halstead held his rifle in both hands as he crawled through the snow away from the horses as much as possible. He knew he was plowing a clear track in the snow as he moved, but protecting the animals was more important than stealth. Five miles was not long to walk on foot in good weather. In winter it could be a death sentence.

He could not remain where he had fallen. The shooter might take a second shot to make sure Halstead was dead. This time, he would not miss.

Halstead stopped crawling when he heard a man call out, "I think you got him, Mac. I saw him drop."

Halstead remained still. Listening. He had to know where Mac and his partner were hiding among the pines. Mac was the more important of the two since he was the shooter. And since the second man was shouting to Mac, it meant they had split up.

"You hear what I told you?" the second man shouted to Mac. "He's down."

But Mac did not answer. Halstead knew he was careful and smart. An experienced hunter who would not risk marking his position while he stalked his prey. A man with a Winchester might have kept firing at Halstead after he had fallen. There was a good chance the man was using a single-shot Springfield, just like the rifle Luke had held on him back at the shack. That meant these men were likely trappers, too.

Halstead slowly used his elbows and knees to inch his way forward through the deep snow. He felt the cold begin to seep up from the ground and into his clothes. He hoped he saw something to shoot at soon before he started to shake.

He had gotten close to a slender tree when he heard a branch snap off to his right.

He listened as the cold bled away his energy with each agonizing second. Mac was patient. Halstead had to be even more patient.

A second branch snapped, this time from his left. Halstead saw a dark form move behind a clump of bare bushes thirty yards away. He brought his rifle to his shoulder, aimed at the center of the bushes, and fired.

A man cried out as the form fell backward. Halstead knew he had scored a direct hit, but the job was only half done. He still had at least one man off to his right. He had to move. *Now.*

Halstead began to roll to his left when pistol fire echoed through the forest from his right. The second man bellowed as he charged toward him through the trees.

Halstead stopped rolling when a skinny man in a bowler hat tied to his head with a scarf broke into the clearing. His pistol clicked dry as Halstead levered in a fresh round and leveled his Winchester at him.

The man slid to a stop in the snow, a look of wild rage in eyes too large for his narrow face.

"Don't move," Halstead ordered. "Your gun is empty. Drop it."

The man slowly raised the empty pistol. Not to fire, but as if to throw it at him. "You killed Mac!"

"I don't know if he's dead and neither do you," Halstead told him. "Drop that pistol and let's go check on him together."

A gunshot from his left pierced the air as a bullet shot through the space between Halstead and the second man, causing Halstead to flinch.

The second man threw his pistol, striking Halstead on the shoulder as he dove at him. He landed on Halstead's back and began to clutch for the Winchester. Halstead struggled to keep it out of his reach as the man began to dig his fingers into Halstead's eyes.

Halstead lost his hat as he ducked his head

under his arm and fired an elbow back into his attacker's side. Their coats muffled the blow but managed to weaken the man's grip.

Another elbow knocked the second man off his back as Halstead fell on him, trying to bring the rifle down across his neck. The thin man tried to push him off as Halstead put all his weight on the rifle.

Another shot hit a tree next to where they were struggling as the second man brought up a knee into Halstead's ribs, causing him to roll onto his left side.

The man rolled with him, still clutching the rifle now that he had the advantage. As he tried to force the rifle down on his throat, Halstead fired his knee up into the man's crotch, weakening his grip enough for Halstead to push him over.

Halstead was about to get up when a man shouted from the clearing. "Don't move!"

Halstead saw a man aiming a Springfield rifle at him with one hand. His left arm hung limply at his side. Blood had already begun to stain the bear hide coat he wore. He was weaving on his feet and struggling to breathe.

"We've got him now, Barry," Mac said to the second man, who was still writhing in pain on the ground. "We've gone and corralled Jeremiah Halstead himself."

Halstead did not risk moving his Winchester. His coat was bunched beneath him, making a play for either of his pistols impossible. Mac might be wounded, maybe even dying, but could still easily hit him at this distance.

Halstead tried to bluff Mac. "You're hurt bad, mister. Set the rifle down and I'll tend to that wound. You'll bleed to death if I don't. I think I nicked your lung."

Mac staggered but did not fall. "Barry here will do any tending I need, won't you Barry?"

Whatever Barry said was muffled by the snow and his agony.

"If I die out here," Mac said, "I don't aim to do it alone. I'll be taking you with me unless you do what I say." He inclined his head to the right, which seemed to make him dizzy. "Toss that rifle over there. And don't try anything fancy. I already reloaded before I stepped out here."

Halstead threw the Winchester just out of reach.

"That's good." Mac's speech was beginning to grow thick from the loss of blood. "Now lean over to your right and put both hands flat on the ground."

Halstead could see Mac was weakening, so he tried to buy himself some time. "Why?"

"Because I don't want you making a play for them fancy guns I hear you carry." Mac renewed his one-armed aim on Halstead's chest. "You'd best do it right now before I lose patience."

Halstead placed his right hand on the ground then leaned over to do the same with his left. He felt ridiculous, which was the point. Mac knew how to keep a man out of position.

Mac said, "That's good. Singe and the others find you yet?"

"Yeah."

"You kill them?"

"Yeah."

"They're no loss," Mac said. "Get your feet under you and get up nice and slow. Make sure you keep your back to me when you do."

Halstead began to do as he was told. "Too afraid to shoot a man while he's facing you?"

"I don't plan to shoot you at all unless you do something stupid."

Halstead followed his directions and got to his feet. His coat now hung open as he stood. The butt of one of his Colts jutted out from his left side within easy reach.

But drawing, turning, and firing before Mac shot him would not be so easy. He slowly shook the snow from his hands so Mac could see they were empty.

"That wasn't so hard, was it?" Mac was having trouble forming words. "Keep on doing what I tell you and Deputy Fremont will have you in a nice warm cell in no time. The next part's my favorite. I hear you're fast with them pistols. I hear that right?"

Halstead kept his hands raised. "Don't believe everything you hear. I'm better with my rifle."

44

"I'll bet." Mac tried to laugh, but it sounded more like a cough. "But if it's all the same to you, we're going to pull them fangs right out of your head. They'll make a fine addition to my collection," Mac slurred. "Now, I want you to—"

Halstead heard Mac's boot scrape the snow. He was having trouble keeping his balance.

Halstead drew his Colt as he turned in a crouch and fired.

The bullet struck Mac in the forehead.

A shudder went through Mac as he collapsed backward, still clutching his rifle.

Barry rolled out of his agony and reached for the Springfield.

Halstead yelled, "Don't do it, Barry. You don't have to die, too."

Barry stopped but did not withdraw his hand. "You tell the same thing to Singe and the others before you killed them?"

Barry made a final stab for the Springfield, but Halstead cut him down before he reached it.

Halstead remained in a crouch as he listened for any sign that someone else might be out there hunting him. Since Mac and Barry knew of Singe and his friends, others would be looking to collect that five-thousand dollars. Five men had already left warm beds and shelter for a chance to get rich. Others would surely follow. Going to Barren Pines had never been his first choice, but it remained the only choice he had.

Confident no one else was waiting among the trees to shoot him, Halstead began to search the bodies for anything he could sell in town. He normally made a practice of dumping his spent brass on the bodies of whoever he killed, but his supplies were too short for such ceremony. He decided to keep the spent rounds in case he found a gunsmith who could reload them for him.

He holstered the Colt and checked the bodies. Neither man had been carrying anything of value except for Mac's Springfield. He carefully traced Mac's tracks in the snow back to where they had left their horses hitched to a tree. His search of their saddlebags proved disappointing save for some dirty laundry. He found a box of twenty bullets for his Colt, pocketed the spent rounds and quickly reloaded. He slid some into the loops on his gun belt and stowed the rest in his right coat pocket. He was sure he would be needing them soon.

He left Mac and Barry's bodies where they had fallen as he led their horses to the others. At least he had a decent number of animals he could use to trade for bullets and supplies in town. He climbed onto Col and pulled the small herd behind him as he rode through the clearing.

Five men had ridden out from Barren Pines looking to kill him. It stood to reason that there were more men in town who would look to try their hand at earning that reward. Halstead would have preferred to avoid the place all together, but it was the only hint of civilization within an easy ride.

And Deputy Jason Fremont was its law. Mac and Singe had mentioned him, which said something about Fremont. Halstead would do his best to stay out of his way for as long as he was in town, but trouble had a knack for finding him.

Halstead thought about doubling back the way he had come, maybe look for another trapper shack around the base of the mountain. But as he looked back toward the Flatheads, he saw a thick band of dark clouds rolling his way. If he squinted hard enough, he could make out the heavy snow falling to block his path.

Halstead knew there was no going back and no way he could survive out here. Barren Pines was a poor choice, but it was his only choice. Going there might even cost him his life, but it was his best hope for survival until the weather cleared. At least he had a chance there. And a chance was all he had ever needed.

He slapped his heels into Col's flanks and set the horse moving toward whatever destiny awaited them in town.

Chapter 4

A heavy snow had begun to fall when Halstead and his horses reached Barren Pines.

It was clear to see how the place had earned its name. The town was surrounded by a stretch of charred pine trees that reached up to the gray sky like talons. He did not know what had turned them black and did not particularly care.

The town was bigger than he had expected it to be. It was not exactly Helena or Silver Cloud or even Battle Brook, but not just a settlement, either. Crooked shops and saloons huddled together on either side of the long thoroughfare. Carts, wagons, and horses had plowed a nasty brown scar through the deep snow down the middle of the street. More squat buildings and canvas huts formed crooked lines behind the buildings on the main street, which Halstead took as shelter for the residents.

The streets and boardwalks were empty, giving the town a peaceful look. But come the thaw, he was sure the place turned into an impassable mud pit. He did not plan on remaining around long enough to see it. He only hoped he managed to remain alive long enough to see another day.

As Halstead steered Col and his small herd of horses down the thoroughfare, he was surprised to see the boardwalk in front of every building was clear of snow and ice. The citizens of Barren Pines obviously took great pride in their town.

Back when he had still been a deputy U.S. Marshal, he would have taken this as a good sign. Fastidious citizens were usually eager to fight for their homes and could be relied upon to help in times of trouble.

But the world looked different to him now that he was a fugitive from justice. Clean sidewalks meant the townsfolk were not likely to turn a blind eye to a stranger, especially one looking to trade horses that had once belonged to five dead men. Men they probably knew and may have liked. Singe had said he, Luke, and Duro kept to themselves, but Halstead had to assume that was a lie until he knew otherwise. Mac and Barry, too. Just because a man was dead did not mean he was not dangerous. Ed Zimmerman had taught him that lesson.

Halstead took notice of every building he passed. Most were just one-story structures except for The Barren Pines Hotel, which had three. The rest were the kinds of businesses he would expect a town to have. A barber that offered warm baths. A saddlery and livery and a blacksmith. A couple of law offices and a slumped building he took for a saloon, but the sign out front proclaimed it was Town Hall. Restaurants and cafes lined both sides of the street, along with a few saloons with names like The Bull Moose, The Dark Forest, and Wild Bill's.

He peered through the thickening snow to see a sign at the far end of the thoroughfare. "Barren Pines Jail." It swung back and forth on a thin chain in the chilly morning wind. Halstead would make a point of avoiding that part of town.

Halstead drew rein in front of a wide building with "Armand's General Store" printed on the shaded windows. He climbed down from the saddle and wrapped Col's reins around the hitching rail, then knotted the lead rope with his five horses beside it. He took down his bag of ill-gotten gains and carried it into the store.

He stomped the snow from his boots before heading inside. A bell above the door offered a gentle ring when he entered.

A short, bald man in overalls and a crown of white hair looked up from a ledger as Halstead shut the door behind him.

"Morning, stranger," the man said as he set his spectacles on the ledger. "I'm David Armand, owner and proprietor of this place." He looked over Halstead from the heels of his boots to the top of his hat. "Don't reckon I've seen you in here before. I'd have remembered you if I had. Not much happens around this town without my notice, especially this time of year."

"I just got into town. My first time here."

Armand continued to study him. "I thought so. I'm not just a shopkeeper, but the postmaster, too. And given the amount of credit people around here owe me, I could be forgiven for adding banker to my list of responsibilities."

"Sounds like you keep yourself busy." Halstead could tell Armand was a busybody, so he wanted to keep his dealings with the man as simple as he could. He had already made an impression on the shopkeeper. "I was just passing through when the weather caught up to me." He lifted his bag for the old man to see. "I've brought some goods I was hoping to trade for supplies."

Mr. Armand looked over the bag. "For money or goods?"

"Whichever you'd like."

Mr. Armand beckoned Halstead to follow him to a side counter at the left side of the store. "Just put it up here, young fella, and we'll see what you've got. What did you say your name was?"

Halstead ignored the question as he set the bag on the counter and untied it. He began to list the items he was showing him, hoping to distract Mr. Armand from his question. "I've got four rifles, three good knives here. Some rounds for the Springfields, too. Nearly a whole box."

Mr. Armand stroked his white beard as he looked over the goods. "A decent haul, young man. Where'd you get all this stuff?"

"Picked them up here and there in my travels."

51

The shopkeeper seemed content to accept the answer. "Got anything else to trade?"

Halstead threw his thumb over his left shoulder. "Horses. Five of them hitched up outside right now. Every one of them in fine condition. Saddles, bridles, and everything."

And the more he talked, the more Halstead realized he was not much of an outlaw. He had just talked his way into putting a noose around his own neck.

"Saddles, bridles, and everything, eh?" Mr. Armand's bushy eyebrows rose. "That's mighty interesting. You find them walking around like that or did you trade for them?"

Halstead had no choice but to carry on with the lie he had started. "You might say trade. I won them in a card game."

"Is that so?" Mr. Armand smiled. "Well, if cards are your game, you've come to the right place, Mister . . . what did you say your name was again?"

He had never been much of a liar but said the first name that entered his mind. "Ramsey. John Ramsey."

Mr. Armand looked him over again. "You don't look like a Ramsey to me. I hope you won't take offense by my saying you could be taken for having a touch of injun blood in you."

Halstead thought fast. "Given name's Ramirez." It had been his mother's maiden name. "Juan

Ramirez, but I go by Ramsey in these parts. It's easier for folks to remember. I'm out of Fort Worth. That's in Texas."

"I know where it is." Mr. Armand laughed and touched the side of his cheek. "That explains your skin tone. I'm glad you said something or else I might've taken you for a half-breed. Only a fool trusts a half-breed. But you Mexicans are good people. Hard workers, too."

Halstead forced a laugh and pointed at his thick beard. "You ever know an Indian with hair on his face."

"Nope, can't say that I have," Mr. Armand agreed. He went to the window and lifted the shade to take a good look at the horses before lowering it again. "I can't say I know much about horses, either, Mr. Ramsey, but my brother Moses does. You can bring them over to his livery right across the street and let him look them over. Just don't get startled when you see him. We're twins, him and me, but in appearance only. He's an ornery one, my brother. I'm the nicer of the two."

"I'll be sure to remember that." He sensed a change in the man, like he was trying hard not to say the wrong thing. "What about do you think you could give me for these rifles and knives right here on the counter?"

Mr. Armand picked up one of the knives and examined the blade. "You're right about them being in fine condition. The Springfields, too. I'll give you thirty dollars for the whole bundle. It's a fair price, one no one in town will beat."

Halstead knew that was not his best offer. The Springfields alone were worth twenty dollars apiece. He was in no position to haggle, but he would be more memorable if he folded too quickly. "I was hoping for more. I understand these rifles are popular with trappers around here."

"They certainly are." He looked over Halstead again. "You a trapper, too, Mr. Ramsey?"

"Trader would be closer to the mark."

"Nothing wrong with that. You look like you're toting pistols under your coat." He glanced at the wall of ammunition boxes stacked on the shelves behind the counter. "What kind do you carry?"

Halstead remembered the wanted flyer had mentioned his pistols. "A pair of Long Colts."

Mr. Armand brought his hand down on the counter like a judge in a court room. "Sold. I'll throw in a box of bullets for your pistols to sweeten the pot." He held out his hand to him. "What do you say?"

"Make it two boxes and you've got yourself a deal."

"Fair enough." The two men shook hands on it. "You want your money in cash or store credit? Credit's a wise investment for a gambling man such as yourself. You'll be needing supplies to get on your way when the weather lets up. You can't lose what you don't have."

Halstead wished that was the case. "I'll take half in money now and keep the rest on account."

Mr. Armand pulled a notebook toward him, licked the tip of a pencil, and began to write out a receipt. "Fifteen dollars won't get you a room at the hotel. They're all sold out, I'm afraid. It's the weather, you see? But a couple of the saloons in town might have a room for you for a few cents a night. Not including drinks, of course. Or feminine companionship. That'll cost extra."

"It always does." Halstead watched Mr. Armand write the receipt. He noticed the handwriting in another notebook beside him. His hand had been steadier then. There was a bit of a shake to it now.

Mr. Armand tore off the receipt and handed it to Halstead. "There you go, Mr. Ramsey. I'll be right out with your bullets. We just ran out of them this morning but I've got a few fresh boxes in the back."

Halstead watched him practically run toward the back of the store before calling out to him. "Wait."

Mr. Armand slowly turned around. "Did I forget something?"

"You didn't write down my credit in your ledger. I wouldn't want you to forget it. Fifteen dollars isn't much, but it is to me."

"Oh, that." He began to breathe again. "Don't worry. I won't forget." He tapped his temple with a crooked finger. "Got a mind like a steel trap.

I never forget anything. Besides, you've got that receipt, don't you?"

"Yeah," Halstead said. "I guess you have a point."

"I'll be right back out with your bullets."

He waited for the old man to duck behind the curtain before he moved. He went behind the counter, crossing in front of the curtain before reaching the other side. He drew his Colt from his belly holster and waited.

A double-barreled shotgun parted the curtains before Mr. Armand stepped through. "Put your hands up you—"

Halstead placed the barrel of his Colt against the shopkeeper's temple. "Ease down those hammers, old timer. Right now."

Mr. Armand swallowed as he uncocked the shotgun.

Halstead snatched the shotgun from him and put it on the counter. "And here I was thinking this was a friendly town. Why'd you pull a gun on me?"

Mr. Armand swallowed hard again. "On account of you selling Springfield rifles I sold to some trappers over the years. I recognized those knives and horses, too. And because you match the description of Jeremiah Halstead. The Butcher of Battle Brook. As cold-blooded a killer as there ever was in this territory, from what they say."

Halstead kept the pistol against the shopkeeper's temple. *The Butcher of Battle Brook? Who pinned that name on me?* "What would've put that thought in your head?"

"You fit the description on the flyer the sheriff's been handing out all over town." Mr. Armand closed his eyes. "No fewer than five men rode out after Halstead the past two days. Trappers. Tough fellas. Tough and mean. You riding into town like you have with that many horses got me to worrying is all."

"If I was a cold-blooded killer like Halstead, I guess I could be forgiven for shooting you right now."

Mr. Armand swallowed. "I'd be grateful if you didn't."

"Then today's your lucky day because I'm not Halstead." Halstead withdrew the Colt and slid it back into his holster. "The name's Ramsey, remember? And I lied about winning those horses in a card game. I found them on the trail as I was riding in here. The goods I've come to trade were in their saddlebags and on the ground. I guess that doesn't make me exactly honorable, but these aren't honorable times."

"No." Mr. Armand pulled at his collar. "I guess they're not."

"I didn't see any sign of this Halstead out there, either. Because if I had, I'd be dead, too. Wouldn't I? A dangerous man like that isn't shy about killing strangers."

"You surely would." He did not sound like he believed that. "I can see that now. Sorry for the confusion, deputy."

Halstead caught that. "Not deputy. Mr. Ramsey, remember?"

"Of course. Mr. Ramsey. I won't forget it again."

"See to it that you don't." Halstead pulled Mr. Armand's ledger across the counter. "Now, I'd feel a whole lot better about things if you wrote down my account in your ledger here. Make sure you use my name. John Ramsey. I don't want anyone else, like maybe Deputy Fremont, making the same mistake you just did."

Mr. Armand took the pencil from behind his ear and wrote down the fifteen dollars in store credit that Halstead still had. "There. It's settled. Hope you won't hold this against me, Mr. Ramsey. Out here, a man can't be too careful. Not with the likes of Jeremiah Halstead running around on the loose."

"It pays for a man to be careful." Halstead took the shotgun with him as he went over to the shelves where the ammunition was kept. "Looks like you were wrong about those bullets for my Long Colts being in the back. You've got a whole stack of them right here. I'll be taking two boxes, just like we agreed."

Mr. Armand kept both hands on the counter. "Guess I was too nervous to notice. Sorry for the mistake."

"No harm done." Halstead opened the shotgun and dumped the shells on the floor, before setting the empty gun on the counter. "No harm at all."

He plucked two boxes of forty-one-caliber rounds and stepped out from behind the counter. "Pleasure doing business with you, Mr. Armand. I'll be sure to be back for those supplies when the weather improves."

"I'll be looking forward to it. Mr. Ramsey."

Halstead pocketed the bullets as he left the store and climbed into the saddle again. He did not believe Mr. Armand would be looking forward to it at all.

Chapter 5

The wind and snow had picked up considerably since Halstead had been in the store. He rode over to The Barren Pines Livery, which was as large as the general store except that it had a second floor. He brought his horses through the wide entrance and was greeted by the smell of burning wood mixed with the smell of horses kept in stalls.

As Halstead climbed down from the saddle, he heard a door open and the sound of men's laughter somewhere in the building.

He saw a rounder version of David Armand standing in a doorway holding a mug of coffee. Moses Armand's beard was just as white as his brother's, but fuller and longer. Faded braces held up filthy britches over an even filthier shirt. He was stockier than his brother and did not seem to mind the cold.

Halstead stood with his left shoulder facing Armand. He could draw his belly gun quicker that way if it came to that, though the man appeared to be unarmed.

"You Moses Armand?" Halstead asked.

"That depends on who you are," the liveryman answered.

"John Ramsey." Halstead looked past him into the office and saw the source of the laughter. Five men sitting around a pot belly stove. Cigar and cigarette smoke wafted out, mingling with the smell of wood, hay, and manure. "Your brother over at the general store sent me here. I've got five good saddle horses to trade or sell. He told me you'd give me a good price, assuming you're Moses."

"I'm Moses," Armand said. "And if what you say is true, it'd be the first good thing he's said about me in thirty years." He looked over Halstead with the same scrutiny his brother had in the store. "You said your name's Ramsey?"

"John Ramsey," Halstead lied. He tried to sound convincing but was not sure he had pulled it off. "And no, I'm not a half-breed. My mother was Mexican. My given name's Ramirez."

Moses glanced at the horses. "I've seen these animals before, mister. I turned out three of them yesterday and two of them early this morning. The men riding them were trappers out looking for a fella by the name of Jeremiah Halstead."

Halstead hooked his right thumb on the buckle of his gun belt. The butt of his Colt was only inches away. "Guess that explains why I found these horses on the trail."

"It surely would," Moses nodded. "It was the reward that sent them looking for him. Five-thousand-dollars. Quite a sizable sum. A man could buy an awful lot of comfort with that kind of money in his pocket. Live the good life for a while."

"If he lived." Halstead looked past Armand at the men inside. None of them seemed to be wearing pistols and he bet none of them had brought rifles. No need for them in town. "I found these horses wandering among the pines as I reached town. I'd say they either found Halstead or he found them. Either way, I don't think you'll be seeing them again."

Moses sipped some coffee. "You see Halstead out there, mister?"

Halstead shook his head. "If I had, I wouldn't be here."

"You certainly wouldn't. There's a knack to it, you know. Living, I mean. There's a knack to it if a man expects to live way out here in any kind of peace. It was that reward money that cost those boys dearly. I guess I ought to count myself lucky that I'm already settled in life."

Halstead understood what he was trying to say. "That so?"

"Yes, sir. I've got money in the bank, wood for my stove, and friends to enjoy it with. I've got my livery and blacksmith business on the side. I wouldn't know what to do with all that reward money if someone just up and handed it to me. I'll take my comforts over riches any day of the week and twice on Sunday."

Halstead dropped his right hand to his side. "I like the way you think, Mr. Armand."

"My brother's Mr. Armand. I'm Moses. Mind if

I call you John? We don't go much for formality around here."

"It's my name, isn't it?"

Moses grinned. "It certainly is." He walked over to the horses and took a closer look at them. "You said you found them just wandering around on the outskirts of town, did you?"

"Found three last night and two this morning just off the trail. Looks like Halstead has been busy."

Moses patted one of the horses on the flank. "I told them they were crazy for going out after a man of such a reputation. Trappers are a hard breed, but it takes more than toughness to go up against the likes of Halstead. Hunting an animal is different than hunting a man. A bear is a fearsome animal, but it can't shoot back and, from what I've heard, Halstead lives by the gun."

"Yeah. I've heard that, too."

Moses moved to the next horse as he kept talking. "He survived an outlaw bounty on his head and killed every man who tried to collect it. Best to stay away from him. Back when he was a deputy marshal, he ran Ed Zimmerman to ground and saw him swing for his sins. In my experience, it's best to avoid a man like that if I can."

Halstead liked the way he thought and appreciated the effort he put into lying. "Mine, too. Hope the rest of the people here in town feel the same way. I'd hate to see anyone else wind up like the trappers who owned these horses."

Moses waved him off as he took another sip of coffee. "Halstead's got nothing to worry about from them. When word gets out about what happened to these boys, and my brother will see to it that it does, they'll realize they're better around hearth and home than trying for any reward money." He moved to the next horse. "By the way, how was he when you left him? My brother, I mean. Still in good health?"

Halstead understood the true question. *Did you kill him?* "He was tending to his books when I left." He dug the receipt out of his pocket and showed it to him. "He even gave me this. Store credit for goods when the weather clears."

Moses glanced at the receipt before Halstead put it away. "Good to hear. My brother's the talkative kind. Always was, even when we were kids. He'll tell every living soul that walks into his store about you finding these horses. We don't get many strangers around here this time of year. Just trappers looking to ride out the winter. We live off them. Got a few ranches scattered around, too, but they've already stocked up until spring. They'll be holed up in their bunkhouses until the thaw."

In his own way, Moses was telling him the lay of the land. "Heard you've got a deputy around here. Jason Fremont."

"He's a nice young fella as far as it goes,"

Moses said. "Sheriff Langham down in Missoula always sends a deputy to spend the winter with us and, this year, it's Fremont's turn. Jason's young and awfully pleased with himself, but he's mostly harmless. You being a newcomer and all, he's likely to take an interest in you."

Halstead remembered Singe had told him about Fremont. "I don't mind a bit of interest as long as he doesn't push too hard."

"He'll sniff around you some at first, but he'll probably leave you alone," Moses said. "He's sweet on this gal who sings over at The Town Hall."

Halstead remembered seeing a sign for the place on his ride into town. "You use your town hall for singing."

Moses laughed. "We don't have any mayor around here. Town Hall is the name of the nicest saloon and gambling hall in town. Glenda likes to bring her show here each winter before she moves on. She's good for business and easy on the eyes, assuming you like that sort of thing."

Halstead remembered the picture he had found among the dead trapper's possessions. Glamorous Glenda. "I doubt I'll be here long enough to see her show. Never liked saloons much. I plan on pushing on as soon as the weather lets up." Moses seemed harmless enough, but he was still a stranger. Halstead did not like telling strangers his plans. "What kind of price will you give me for these horses?"

Moses said, "I'll give you an even hundred for the lot of them."

"A hundred?" Halstead was almost insulted. "These are saddle horses. They should bring at least two hundred a piece. Each saddle's worth at least sixty."

"That's true," Moses allowed, "but this is the beginning of winter. Everyone's already holed up for the season. Not much call for horses right now. And I'll have to feed them and tend to them until the thaw, which doesn't come for another few months yet. There are other factors to consider, of course."

"Like what?"

"Like how you came to find them," Moses explained. "Dead men's horses, I mean. Some folks might look poorly on buying such an animal. Might think there's bad luck using a dead man's saddle, too. I'm sure you understand."

Halstead understood. Moses knew who he was and how he had gotten the animals. He could not expect full value for them. He was getting the outlaw price and there was nothing he could do about it.

"Can you at least put up my own horse as part of the bargain? Col's seen some hard riding and I'd like to see her tended to properly while I'm here."

Moses looked her over. "She's got a bit of a wild streak in her. Mustang unless I miss my guess."

He was not surprised the liveryman had an eye

66

for horses. "I rode her all the way up here from Texas. She's a good animal."

"I'll not only put her up for free but I'll even put new shoes on her when you're ready to leave. I can put you up, too. There's a room upstairs in the loft you can have. It's a nice quiet place and you won't have to bother with any of the locals. They're all like my brother. The curious type." He held out his hand to Halstead. "How's that strike you? Deal?"

Halstead regarded the hand for a moment. "Why are you being so nice to me?"

"A man in my line of work sees all kinds of men, Mr. Ramsey," Moses explained. "You look like a man who's made some mistakes. I've made one or two myself. Had kindness shown to me when I needed it most. Look at this as me just returning the favor."

Halstead gladly shook the man's hand. "I'm grateful, Moses. I truly am."

"You also look hungry," Moses observed. "I've always got coffee on the stove, so there's no charge for that. I'm not much of a cook, so don't go expecting me to feed you. I take most of my meals at Millie's Kitchen just up the street. It's not the most popular or fanciest place in town, but I don't think you'll mind that. The food's good, and they serve breakfast all day, even for supper. It's a nice quiet place I think you'll enjoy after your journey."

Good food and quiet were exactly what Halstead needed. "I'll help you get these horses settled and get myself something to eat."

Moses set his mug by the door and began to undo the saddles. "I sure hope they go easy on that Halstead fella if they ever find him. From what little I've heard about him, it sounds like Zimmerman and his men needed killing."

Halstead undid the cinch of Col's saddle. "Sounds like it."

At the back table in Millie's, Halstead finished the last of the biscuits on his plate. They were almost as hard as the ice out on the thoroughfare, but the egg yolk made them reasonably edible. The coffee was weak, little more than beige water, but better than nothing. Billy Sunday could teach them a thing or two about brewing a good pot.

He ignored the curious looks he drew from the four other patrons as he ate. Two couples at separate tables. Their dress was formal and he took them to be travelers from The Barren Pines Hotel, not locals or trappers. He did not know if they looked at him because he was a stranger or because they took him for a half-breed. Maybe both. None of them were armed, so he paid them little mind.

He had seen his wanted poster in the front window when he walked in, but thought his full beard and moustache did a decent job of masking his appearance.

Millie had taken his order and brought it to him. She was a pinch-faced whisp of a woman with graying curly hair. She had barely looked at him when she had come to his table but he had caught her stealing looks at him from the counter. It was not out of admiration but out of curiosity. A bell sounded from the kitchen whenever a meal was ready. That meant there was at least one other person in the back. Maybe another who washed dishes, bringing the total to three.

That meant there were seven people in the place. None of them dangerous. That was good.

Halstead had made a point of keeping his hat on and his head down while he ate. The brim did a good job of concealing his face. He decided it would be best if he spent as much time in Hank's loft as possible. He would only eat once a day and at off times when most of the town was working or busy doing whatever they did during winter. Saloons were out of the question, especially Town Hall.

He noticed the place had a back door that led out to an alley. He would only use it if he had to make a fast escape.

He made a point of not looking up when he heard the café door open.

Millie was busy clearing plates from a table when she greeted the new customer.

"Morning, Jason. We weren't expecting you back here so soon. Still hungry?"

So that was Jason Fremont, the deputy sheriff of Barren Pines. Halstead kept his head down but eyed Fremont's boots as he stepped inside. They were wet from snow, which meant he may have crossed the thoroughfare before coming to Millie's. He had probably just left Mr. Armand's General Store.

"How could I be hungry after that big feast you gave me this morning?" Fremont said with a smile in his voice. "I heard we have a stranger in town and figured I ought to look him over for myself. I understand he's here."

Millie set the dishes back on the table and began to whisper to the sheriff. The tips of his boots were facing Halstead, so he knew he'd be coming back to see him once Millie finished gossiping.

Halstead wiped his mouth with the napkin and tossed it on the table as he took his first full look at Jason Fremont. He judged the sheriff to be around the same height as he and just as lean. The lines on his face told him he was a few years older, which put him just north of thirty.

But where Halstead had dark hair and features, Fremont had sandy hair and green eyes. Halstead imagined the ladies of Barren Pines found Fremont quite becoming, and he carried himself like a man who knew it.

Fremont sported a Peacemaker in a holster on his right hip, but the leather looked brand-new. Halstead wondered how much call Fremont had to use it and decided it was not often. The tan, flat-brimmed hat he wore looked new as well. Moses had been right about him. The deputy seemed quite pleased with himself.

Fremont eyed Halstead while Millie continued her hushed report. Halstead did not know how much a woman could know about a man simply by watching him sop up yolk with biscuits, but she seemed eager to tell Fremont anyway. Perhaps she was telling him about the stranger's quiet nature or how he didn't seem to mind being the center of attention. He was certain she was telling him about the Colts he sported. Even if they gave away his identity, he would not dare walk around without them.

When she had finished speaking her mind, Millie picked up the dishes and scurried back to the kitchen without looking Halstead's way. Whatever she had told Fremont must not have been good.

The sheriff thumbed his hat farther back on his head as he began to walk toward Halstead's table. The easy smile he offered did not match the flat look in his eyes.

Halstead sat back and rested his elbows on the arms of his chair, folding his left hand over his right without interlacing his fingers. A contemplative pose, but also a practical one. The handle of his Colt was within easy reach if he needed it.

Fremont stopped in front of Halstead's table and parted his coat as he hooked his thumbs in his gun belt. Halstead noticed the star pinned to the vest beneath it. That was the point.

"You must be Mr. Ramsey."

"And you must be Deputy Fremont."

His eyebrows rose. "You've heard of me."

"I certainly have." Halstead decided a bit of flattery could not hurt while he got a sense of the kind of man the deputy was. "A man can hardly spend a day in this part of the territory without knowing who Jason Fremont is. Every trapper from here clear on up to Canada says the same thing. Keep your nose clean if you go to Barren Pines for Jason Fremont doesn't tolerate troublemakers of any kind."

Fremont's smile grew wider. "They say all that, do they?"

Halstead nodded. "They surely do."

"Which are you, Mr. Ramsey? Trapper or trouble."

"Neither one. I'm just a man waiting for the weather to lift so I can be on my way."

"We're a state now, you know," Fremont told him. "Montana, I mean. We got ourselves admitted to the Union a few months back."

"Congratulations," Halstead said. "I don't pay

politics much mind. I'm never in one place long enough to give it any thought."

"A traveling man, are you?" Fremont did not wait for an answer. "Trapper? Trader? Indian agent?"

"I've been all three at one time or another," Halstead said. "I came to town to trade, but you already know that since you know my name."

"I know the name you gave Dave Armand. Saw it in his ledger myself. John Ramsey out of Fort Worth, Texas."

He was glad to have made the shopkeeper write it that way. But he had undoubtedly told him more than that. "I look forward to cashing my credit with him for supplies as soon as the snow stops. I'll be needing supplies when I leave. He's got a nice store."

"That's because Barren Pines is a nice town," Fremont said. "And it's my job to keep it that way." He gestured at the chair across from Halstead. "Mind if I take a load off?"

"Not at all."

Fremont pulled the chair out, but instead of sitting down, rested his left boot on it. His right hand slid back toward his hip, closer to the Peacemaker. It was a casual gesture, but far from subtle.

Halstead kept his hands where they were.

Fremont took notice of his guns. "We get a fair number of trappers and traders who come through here, but I can't recall any of them toting two pistols like you. They usually prefer a knife and a rifle. The kinds of rifles you brought to Dave Armand for trade."

"They make you nervous, sheriff? My Colts, I mean."

"Curious more than anything," Fremont said. "Why do you tote so much iron, Mr. Ramsey?"

"Because it's a dangerous world and Montana is dangerous country. I like to be able to defend myself."

"Need two guns to do it?"

"From time to time."

"And were you defending yourself just now when you put a gun to David Armand's head?"

"I was." He was not surprised that the old man had told Fremont about that. "But I'd call that just a misunderstanding. I thought he was acting strange and when he came out from the back with a shotgun. I was right. I drew my pistol first. It turned out well in the end. No harm done. I'll be happy to show you the receipt he gave me if you like."

Fremont leaned on the chair. His smile a distant memory. "If I want anything from you, I'll take it."

"You're welcome to try."

Fremont slid his boot off the chair and stood on his own two feet. "You fit a lot of descriptions, Mr. Ramsey. The one in the window over there, for instance. Jeremiah Halstead. The Butcher of Battle Brook."

Halstead shrugged it off with a smile. "The world's full of tall dark strangers, deputy. You plan on arresting every single one of them who happens into town?"

"Only if they're Halstead, which I think you are."

Halstead had enough time to prepare himself for hearing his own name used against him. "So that's what this is about. You think I'm Halstead. You're wrong."

Fremont stood to his full height. "I know that over the last two days, five men rode out looking for Halstead and none of them have come back. I know you've ridden into town with their horses and their knives and rifles to trade."

"I told Mr. Armand I found those horses and those rifles out on the trail."

"He passed on your lies," Fremont said. "Those men who went looking for you weren't exactly choir boys. They were rawboned and meaner than hell. Only a man like Halstead could kill them."

"That may be, except I'm not Halstead. And you can't prove otherwise."

"Maybe not right now, but I can throw you in a cell until I can get word to Missoula about you. See what Sheriff Langham wants to do about it when I could get word to him."

Halstead slowly shook his head. "Prisoners need feeding and tending to. I'm not going anywhere for a while. Why go through all that trouble?"

Fremont grinned. "You don't think I could take you, do you?"

The deputy was easy to rile. Halstead would remember that. It could come in handy at the right time. He decided to push him a little further. "There's no reason for you to try. You've got a whole town to look after, deputy. You have better things to do than spend your days looking after me. And, from what I've heard, your nights, too." He winked. "Glamorous Glenda is quite a gal and you're a lucky man. You're right to be careful."

Fremont's eyes drew narrow as he swallowed. The boy had a shorter fuse than Halstead thought. "You make careful sound a lot like cowardice."

Halstead shook his head. "I can't help what you hear. Careful means careful."

"And what makes you think I'm so careful?"

"Because you weren't dumb enough to ride out with those boys when they went looking for Halstead. If you had, you might be out there with them right now. You're not just careful, deputy. You're smart. It's a good way to be."

Fremont set his hands on his hips and looked away in frustration. Halstead could tell he was not used to being challenged. His charm probably settled most disputes, and when that failed, he used his authority. People followed him because of the star on his chest, not because of who he was, and he knew it.

"I have half a mind to lock you up right now on suspicion of murder."

Halstead kept his hands where they were. "You're welcome to try."

A plate shattered in the kitchen. Millie had been listening and did not like what she heard.

Fremont took a step back. "That does it. Get up."

The deputy's hand moved back to his Peacemaker, but not before Halstead drew his Colt.

The sheriff flinched. It was clear he had never seen a man pull so fast.

"It's only you and me in here, sheriff, so you've still got your pride. Back up, turn around, and walk away. Leave me alone, and I'll do the same. I'll be gone as soon as the weather lifts. You've got my word on that."

"The word of an outlaw?" Fremont managed to keep most of the tremble out of his voice. "The word of a butcher like you?"

"If I was an outlaw, you would've been dead by now."

Fremont's right hand grew red as it hovered above his pistol. Halstead had been in his position before. He knew how it felt when fear, anger, and pride boiled together at once.

"I'm the law around here," the deputy said. "I have a *duty*."

"Can't do your duty if you're dead." Halstead nodded toward the door. "Do what I told you. Leave. Now."

Halstead holstered his Colt after Fremont slid his hand closer to the buckle of his belt. Both men had made their point. There was no use in pushing it further.

The deputy asked, "I want to know where you're staying while you're here."

"Moses Armand's loft. I'll be there until the weather breaks."

Fremont did not look like he believed him. "I've never known him to do that before. He must be getting generous in his old age."

"It's a fair trade. After all, I brought him five good horses."

Halstead did not flinch when the sheriff pointed his finger at him. "Since you like to trade, I've got one for you. Stay out of my way. Keep to the livery and Millie's and I'll leave you alone. No saloons and no trouble. You take one bad step, and I'll throw you in jail with five counts of murder. I can get ten men with rifles to back me any time of day or night. If you doubt that, you'll regret it."

Halstead kept his hand flat on the table. "Wouldn't it be nice to think so."

"As soon as the weather clears, I want you gone."

"Understood."

He watched Fremont back out of the restaurant, go outside, and walk back toward the jail through the driving snow at a brisk pace.

Halstead took a sip of coffee. *So much for a nice quiet meal.* He was glad the sheriff had not made him kill him. The weather was getting bad and he would have hated to travel in it. He would have hated to kill another law man simply for doing his job.

But I'm not a law man. Not anymore.

He saw Millie poke her head around the corner like a prairie dog. He lifted his mug with a smile. "I'll take some more. And the check when you get a chance."

She ducked out of view and Halstead finished off his coffee. She had heard their exchange and would waste no time in telling anyone who would listen about his run in with Fremont. The deputy might be pushed to do something to save his pride and reputation. He had no doubt it would lead to more trouble, but if life on the run had taught him anything, it was to worry about the present. Tomorrow would take care of itself. All he could do was be ready to meet whatever happened next.

Millie delivered a new cup of coffee to him and left the check as she picked up his plate. She did not look at him this time, either.

Chapter 6

Halstead finished his coffee and left the money for his meal on the table before leaving Millie's. The weather had taken a bad turn, and the boardwalks were still deserted. A strong wind might have taken his hat had he not managed to grab it in time. Snow had begun to mix with sleet and pelted the boardwalk.

He raised the collar of his coat against the biting cold and noticed a man waiting just inside the entrance to Armand's Livery. He wore a long gray overcoat and a wide-brimmed hat pulled low on his head. He kept his hands away from his sides and held up gloved hands to show they were empty. He pulled down his scarf to reveal an iron gray Van Dyke beard and a moustache that had been waxed into a curl on each end.

Halstead recognized the man immediately. "Lance McAlister? From Silver Cloud."

"The one and only," the gambler said as they shook hands and moved inside the livery and out of the elements. "Glad to see you're still alive, my friend. I've been reading about your hardship in the papers. Sounds like you've had a rough time of it."

"You don't know the half of it. What are you doing all the way out here?"

"I like to spend the winter here whenever I can," McAlister said. "It's quiet, and the trappers make for good pigeons for an old card sharp like me. They play big and lose big, especially early in the season." He took off his hat and shook off some of the icy snow that had begun to accumulate on the brim. "I heard a rumor that you might be in town. I figured you could stand to see a friendly face."

McAlister had been one of his few allies back in Silver Cloud during his first run-in with Zimmerman and the Hudson Gang. He was the closest thing to a friend he had seen since fleeing Helena. "A lot's changed since the last time I saw you."

"I've read all about it. You've gone and gotten yourself something of a reputation. What should I call you now? Ramsey or by your real name."

After his confrontation with Deputy Fremont, there was no reason to carry on the weak pretense of being John Ramsey. "Might as well use my real name. John Ramsey wasn't very convincing anyway."

"A man can only hide who he is for so long," McAlister said. "I ought to know. I've been trying to do it for near sixty years now without much luck. I heard you were at Millie's having breakfast. I was going to see you when I saw you and Fremont having a talk. Seeing as how the deputy and I don't get along, I decided not to interrupt. I figured I'd wait for you here. I imagine you two had quite a conversation."

"One for the ages." Halstead winced at the memory. He did not hate Fremont. If he had still been a deputy marshal, he would have wanted a man like him on his side. "He's a good man. I can't blame him for not wanting me around."

"Not everyone in town thinks the way he does," McAlister said. "You could say that's part of the reason why I'm here."

Halstead grew suspicious. "That so?"

The gambler nodded. "There's someone who wants to make your acquaintance. In fact, she asked me to come bring you over to see her right now."

"She?" Halstead repeated.

"The Queen of Barren Pines herself," McAlister told him. "Miss Glenda Younger. Our glamor girl."

Glenda certainly had her share of admirers. "What does she want to talk about?"

"She didn't tell me," McAlister said, "but Glenda rarely explains herself. She lets me run the gambling over at The Town Hall. Gives me a piece of the house take as long as I keep an eye on the cheaters. She's quite a woman, Jeremiah, but I wouldn't waste much time worrying about her reasons. Many men have gone crazy trying to understand why she does the things she does. All they got for their trouble was misery and heartache. I suspect she has her reasons now. I can't make you talk to her, but I've found she usually has something to say."

Halstead imagined his recent reputation as an outlaw must have had something to do with it. "Where and when does she want me to see her?"

"At your earliest convenience in her dressing room over at The Town Hall."

Halstead may have had nothing but time to kill until the weather improved, but he remembered Fremont's edict. "The deputy and I agreed that I'd keep out of sight while I'm here. I don't want to go tweaking his nose any more than I already have. I damaged his pride just now, and he'll be looking for a reason to do something about it."

"There won't be any trouble from him or anyone else," McAlister assured him. "Glenda makes the rules in this town, and she's got Fremont wrapped around her little finger. Like I said, she's quite a woman."

"Sounds like it." Halstead knew Moses and McAlister were the closest people he had to friends in Barren Pines. It would not hurt to find out if Glenda might be one of them. "Is there a back door I could use? I don't want to walk through the saloon. Some drunk might get to thinking about taking a chance at that reward money."

"I'll take you in the side door. A big Chinaman named Joe keeps an eye on it for her, but he's expecting you. I swear, he's just about the biggest Celestial I've ever seen. Didn't know they grew them so big over there. Guess you learn something new every day."

Halstead gestured toward The Town Hall Saloon. "You and me both."

Emil Riker almost spilled his whiskey as the train rocked back and forth on the tracks. But almost did not count much in life and he managed to swallow it down whole.

He set the glass on the table and told the man sitting across from him, "Again."

"You ought to take it easy on that stuff, boss," Keane said as he poured more whiskey from his flask. "You're apt to regret it something fierce when we reach Missoula tomorrow afternoon."

Riker already had a belly full of pain and regret no hangover could match. "I don't pay you to think, Keane. I pay you to do what you're told, and I'm telling you to pour."

"You ain't paid me and my men anything yet," Keane reminded him, "except for provisions and train fare for me and my men."

Riker hated whiskey almost as much as he hated conversation, but at least the whiskey helped dull the ache in his missing right arm. It dulled the constant insult of knowing he would spend the rest of his life as a cripple.

The cold only served to make the phantom pain

grow worse. Doc Potter had told him the feeling would subside in time, but Riker knew some wounds never healed. Only one thing could cure what ailed him. The sight of Jeremiah Halstead's dead body swinging from a tree branch.

As the whiskey hit home, Riker remembered Doc Potter's tense fear the day he told him there was no choice but to amputate his ruined arm. His shoulder had been destroyed by Halstead's bullet, and the wound had gradually become infected. Keeping it would cost him his life. The good doctor had not understood that taking the arm had cost him his life anyway. The life he had known. The man he had been.

He looked out at the snow falling just outside the train window. *Amputate.* An elegant word for butchery. Doc Potter may have surgically removed his arm, but he might as well have used a meat cleaver. The result had been the same.

Each waking moment from that day on had been a new humiliation for Emil Riker. He had been forced to give up his position as sheriff of Battle Brook, though Hubbard and Mannes had not reduced his share of the profits from the towns. They said it was the least they could do after all he had lost. After he had helped rid them of Halstead in his own way. They called it severance. Riker called it what it was. Charity.

He knew all the money in the world could never make him whole again. He would never fire a rifle or cut a steak or any number of the dozens of other mindless tasks he had taken for granted back when he had been whole. Even buttoning his shirt and unbuttoning his britches took considerable effort.

The sympathetic looks he drew from strangers who saw his empty sleeve made him feel as if he had been shot all over again. The pain of his missing limb only served as a constant reminder of what he had lost. Of all that Jeremiah Halstead had taken from him. Riker had left more than his arm and his brother back in Battle Brook. He had left a piece of whatever soul he still had left. His dignity.

He had come to Montana at Zimmerman's invitation with the promise of gaining revenge on Halstead for killing his father. He had come out of greed for the riches the growing town had promised. His desire for vengeance and money had cost him dearly.

But not as much as it would ultimately cost Halstead. He had seen to that.

Riker asked Keane, "You know anything about this man we're supposed to meet in Missoula? Vander-something?"

"Vandenberg," Keane said. "Hy Vandenberg. He's a reporter for one of the local papers. Mr. Hubbard wired him a couple of days ago to tell him we were on our way."

Riker had not wanted to tell anyone he was

going to Missoula to hunt Halstead, much less a fool reporter, but Mark Mannes had insisted on using him. He had assured him that Vandenberg was a good man who knew all that was worth knowing in the area. If Halstead was around, Vandenberg would know about it. "Expecting a reporter to keep his mouth shut doesn't sound like a good idea to me."

"We don't need him to keep his mouth shut," Keane reminded him. "We just need him to tell us where Halstead might be. Mr. Mannes is confident he'll be useful."

Of course, Mannes would think that. The lawyer thought men could be bought simply by giving them money. Family connections and influence had served Mannes well, but given money was soon forgotten.

Riker knew newspapermen usually caused more problems than they solved. He could have gotten as much information from a bartender or one of the sporting ladies working in a saloon. "Vandenberg won't care who brings in Halstead as long as he's there with a photographer to take a picture of the body."

"Mr. Mannes said he's paid Vandenberg enough to make sure he only deals with us."

Keane was starting to sound like a parrot. " 'Mr. Mannes says.' If you knew the man, you wouldn't bother calling him 'mister' anything. At least the miserable weasel had the decency to ride to Helena in his own private compartment. It spares me the burden of suffering his company."

"I don't know about that," Keane admitted. "I also don't know about that fancy lady you said you've been writing to. The one who's supposed to help us find Halstead."

Riker cursed himself for the misstep. He had too much of Keane's whiskey the night they boarded the train in Wellspring. He had been awash in drunken glory and mentioned the woman Mannes had helped him find. A woman Riker was sure could play a part in his revenge before all was said and done.

He had already been foolish enough to tell Keane too much. If he told him more, the mercenary might not have any further use for him. He could easily cut Riker out of the scheme for a greater share of the five-thousand-dollars Halstead would bring. Riker had no interest in the money. Halstead's corpse was all the payment he sought.

"You'll learn more about her when the time is right," Riker said. "We might not even need her. Only time will tell."

Keane screwed the cap back on the flask and slipped it into his coat pocket. "I don't even know why you think he's out here. It's a long way to travel with an awful lot of men just on a feeling."

Riker grabbed his aching right shoulder. "Because he was seen heading into the Flatheads and no one has seen him anywhere else since. I've spent a small fortune sending telegrams to every town from here to California. No one has even heard a rumor that he's there. Now that the snows have started, he'll be coming off the mountain. He won't dare go back to Helena, so he's bound to be somewhere near Missoula. Halstead's always been a town man. He won't be able to last long in the mountains now that the weather's turned ugly."

"If he's still alive."

Riker rubbed his shoulder. "He's still alive. I'd know it if he wasn't. He's tougher to kill than you think. I ought to know."

Keane's frown showed he was not convinced. Riker did not usually care what men thought of him, but a one-armed man had to work even harder to prove himself, so he added, "I'm not the only one who thinks Halstead is in Missoula. Mackey thinks so, too."

"Mackey?" Keane and his gang had a reputation for ruthlessness. It was what had brought them to Valhalla in the first place, but the mere mention of Aaron Mackey was enough to give even the hardest man pause. "You didn't say anything about him being part of this."

"He's not," Riker assured him, "but my people at the railroad tell me he's sent a deputy to Missoula. I think he's sent him to bring Halstead back home."

Keane continued to look worried. "Not Billy Sunday."

"No. Halstead's friend Joshua Sandborne. I wouldn't have thought anything of it if he'd sent anyone else, but I don't think he'd send Sandborne on a lark. Mackey either knows where Halstead is or he thinks he's somewhere near Missoula. It's a good enough reason for us to go looking for him. We'll stay on his back trail while he does all the work. I intend on being there when he finds him."

Keane tossed his thumb behind his right shoulder. "You've got men, horses, and provisions back there right now ready to ride into a blizzard on your say so. And you're telling me the best you've got is a guess?"

"They're riding back there for the same reason why you're up here with me," Riker reminded him. "I'm paying you good money to do it."

Keane took out the flask and poured some whiskey in his coffee. "Won't do us much good if we freeze to death first."

Riker looked out the window as the train raced through the white countryside. He knew there were worse things than death. And he had his hate to keep him warm.

Chapter 7

McAlister pointed out the side door to him before he went into The Town Hall through the front entrance of the saloon.

Halstead went inside and found a large, bald Chinese man with no eyebrows waiting just inside the doorway. McAlister had not been exaggerating. He was at least half a foot taller than Halstead and was wide enough to fill the narrow hall.

Halstead said, "Miss Glenda sent for me. My name is Halstead."

Halstead remained where he was while the giant went to knock on a door at the end of the hall. He opened it and nodded in Halstead's direction.

"Let him in, Joe," a lady's voice sang out. "I've been expecting him."

The large man stood aside and beckoned Halstead to approach. He pulled the door behind him as he walked back down the hall to the saloon.

Halstead found himself in a large dressing room with gowns and costumes of bright colors draped across every piece of furniture.

Glenda Younger was sitting at a mirrored table as she patted powder on her face with a soft brush. Her features were much softer than she had appeared in the photograph he had found among the dead trapper's belongings. Her skin was pale and white to the point of almost glowing. She had high cheekbones and long red hair swept high, held in place by several pins. Her neck was long and inviting, and her robe did little to hide the alluring curves beneath it.

Her green eyes sparkled as she smiled at Halstead's reflection in her mirror. "There you are," she said in passable Spanish. "A pleasure to meet you. Forgive me for not shaking hands, but my performance starts in a few minutes."

He replied in English. "Your Spanish is very good, Miss Glenda."

"You can drop the 'Miss,' " she told him. "I ran a show in Mexico City for more than a year. I not only fell in love with the place but the language as well. I try to speak it whenever I can, just to keep in practice. Not too many people around here speak Spanish, so I'm sorry if I'm a bit rusty."

"Mine is just as rusty as yours." He could see why men prized her picture. She was as charming as she was beautiful, but not enough to make him forget why he was there. "Lance McAlister said you wanted to see me."

She offered a pout he was sure had melted the hearts of many men over the years. "Business so soon, Jeremiah? You should relax. Have a drink while I get ready. I was hoping we might be able to get to know each other after my show. It won't be long."

But with a price on his head, Halstead did not want to remain in one place for so long. "I like to know why I'm doing something before I do it. I can come back later if you want."

"I've always admired direct men." She undid the pins holding up her hair and allowed it to flow down around her shoulders. She picked up a brush and began to comb it in long strokes. "Tell me, did you know you would be wanted for murder when you shot those men at that train station in Wellspring? I'm always curious about such things."

"Let's just say I knew what I did and why I did it. That's why I want to know why I'm here now."

She hummed a tune to herself as she ran the brush through her hair. "Do you enjoy being a wanted man? I imagine it's quite romantic."

"There's nothing romantic about almost freezing to death. Or about having a price on my head."

She looked at his reflection as she combed her hair. "You seem to be handling it well, though I'm afraid that beard doesn't suit you at all. I prefer a clean-shaven man. Be sure to stop by the barbershop when you leave here. Sam Rivers runs the place. Tell him I sent you. He'll get rid of that pelt you're wearing for you free of charge. Sam's a darling that way."

"No need for that. I don't plan on being in town long enough to keep up with shaving. As soon as the weather clears, I'll be on my way."

She stopped combing. "Where will you go?"

"Somewhere no one's looking for me," Halstead said. "That leaves anywhere but Montana."

She resumed combing her hair. "I guess you plan on staying away until they quit looking for you, is that it?"

Halstead wished it was that easy. "They won't quit until someone tells them to quit."

"Maybe someone could arrange that. Someone like me, for instance."

Halstead might have left if he'd had somewhere else to be. But it was warm in her dressing room, and Glenda was beginning to become interesting. "The only one who could do that is the governor of Montana. And if he was willing to do that, this would've ended weeks ago. My boss works just down the hall from him."

"I doubt Aaron Mackey knows him as well as I do. I got to know him in far more informal conditions."

Halstead understood her meaning and felt himself begin to blush. "Is that so?"

"I'll be more than happy to write to him on your behalf this very day if you'd like. I'll tell him to end all this wanted nonsense immediately if he ever hopes to enjoy my company again.

He'll listen, too. He's always been one of my most ardent admirers."

She laughed as she turned to look at him, not his reflection. "My, look at you blush." Her eyes glistened. "I can be a lot more persuasive than the marshal. Don't you think?"

"I'm sure you could. The question is why you'd want to do that for me."

"I have my reasons. A woman always does."

"Since it concerns me, I'd like to know what they are."

She began combing the other side of her hair. "Because I've got a lot of friends like the governor, but I won't have them for much longer. Time waits for no man and it's even more impatient with us women." She swept her brush above the jars of powder and face paint lined up in front of her mirror. "When I first started in the business, I only had one jar of rouge to give my cheeks a bit of color. I could stay up all night and most of the morning and get myself ready for a show in no time at all. Now, it takes all this just to make me presentable to all those charming faces you saw out there. They don't seem to appreciate the effort, but I do. I can't expect to be a showgirl forever and, with your help, I won't have to."

Halstead moved aside one of her gowns and sat down in a plush chair. "I don't know anything about being an entertainer. I can't even remember the last time I saw a show."

She set her comb on the dresser. "If you do things my way, you won't have to."

Halstead closed his eyes. He had heard this kind of story before. He had seen what ambition did to people. "Let me guess. You've got some money squirreled away and you're going to make a big name for yourself. Have your name on a town somewhere so you can run it and everyone who lives there like it's your own personal kingdom."

"A town? What would I want with a whole town? I like traveling way too much to be cooped up in one place for very long. They don't put your name on a building or a street until after you're dead, and I intend on living for quite a while yet. I'm talking about you and me doing something a lot more fun than owning a patch of dirt way out in the middle of nowhere. Maybe a traveling show of my own. Glamorous Glenda and Her Glamour Girls. You could help me run it. A man of your renown could help bring investors. I might even make you part of the show if you wanted. People would pay a lot of money to see a man like you. Bill Cody has made a small fortune with that ratty old show of his. There's no reason why we can't do the same. Maybe even tour Europe. What do you think of it?"

"I wish you the best of luck with it. But I don't know what it's got to do with your reasons for helping me."

"Because you've got something all the money

in the world can't buy. You have a name. Fame. A reputation. That's invaluable in this business, and don't let all the powder and perfume you see here fool you, Jeremiah. This *is* a business."

"I'm sure it is. But it's not my business."

She offered a crooked smile. "Not yet, but it will be." She got up from her seat and whipped off her robe. He got an eyeful of her beauty before she stepped behind a dressing screen and began to pull down the undergarments strewn across the top of it.

She spoke to him as she began to get dressed. "Don't be modest, Jeremiah. Jason is mighty impressed with you and that's saying something. It takes a lot for a man to leave a mark on him. Jason's quite taken with himself. Big fish in small ponds usually are, I suppose."

Halstead was beginning to see things clearer. "So that's why he stopped by the café. He was testing me for you."

"Most of what he does is for me," she said from behind the screen. "He's got big dreams that go far beyond Barren Pines or Missoula. He thinks he might be governor someday. Maybe even a senator, though I think Sheriff Langham will beat him to it."

"Fremont's got the look for it. I wish the both of you luck."

"Luck." She laughed over the whispered rustle of fabric. "Smart people make their own luck by taking advantage of the opportunities they have. Do you think luck put a warrant out for your arrest? Do you think luck set you on the run or brought you to Barren Pines?"

"The worst kind of luck there is. Bad luck."

When she stepped out from behind the screen, she was wearing a flowing green dress that brought out the color of her eyes. It made her hair appear even redder than it already was. "Do I look Irish enough? The boys are always a sucker for Irish songs this time of day. I don't sing them at night because it only makes them melancholy and melancholy trappers are hard on the furniture."

"You look fine," he told her. "I'm sure you'll make every man who sees you forget about his troubles."

She raised her chin as she looked at her own reflection in the mirror. "What do you say, Jeremiah? Will you let me help you forget your troubles? We can talk about it later over supper if you'd like. My treat."

"Sounds nice, but I'm pretty sure Fremont wouldn't like that."

"Don't tell me you're afraid of that old braggart." She ran a hand over her neck. "He's not half the man I've heard you are."

Halstead had learned to never trust flattery, especially from a beautiful woman. "I've already had enough trouble for one day. I'll be spending most of my time in my room waiting for the snow to stop."

She picked up her comb and ran it through her hair a final time. "You'd find it much more comfortable in here with me."

"I'm sure I would." Halstead opened the door and stepped outside. "But my fiancée wouldn't like it, and I'd hate to disappoint her more than I already have."

"You really think you'll be seeing her again?" Her laugh was different this time. Not as musical, but flatter. She was laughing at him, not with him. "You've got a mighty bright outlook for a man in your situation, Jeremiah Halstead. Think it over and don't be hasty. I think we could do each other a world of good if we work together."

Halstead had heard that before. "The last time someone said that to me, I wound up in a cell for three years. But thanks for the thought. And good luck with the show. I'm sure they'll love it."

"You should stay and see it for yourself. I'm quite good, you know."

Halstead did not doubt her performance onstage would be even better than the one she had performed for him here in private. He did not know what she had been trying to do, but figured it had nothing to do with him joining her show. It probably had something to do with the price on his head. Five thousand dollars was a lot of money for a trapper. It was a lot of money for a showgirl, too.

He left by the side door and went back to his room at the livery, far from the limelight of Glenda's stage. Whatever she was planning, he wanted nothing to do with it.

Chapter 8

It was already well after dark by the time Joshua Sandborne rode his bay gelding into Missoula. He led a pack horse loaded with supplies close behind. His train had been due to arrive earlier that morning, but it had taken the crew and several passengers to clear a small avalanche of snow from the tracks. He had hated the delay it had caused but welcomed the distraction of hard labor to take his mind off Halstead's plight for a while.

Sandborne had spent most of the long ride from Helena worried about his friend, wondering if he was still alive. Wondering if he would be able to find him in the expansive wilderness surrounding Missoula.

Sandborne was not sure he wanted to find him at all. Except for Aaron Mackey and Billy Sunday, Jeremiah Halstead was the toughest man Sandborne had ever known. But he knew time alone on the run through rough country and brutal weather could change a man forever. Halstead had already endured quite a bit in his young life, but even the toughest men could be broken. He hoped he could reach his friend in time to pull him back from the brink of his limits.

Sandborne was glad he had worn his heaviest

coat to brace him against the cruel winter gale that struck him as he steered his horses around wagons filled with passengers and goods from the train. He had not known what to expect from Missoula but was glad to see the place had a sense of permanence to it. Gas lamps cast a flickering light on the townsfolk and visitors who braved a frigid night as they quickly walked along the boardwalks of the thoroughfare.

The Missoula Hotel was a large building in the center of town with a bustling saloon right beside it. A sign in front of the hotel promised an attended livery for all guests at all hours of the day and night. It looked like an expensive place, but as Sandborne would be spending most of his nights outdoors, he figured Mackey would not raise an eyebrow at the cost for one night. He was less concerned about his own comfort than he was about his horses. Grant, the name he had chosen for the bay gelding, had not enjoyed his train ride and could use tending to before they began their search for Halstead the next morning.

After passing off his animals to the attendant in the livery, Sandborne went into the hotel to see about a room. The clerk at the desk barely looked up from his register when Sandborne approached.

"Name?" the clerk asked as he opened the guest book and prepared to write.

"Joshua Sandborne, Deputy U.S. Marshal out of Helena."

The clerk wrote it down as a man slowly rose from one of the several overstuffed chairs arranged throughout the lobby. "Deputy, did you say?"

Sandborne turned to see a lanky man whose thin face seemed too small for the rest of his long, wide body. He had a full brown beard that only bore a few stray gray hairs. The star pinned to the lapel of his coat said he was the sheriff. "That's right. Who are you?"

"Sheriff Henry Langham." The two law men shook hands. "I'm the sheriff here in Missoula and of the entire county, too. I had heard Marshal Mackey was sending one of his men here to Missoula, but I wasn't expecting the famous Joshua Sandborne to grace us with his presence."

Sandborne had learned to never trust compliments from strangers. Just because folks knew about him and Halstead did not mean he was famous. "I hope I won't have to trouble you much while I'm here. I'll be riding out first thing in the morning."

"You won't be any trouble at all," Langham said. "In fact, that's why I'm here. I wanted to offer my help."

Sandborne had expected a bounty hunter or two to be on the hunt for Halstead. He had not counted on having to worry about a sheriff. "Be careful what you wish for, sheriff. You don't know why I'm here."

"Why, to bring Halstead in, of course." Langham tucked his thumbs into his vest pockets. "Can't be any other reason. First, Halstead's wanted flyers show up. Now, you're here. That's a mighty big coincidence."

Sandborne would not tell this man anything until he knew him better. And, from what he saw, he seemed to be eager to jump to his own conclusions. "Lots of wanted men in Montana besides Halstead." He knew he risked saying too much if he kept talking. "I don't mean to cut this short, but I've had a long day and the promise of an even longer one ahead of me tomorrow."

Langham leaned against the desk. "I imagine you do. And if you'll just give me a few moments of your precious time, I'd like you to listen to what I have to say. You may find it interesting."

Sandborne wished the clerk would hurry up and give him the key to his room. "The only thing I'm interested in is a bed and some sleep. We can talk some other time."

But Langham continued. "I hate to insist, but I was hoping you and I could reach something of an understanding while you're here. It won't take long. You have my word."

Sandborne could remember a time not too long ago when he might have been eager to have a stranger like Langham think well of him. But time spent with Mackey had taught him to regard people carefully, especially when they were trying hard to make a point. Billy had taught him that not every smile was friendly and a bullet or a punch often followed. And Halstead had shown him that few people ever helped a law man purely out of kindness. The most complicated questions were often the shortest. "Why should I?"

Langham shrugged. "Call it professional courtesy."

"Professional courtesy would be you letting me get some sleep."

"Five minutes is all I ask of you," Langham pressed. "You'll find that it pertains to the reason for your journey here."

Sandborne made a mental note to add "pertains" to his list of words. He kept track of new words that interested him and made sure to look them up in the new dictionary Katherine Mackey had been kind enough to give him for Christmas the previous week.

Sandborne knew Mackey or Halstead might have been able to get away with offending a sheriff, but they were not there. He was on his own and all alone. He might need Langham's help while in the county. Offending him now could prove expensive later. "I'll join you as soon as I get the key to my room."

As if on cue, the clerk produced a key immediately. "It's at the top of the stairs and to the left. Our finest room, save for the Missoula

Suite, which is currently occupied by a most esteemed guest."

Sandborne took the key. He did not care how esteemed they were. He just hoped they were quiet.

Langham crowded Sandborne to one of the sofas and sat down across from him. "What do you make of our fair city so far, deputy? I know it's a far cry from Helena, but we're making progress."

Sandborne was not used to such a soft couch and felt as though the cushions might swallow him whole. He moved himself to sit on the edge of it instead. "Not much to see considering it's going on midnight."

Langham forced a laugh. "Well, of course, but whether you can see it or not, Missoula is a town on the rise. I've been in my share of boom towns in my time, but there's a sense of permanence around here the likes of which I've never seen. Never even heard of, actually. Why, we've got ourselves a logging operation that rivals any in the state, and I'm confident that it'll only improve in the years ahead."

"I'm sure it's a fine place." Sandborne did not bother to hide the yawn that rose within him. "What's any of this got to do with me?"

Langham remained focused on what he had to say. "A town needs more than just a thriving industry to become an important place these

106

days, deputy. People from back east are always looking for new places to invest. They expect towns like ours to have a certain patina to them. A rustic quality. A certain charm."

Sandborne would remember to look up "patina," too, if Langham ever let him get to bed. "Patina?"

"A certain flair if you will. Missoula's a fine town, but it's a hardworking place filled with good, hardworking people. What it lacks is character. Not character in terms of civic duty or decency, of course, but the kind of aspect people back east look for in places such as this."

Sandborne felt his eyes begin to close. "I wish you the best of luck in finding it. Now, if you'll excuse me . . ."

He began to get up, but Langham gestured for him to wait. "I can see you're tired, so I'll get right to the point. We don't have many men like you come through town, deputy. At least not to stay for any length of time. That's what I wanted to talk to you about. I know you've come to hunt down Jeremiah Halstead and bring him to justice."

Sandborne knew he had to be careful. Langham was a smooth talker. A politician who used words like Halstead used his Colts. "You don't know why I'm here because I haven't told you yet. And I'm not going to, either, because it's none of your business. If it was, I'd ask for your help."

"Joshua Sandborne ask for help?" Langham waved off the notion. "I wouldn't expect a man of your renown and reputation to ask a lowly county sheriff for help at all, except maybe for the use of our jail to house a prisoner." He moved to the edge of his sofa. "That's why I'm asking you for a favor. Not just for me, but for the town and for yourself, as well. I'm asking you to bring me with you when you ride out after Halstead tomorrow."

Sandborne was not used to speaking to his elders in a disrespectful manner, but Langham was beginning to make it easy. "I never said I was looking for Jeremiah."

"You didn't have to," Langham explained, "and I don't expect you to say it now. But any man with two good eyes can read a map. I've heard how he fled up into the Flatheads after escaping Helena. With the weather being as bad as it's been, he's got no choice but to come down from there eventually. Your being here tells me you and Mackey think he might be close by. I happen to think you're right, not that my opinion counts for much with you."

"You're right. It doesn't." This time, Sandborne did not let the sheriff stop him as he stood up. "And since we've got nothing to talk about, I'm going to bed."

Langham stepped in front of him and lowered his voice. "Not everyone thinks Halstead *escaped* into the Flatheads, deputy. There's some nasty talk going around that he had provisions waiting for him when he ran out of Helena. That means someone knew about the warrant and helped him get away. People have too much respect for Aaron Mackey to say he cut his friend a break, but there's been talk of it. Whispers, you might say. Whispers that could grow into shouts if we don't try to stop them."

Sandborne was beginning to grow annoyed. "The marshal has never cared what people say about him, Langham. And what they say behind his back, they rarely say to his face. Get out of my way."

Langham remained where he was. "You've got it all wrong, deputy. You're the one who's in my way. You're in my town's way. Hunting a fugitive like Halstead and bringing him in could bring a lot of attention to Missoula. Plenty of newspaper men from all over the country will be interested in what happens here over the next few days. Some have already begun to arrive here looking to cover it. I understand more are on the way. Seems we're not the only ones who can read a map. Reporters tend to grow bored when they're just sitting around waiting for a story to break, and I'd hate to see them write about those nasty rumors about Mackey helping his friend flee from justice."

"I'm sure you would."

Langham continued. "I think a story about Sandborne and his posse braving the elements to bring the Butcher of Battle Brook to justice would be better for everyone. Attention like that would be good for Missoula."

Sandborne felt his neck begin to redden. "Good for you, too."

"Good for all of us," Langham said. "I imagine a picture of you and me and my men leading Halstead into my jail could make us all famous. I know you're going to get him eventually. All I'm asking is a chance to be with you when you do."

Sandborne looked the man over. He had never met him before but knew the type. "You're a scavenger. Just an old buzzard circling around waiting for something to die so you can feed on it."

Langham hooked his thumbs in the pockets of his vest again. "We all feed on death and despair, Sandborne. I'm not asking you to let me in out of the goodness of your heart. There'll be plenty of money in it for all of us."

There it was. It always came down to money. "We're not eligible for that reward, Langham."

"True, but newspaper men aren't shy about paying for a good story, especially if it's an exclusive. I know how much Mackey pays you as a deputy. You could make more than a year's salary just by giving a reporter a few minutes of your time when it's all over with."

Sandborne decided the less he said to Langham, the better for all concerned, especially Jeremiah. "You'd best step aside."

"And you'd best listen to reason," Langham said. "You can either take me and my men with you, or we can follow your back trail wherever you go. Me and my boys know this country a lot better than you and we'll have no trouble keeping up with you."

Sandborne had never thought of himself as having a temper, but Langham was testing the limits of his patience. "Don't let my lack of gray hair fool you, sheriff. I'm not so easy to track."

"Everyone's easy to track in the snow, son," Langham said. "There'll be five of us riding behind you. I'd prefer it if we were riding with you. None of us wishes you or Halstead any harm. And if you let us ride with you, we'll do everything your way. If we're on our own, we'll have to do it my way, and I can't speak to what'll happen if we do. People could get hurt. Halstead. Maybe even you."

Sandborne made a point of keeping his hands flat against his sides. "I'm even harder to kill than I am to track."

"I know you are. I heard about what happened to you back in Battle Brook before Halstead brought you back. You deserve a lot of credit for healing as quickly as you did. I'm not looking to fight you, son. I'm just asking for you not to fight me. There's glory to be had here. If you don't want it, that's fine, but I'd like a piece of it. It'll cost you and Halstead nothing. That's all."

Langham finally stepped aside, moving out of Sandborne's way. "The choice is yours."

Sandborne wanted to go to his room and go to sleep. He hoped he could forget about his encounter with Langham by morning and go about finding Jeremiah on his own.

But he knew it would not be that easy. He could not wish away a problem like this. And with neither Mackey nor Billy nor Halstead there to give him advice, he would have to decide on his own. Since he could not stop Langham and his men from following him, he decided it was better if he kept them close so he could watch them. It would also be good to have someone with him who knew the land and its people.

"I'll be riding out after first light."

"Me and my men will be ready," Langham assured him.

"How many men will you be bringing with you?"

Langham looked happy enough to burst. "Five deputies. They've been with me on rides like this many times before. You won't have to worry about them."

Six-to-one were miserable odds. "You'll bring two."

Langham looked like he might argue but did

not. "Fine. I'll bring my two best men." He held out his hand to Sandborne. "You won't regret this, deputy. I can promise you that. Tomorrow, after you swear us in, we'll be . . ."

Sandborne pushed the sheriff's hand aside as he moved past him toward the stairs. "There'll be no ceremony and no swearing in. You'd better not expect a dime from the marshal, either, because you're all volunteers. Any man who can't keep up is on his own. I'm not slowing down for anyone. And if we find Jeremiah, you do what I say. You won't like what happens if you go against me."

Langham called after him as Sandborne climbed the stairs. "You can count on us, deputy. We'll be ready to hit the trail first thing in the morning."

As Sandborne went up to his room, he wondered if Langham had said that last part for his benefit or so someone else might hear him. He decided it did not matter. He could not remember the last time he had felt so tired as he rounded the final landing up to his room.

But when he saw a man's shadow fall upon the stairs from above, Sandborne drew his pistol from his hip. He rounded the corner slowly as he aimed the revolver up the stairs.

A broad man in a bowler hat raised his hands and backed away. "You Joshua Sandborne?"

Sandborne remained on the landing as he kept the pistol on the stranger. "Who's asking?"

113

"My boss is asking," the man told him. "He wants to see you." He nodded to his left. "He's just down the hall from your room."

Sandborne remembered the clerk had said something about an esteemed guest staying on the same floor as him. "Who is he?"

"A man you may have heard of before." The man was smart enough to keep his hands up where Sandborne could see him. "Frazer Rice."

Sandborne's aim did not falter even though the name meant a great deal to him. "That rich fella from back east? The railroad man?"

"The very same. Can I lower my hands now?"

Sandborne kept his pistol on him as he began to climb the last few stairs to the top. "Drop those hands and I'll drop you. Back up."

The man kept them raised, only for Sandborne to see another man down the hall to the right. He, too, had his hands in the air.

The man with the derby said, "No one wants to hurt you, deputy. We're just doing what we're told."

Sandborne gestured to the man down the hall. "Open it and move away from the door."

The second man did as he was told. "You're a bit young to be this jumpy, aren't you?"

"I won't be getting any older if I'm not careful." He told the derby man to move down with his friend, which he did.

A booming voice from inside the suite called

out, "Leave him be, boys. He's got a right to be cautious. He wasn't expecting us."

With the two men crowded at the end of the hall, Sandborne stole a quick look inside the room. A man he recognized as Mr. Rice sat at a table with a silver tea set on it.

He remembered seeing the millionaire at this distance back in Dover Station when Rice had spent a lot of money building up the town. His once-silver muttonchops were white now, and the wire spectacles pinched at the end of his nose made him look like an old man. The blanket across his lap and the cane propped up against the table did not make him look any younger, even if the cane sported a silver handle.

"Come in and shut the door, deputy. As you can see, you're quite safe. No one will harm you unless you find harm in enlightenment, as some men do in this part of the world."

Sandborne slid the pistol back in its holster and closed the door. He would make a point of looking up "enlightenment," too, before he went to bed, though it looked like sleep would have to wait a bit longer than he had planned.

Mr. Rice gestured to the gleaming pot and cups on the table at his elbow. "Do you like tea, deputy?"

Sandborne had never known much about finery, but he would have wagered all that silver was probably worth more than he could make in ten years working for the marshal. "Never had much of a taste for it."

"Neither did I." Mr. Rice's face grew sour. "I still don't. I was always more of a coffee man myself, but my doctors won't let me have it anymore. I'm not inclined to being told what to do, but given how much they charge me, I'd be a fool not to listen to them. I've been relegated to drinking tea each night. It's the only thing that helps me sleep these days. That is if you call staring at the ceiling until I lose consciousness sleep."

Sandborne did not know what to call it, so he held his tongue. He also did not know if he should sit in the empty chair across from Mr. Rice, so he remained standing by the door. It was not always easy to know what to do around men like Mr. Rice.

The older man seemed to understand Sandborne's predicament and gestured to a chair. "You'd better sit down before you drop. I imagine you must be anxious to sleep. I understand removing the snow off the track must've been quite an ordeal."

Sandborne sat in the chair and tried not to look around the fancy room. "How'd you hear about that, sir?"

Mr. Rice smiled. "I own the railroad, son."

Sandborne felt himself blush. He had forgotten that.

Mr. Rice pushed aside his cup and saucer. "My men out there tell me Sheriff Langham got your ear just now in the lobby. What was that imbecile babbling about?"

Sandborne saw no reason to keep it a secret. "He thinks I'm here to hunt down Jeremiah Halstead. He wants to lead a posse with me to find him."

Mr. Rice looked at him above his spectacles. "And will you allow them to come with you?"

"Can't see how I could stop them," Sandborne admitted. "At least I can keep an eye on them if they're right next to me."

"A wise move. Like the man said, 'Keep your friends close but your enemies closer.' It's a sound strategy, provided a man doesn't have many enemies. Is that why you're here? To hunt Halstead down?"

Sandborne shifted in his chair. He supposed a man as important as Mr. Rice had a right to know such things. "The marshal sent me to look for him. That's different than hunting him."

"I'm glad you appreciate the difference. What do you plan on doing if you find him?"

Sandborne had given that considerable thought on the train. "Help patch him up if he needs it. Bring him here and wire the marshal back in Helena. Figure I'll do whatever the marshal tells me to do after that."

"And do you think you can do it, deputy?" Mr.

Rice asked. "Find Halstead, I mean. Bring him here without incident."

Sandborne sat straighter in the chair. "If he's out here, I'll find him, sir."

"Good. That's what I wanted to hear." Mr. Rice took off his spectacles and tossed them on the table. "I remember you were with Mackey after the siege at Dover Station. Had your head bandaged some."

Sandborne had not thought he had made such an impression. There was no reason for a man as important as Mr. Rice to remember a boy like him, especially back then. "You have a good memory, sir."

Mr. Rice grunted. "Sometimes too good for my own good. When you reach my age, you'll realize there are some things you'll wish you could forget. But my time in Dover Station isn't one of them. I'm just sorry my plans failed to work out as I had hoped. Have you been back there since it burned?"

Sandborne had not. "Not much left of the old place to see. I heard they've changed the name, though."

"Yes. To 'Clayborn.'" Mr. Rice frowned. "No idea where they got that name from. Ah well, as Burns wrote, 'The best laid plans of mice and men' and all that."

Sandborne did not know anyone named Burns but he had heard that phrase before. "Yes, sir."

Mr. Rice's eyes narrowed. "I hope you won't take offense when I say I'm sure many people make the mistake of underestimating you."

"I guess it's on account of me being young. I guess young folks aren't supposed to know as much as our elders."

"Age should never be mistaken for wisdom just as youth should never be written off as folly. You and Halstead are about the same age, aren't you? Mid-twenties, I'd say."

"I'm twenty-four," Sandborne said. "Jeremiah's a bit older."

"A good age. I was your age when I joined my father's business. It was just a small concern back then. Ferries back and forth through New York Harbor, a small freight company on land, but I saw great promise in it. I've always had a knack for seeing the promise in things. In people, too. That's why I know you're a good man, Joshua Sandborne, just like I know Halstead's a good man, as well."

"He'd be pleased to hear you thought so, sir." Though Sandborne had never known Jeremiah to care much about what people thought of him. He was like Mackey and Billy in that regard.

Mr. Rice continued. "I know your friend is in a bad way with these murder charges hanging over his head. How do you think he's holding up under the strain?"

"I won't know that for certain until I find him,"

Sandborne admitted, "but if he's still alive, he's doing fine. He's been in tough spots before and has always come through."

"He certainly has," Mr. Rice said. "He's resourceful, which is why I've asked you in here tonight. I was hoping you might be willing to do something for me. For Halstead, too, if you find him."

Sandborne grew cautious. First Langham, now Mr. Rice. "I'll be glad to help if I can, as long as Jeremiah or Aaron don't mind."

"Halstead's career as a law man is over," Mr. Rice stated. "Even if he's acquitted of these charges, he'll always have a mark against his name. Word about his earlier incarceration in El Paso is bound to get out and he'll have a tough time getting people to forget that. Having a convict as a deputy might've been fine when this was just a territory, but now that it's a state, I'm sure people will expect an air of respectability in their law men."

"Jeremiah's the most respectable man I know." Sandborne had not intended his words to have such an edge, but he did not apologize for them.

"Point taken. But even if Halstead can't remain a federal law man, his skills are still in high demand. That's why, when you find him, I want you to tell him I intend to help him."

"How?"

"By getting the charges against him dropped

and by offering him a job with my railroad. He'd be working directly for me."

"That's mighty generous of you, sir."

"Generosity has nothing to do with it. He'll need a job, and I need a man like him. My railroad is still growing, and I need good men who know how to get things done. Men who know how to handle problems before they arise and after. I have too many lawyers and accountants who are always looking to boil down a problem to words and figures. I need a deliberate man who isn't afraid to get his hands dirty from time to time. I believe Jeremiah Halstead to be such a man. What do you think he'd say to such a proposal?"

Sandborne imagined he knew Jeremiah better than almost anyone alive, but he had no idea how Halstead might take such an offer. "I don't pretend to speak for him, but I imagine he'd want to know why you'd go through all that trouble for him. I'd think a man like you would have the pick of the litter as far as talent goes."

Mr. Rice nodded. "A fair question. I have a vested interest in Montana and a personal interest in seeing Aaron Mackey thrive. Montana needs men like him and he can't do his job if one of his best men is being sought for murder. I want to make this burden go away for him if I can. I think everyone's interests will be best served if Halstead comes to work for me."

Sandborne did not know how to deal with

the likes of Mr. Rice, but he knew a chance to bargain when he saw one. "Jeremiah would be more inclined to take the offer if he didn't have a gun to his head. Getting rid of those charges would go a long way to him looking kindly upon your offer."

Mr. Rice surprised Sandborne by cutting loose with a sharp laugh. "That's the spirit, young man! Negotiate and bargain. It's always best to get while the getting is good."

Sandborne suppressed a yawn. "Just answering how I figured Jeremiah would, sir."

Mr. Rice drummed his fingers on the arm of his chair. "You said you and Langham will be leaving after Halstead at first light?"

"That's the plan."

"Good. I'll plan on you being back within a week. I'll get things in motion with the governor. I hope to have a favorable resolution for you by then. How does that sound?"

"Sounds fine to me, sir. Now, if you'll excuse me, morning's coming quicker than I'd like, so I'd best get some sleep."

Mr. Rice looked several years younger than when Sandborne had first entered the suite. "This has been an enlightening conversation, deputy. Thank you for the pleasure of your company and for showing this old swindler a thing or two."

Sandborne left, unsure about who had swindled whom.

Chapter 9

Halstead knew it had to be a nightmare.

The fastest train in the country could not have returned him to El Paso from Montana so quickly. But there he was, back on the broken floor of the same cell where he had spent almost three years of his life. The darkness forbade him from seeing it, but the smells were the same. The humid stench of his own waste in the bucket by the door. Bits of uneaten food allowed to rot for days on end. The sounds of the mice scurrying along the base of the wall. The feeling of roaches crawling across his bare feet.

He was alone once more. Forgotten. Forsaken. Trapped.

He refused to allow himself to panic now, just as he had refused to let fear take hold back then. He had trained himself to not feel anything to survive. Expectation and hope had broken more men than beatings or empty bellies. He had retreated deep within himself to a place where neither the warden nor the guards nor even the vermin could reach. A refuge so small and dark that not even the endless monotony of prison could crush it.

But sweat broke out across his body as he heard a great rumble begin all around him. A force so great that it threatened to shake him to pieces. He felt himself begin to slide across the floor and did his best to make it stop, but his bare feet failed to find any purchase on the floor.

He spread out his arms and cried out when he was able to touch both walls. His cell was tiny, but wider than that. He realized the walls were beginning to close in around him. His feet brushed against the door of his cell and his hair was flattened by the wall behind his head.

Then everything stopped. Blessed silence made him hope the horror had passed. He was cramped, but alive.

Another rumble, greater than the first, was followed by his hands scraping along the walls as the floor began to rise at great speed. The friction burned the tips of his fingers. He cried out as the ceiling dropped toward him. The air rushed out of his lungs as Zimmerman's piercing cackle filled his ears. His nose flattened against the ceiling, and he knew his end had finally come.

Halstead screamed as he threw his arms over his face, only to find himself back on the straw mattress in Moses Armand's loft. The walls were no longer closing in, and the wooden ceiling remained high above him. He sat up and felt his damp shirt clinging to him.

His nightmares often involved being back in his cell, but they had never been like this. The darkness had never closed in on him before. His mother had once told him that dreams were a

124

window to a man's soul. He hoped for the sake of his sanity that was not true.

He heard an argument coming from in the livery and thought it might be a remnant of his dream. But when he heard more voices enter the mix, he realized that it was real. Moses was probably having a dispute with some of his coffee buddies. It was best to stay out of it.

But when he heard "Halstead" among the rising shouts from below, he knew that would not be possible.

He found his pants in the darkness and pulled them on, followed by his boots. He slipped into his gun rig and strapped on his belt before slowly taking the stairs down to the livery. The steps cracked and popped during his descent.

He saw Moses Armand sitting on a bale of hay by the stables as a group of men carrying torches stood at the entrance. Sheriff Fremont had a hand on the liveryman's shoulder as Moses appeared to sob into his hands.

"What's going on here?" Halstead asked when he reached the bottom of the stairs.

The arguments stopped as Fremont turned and went for the pistol on his hip.

Halstead drew the Colt from his belly holster before the sheriff cleared leather. "We've already settled that, Fremont. Don't do anything stupid."

The men with the torches stepped backward into the street.

"What's going on?" Halstead asked again.

"As if you didn't know," Fremont sneered.

"If I knew, I wouldn't be asking." His point made, Halstead lowered his Colt to his side. "What's wrong with Moses?"

Fremont stepped away from the sobbing man. "You honestly expect me to believe you have no idea why we're here. That you don't already know Dave Armand is dead."

Now Halstead understood why Moses was weeping. "I don't care what you believe, Fremont. If he's dead, I had nothing to do with it."

Moses lifted his head from his hands. "I already told you that, Jason. The kid's been up there sleeping all day. He didn't even come down to get supper."

"You don't know that for sure." Fremont kept his eyes on Halstead. "You were in your room when it happened. He could've easily slipped over to the store and killed Dave without you hearing him."

"Not unless he flew." Moses used the heels of his palms to wipe the tears from his eyes. "You heard him coming down those stairs just now. My hearing ain't as bad as being able to miss that racket, even with my door closed. And if I hadn't heard him come down, I sure would've heard him go back up again."

Fremont kept his hand on his pistol. "Don't sell him short, Moses. He's a slippery one."

Halstead could see Fremont was trying to work himself up to something, so he tried to remain calm. "I haven't been anywhere near that store since this morning. I haven't even been on that side of the street."

"That's a lie," one of the torchbearers said. "I saw you leaving Town Hall right around lunchtime."

Halstead realized his mistake. "And I came right back here when I left. Moses saw me when I did. I've got no reason to kill Dave or anyone else in town."

"You held a gun on him this morning," Fremont said loud enough for the men to hear him. "Don't go denying it now."

"Because he pulled a shotgun on me," Halstead said. "But he was alive when I left him. You know he was. You talked to him before you came to see me in Millie's."

Fremont grew still. "I knew I should've locked you up when I had the chance. We'll get this straightened out down at the jail. Let's go."

Moses rose from the bale of hay and got between them. "Don't be a fool, Jason. That boy could bury one between your eyes any time he wants." He spoke to the men with torches in the street. "The same goes for the rest of you. Back away from here before one of you gets yourself killed." He looked at Halstead with red eyes. "But Fremont's right about one thing, isn't he? You *are* Jeremiah Halstead, ain't you?"

"Yeah. I am."

A murmur went through the torch men as they backed even farther into the street.

Moses said, "We've had enough killing around here for one night. Jason, you let this boy be and get your hand away from that gun. Halstead, tuck that iron away and come with me. I want you with me when I see what happened to poor Dave."

Halstead waited until Fremont moved his hand from his pistol before sliding his Colt back into its holster.

Moses pushed through the men in the street as he trudged through the snow toward his brother's general store.

Fremont spoke to Halstead as they began to follow Moses. "I've got my eye on you, Halstead."

"Good. Maybe you'll learn something that way."

As the men with the torches broke apart and went elsewhere, Moses pushed in the door of his brother's store.

Halstead noticed the boardwalk had a new coating of snow. There was only one pair of footprints heading toward the store and away from it. Interesting.

Halstead stopped at the door and examined the splintered wood around the lock. The door had been forced in, but the glass had not been broken. There were no scuff marks on the door, either.

Fremont grew impatient behind him. "You plan on standing out here all night or are you done playing games?"

Halstead ignored him and moved inside as Fremont followed and closed the door.

Several lamps were already burning throughout the store as Fremont said, "You'll find Dave on the other side of that curtain, Moses. You'd best steady yourself because it's not a pretty sight."

Moses pushed both curtains aside, revealing Dave Armand's corpse flat on his back. His vacant eyes half-closed in fatal repose. A single bullet wound had scorched his apron above his heart. A fair amount of blood had pooled beneath the body. Halstead imagined Dave had died quickly. Recently, too, for the blood on the floor had not yet begun to harden.

Halstead knew that meant David Armand had been killed within the hour.

"He looks peaceful," Moses said as he took a knee beside his dead brother and rested his hand on his chest. "His body is still warm. How is that possible? I was tending to the horses before Fremont showed up. I should've heard the shot."

Fremont's voice was hard. "Don't blame yourself for another man's evil."

Halstead squatted beside the corpse and touched Dave's lifeless hand. Moses was right. It was still warm. Pliable, too. The stiffness that always accompanied death had not started.

He asked Fremont, "Who found him?"

"I did. I was making my nightly rounds, checking to make sure the shops were locked up tight. Can't be too careful now that we've got a certain element in town."

Halstead ignored the insult as Fremont continued. "When I saw the door looked like it had been busted in, I came inside to look around. That's when I found Dave just as he is now. Guess he must've surprised a robber and got killed for his trouble."

Moses lowered his head and began to quietly pray beside the body of his dead brother.

Halstead caught a familiar and unmistakable scent in the air. "Was anything taken?"

"I don't know," Fremont said. "I didn't have time to look around."

Halstead lowered Dave's hand to his side. "But you had enough time to round up those men and their torches."

Fremont was silent for a fraction of a second too long.

Halstead rose as he threw an elbow up into Fremont's jaw. The deputy reeled backward as Halstead followed up with a hard right hand that dropped Fremont to the floor.

Moses Armand stopped his prayer as he got to his feet. "What the hell are you doing?"

Halstead closed in on Fremont. "Taking care of your brother's killer."

Fremont cried out when Halstead pinned his right arm to the floor with his boot and bent to pull the sheriff's pistol from its holster.

Moses remained next to his brother. "You don't think Jason did this."

Halstead did not have to think. He knew. "There's only one set of footprints in the snow on the boardwalk and one set leaving here. There should've been two sets. One from Fremont and one from the killer. But there was only one. Fremont's."

Moses said, "It's been snowing all day, Jeremiah. That doesn't mean anything."

Halstead took Fremont's pistol by the barrel and held it out to Moses. "You know anything about guns?"

"I suppose I know enough. Why?"

He gestured for him to take the pistol. "Smell that and tell me what you find."

Moses awkwardly took the pistol with both hands and sniffed at the barrel before recoiling. "Smells like it's been fired."

"That's because it has." Halstead put more weight on Fremont's arm as the deputy struggled to pull his arm free. "I could smell the gunpowder in the air when I crouched next to Dave. Gunpowder and leather, the kind of smell you get when a hot barrel gets holstered too quickly. It was coming off Fremont."

Moses lowered the pistol. "That's not—"

But Halstead was not through. "The hole on Dave's apron is scorched from a powder burn. That's because his killer had his barrel flush against his chest when he shot him. That's why you didn't hear the shot. You know how cautious Dave was. You think he'd let some stranger get that close to him, especially if he thought he was being robbed?"

Fremont yelled, "Don't listen to him, Moses! He's the one who killed Dave. He's just covering up for himself by blaming it all on me."

Halstead kept the sheriff's arm pinned to the floor. "Check the cylinder for yourself, Moses. I'd wager he didn't take the time to get rid of the spent round."

Moses did what Halstead had said and dumped the bullets into his hand before slowly letting them spill to the floor. His expression said it all. "You're right. There's a spent round there."

Fremont screamed, "That doesn't mean anything!"

Halstead kicked aside Fremont's left arm and took him up by the collar. "Dave almost shot me this morning because he thought I was an outlaw. He never would've come out from the back without his shotgun if he heard someone breaking in here this time of night, would he Moses?"

The livery owner slumped against the counter. "No, I guess he wouldn't. He'd never let a stranger get that close to him, either."

Halstead pulled Fremont to his feet, pushed him against the wall, and held him there. "Why'd you do it, Fremont? Why'd you kill Dave?"

"I didn't kill anyone!" Fremont roared. "Don't listen to him, Moses. Are you gonna believe a wanted murderer over me?"

Moses ran his hands over his face. "I guess I am, Jason." He bent at the waist and placed his hands on his knees, trying to catch his breath. "Why'd you kill him? Why'd you kill my brother?"

Fremont struggled to get free, but Halstead twisted his arm behind him. "Guess he doesn't feel like answering questions. Don't worry. There'll be plenty of time to get the truth out of him later."

Moses slowly stood up and steadied himself against the counter. "What'll you do with him now?"

"I'll run him over to the jail and lock him inside while we get this mess straightened out. I'll come back here to help you with Dave when I'm through with him."

"No, you won't," Moses said. "I'll get some of the boys to help me move him. It'll be best if you stay with him over in the jail. There'll be no shortage of men looking to kill him for this. I'll be by to see you later when I'm able."

Halstead pulled Fremont's arm back behind him and kept a tight grip on his collar. "You give me any trouble and I'll break your arm."

He pulled open the door and forced Fremont outside.

He stopped when he saw a dozen or so men and women waiting in the snowy thoroughfare. The hammers and levers of their rifles being worked sounded like crickets on a summer evening.

"Hold it right there, Halstead." It was the same torch man who had spoken against him at the livery. "Let Fremont go before we cut you down."

With one hand, Halstead strengthened his grip on Fremont's arm while the other held him by the collar. "This man just murdered Dave Armand. Don't take my word for it. Ask his brother if you don't believe me."

Moses spoke to them from the doorway of his dead brother's store. "He's telling the truth, boys. Let him pass. Fremont killed my brother."

Their leader stepped forward, his rifle at his shoulder and aimed at Halstead. "I say we lock them both up. Send a rider down to Missoula in the morning. Let Sheriff Langham sort this out when he's able."

"Nobody'll be riding anywhere until this weather lifts," Moses said. "Not you or Halstead or anyone else. Best do as I told you. Halstead is an impatient man."

Halstead made a point of looking each man in the eye before he moved Fremont toward them. They had the looks of trappers and hunters. Stout men with hard eyes and blackened patches of skin they had lost to frostbite. Each one of them was a killer in his own right, but none of them had the look of a killer of men. None of them had the same look Halstead saw whenever he found himself in front of a mirror.

He pushed Fremont past the men in the street and moved along the boardwalk. Each rifle remained trained on him as he moved Fremont in front of him. He thought one of the men might shoot as he steered the deputy through the snowbound thoroughfare, but one by one, each man lowered his gun.

When they made it to the jail, Halstead pushed Fremont inside. It was a small, one-room structure with a desk in one corner and a small cell with iron bars bolted to the floor and ceiling in the opposite corner.

Halstead kept hold of his prisoner's arm as he stopped him next to the desk. "Where's the key to the cell?"

"Go to hell."

Halstead drove his boot hard into the back of Fremont's knee and forced him hard to the floor. He kept him there as he opened one of the drawers and found two keys on an iron ring.

Halstead kept firm hold on his arm as they got up and moved to the cell. Halstead opened it and threw him inside. Fremont rattled the door as soon as Halstead locked it.

"This is going to end bad for you, Halstead," Fremont seethed. "You're as much a prisoner here as I am. You just don't know it yet."

Halstead tossed the keys on the desk. "Take off your gun belt and drop it outside the bars. The belt for your trousers too."

Fremont sneered at him as he followed Halstead's orders. He dropped his gun belt through the bars, then his other belt. "You think I'm going to hang myself? Not a chance. I want to live to see what happens to you."

Halstead grabbed hold of the star pinned to Fremont's lapel and ripped it from his coat. "You're not fit to wear this anymore."

Fremont laughed as he sat on his cot. "And you think you are?"

Halstead examined the star before dropping it in the desk drawer. "Compared to you I am."

Chapter 10

It was still dark outside as Sandborne enjoyed a quick breakfast of coffee, biscuits, and bacon in the hotel dining room. When he had finished the last of his coffee, he went outside to get his horses from the livery out back.

He found Langham and three men waiting for him. Two of the strangers were ready to ride and had brought a separate pack horse loaded down with supplies that appeared to be enough to last three men for a week.

Both men looked capable. One was about forty and sported a thick red moustache but was otherwise clean-shaven. The other man was much larger with streaks of gray in his brown beard and appeared slightly older.

But Sandborne was not happy to see a third man among them. He wore a gray suit and a bowler hat with spectacles like those he had seen Mr. Rice wearing the previous evening. His bearhide coat was dark black and looked as warm as it was expensive.

Langham climbed down from the saddle to greet him. "Morning, deputy. As you can see, me and my men are ready to ride. Buster Stewart and Red Gumbert. Buster was a deputy in Wichita and Red was the acting sheriff in Cheyenne for several months. They're my best deputies, and you'll be glad to have them with us on the trail."

But Sandborne had not taken his eyes off the fourth man. "And what's that supposed to be?"

"That's Hy Vandenberg," Langham told him. "The star reporter of *The Missoula Memo*, one of our many local papers here in town. He'll be serving as our chronicler for our intrepid expedition. He won't be coming with us, of course, but he'd like a word with you before we leave."

"Chronicler? Looks like a reporter to me."

Buster and Red traded glances before looking away.

"That's exactly what he is," Langham said. "His editor thought it would be a good idea to talk to us so he could provide a firsthand account of our quest." Langham lowered his voice. "He's one of those friends we talked about last night. The kind of friend we'll need once all of this is over."

Vandenberg backed away as Sandborne approached him. "I was hoping you could tell me something about yourself, deputy. Like how you came to know Halstead. Maybe a bit about what happened to you back in Battle Brook. I'll just bet you have quite a story to tell."

Sandborne watched the reporter back up until he stumbled off the boardwalk and almost fell in the street. "Any stories I tell will be after I bring Jeremiah back here safe and sound. Anyone who gets in the way of that will answer to me. Now get going."

Langham stepped in, but Sandborne cut him off. "The same goes for you, Langham. I told you no reporters, and I meant it. Cross me again and it'll be me having a word with you. If you don't like it, you and your men can stay behind. You want to argue, I'll walk over to the station and wire Marshal Mackey, but you won't like what he says."

Langham's right eye twitched before he took a step back. "Fine, deputy. We'll do it your way. Your rules."

Sandborne pointed down at the reporter, who was just beginning to steady himself. "Stay in town, Vandenberg. I find you on our back trail, I'll put a bullet in you for your trouble. You can chronicle whatever you want when this is over."

He did not wait for a response as he walked away. "Be ready to ride in ten minutes, boys."

The hotel's liveryman saw Sandborne coming and stopped mucking out a stall to ready his horses. Sandborne wondered how Mackey might have handled the reporter. He probably would not have had to lay a hand on him. He just would have glared at the man until he realized he was not welcome.

No, Sandborne decided. He would not have had to do that much. Had Mackey been there, Langham would not have dared to defy him.

· · ·

Sandborne had enjoyed the two hours of silence since riding from Missoula. Langham had impressed him by showing surprising restraint. He did not think the sheriff would have been able to keep his mouth shut for such a length of time. The lack of conversation had allowed Sandborne to focus on reading the land and choosing their path through the snow.

Red was the first of the group to break the silence. "Mind if I ask you a question, Deputy Sandborne?"

He saw the path they had been following meandered for about half a mile or so straight ahead through open country. If they were going to speak, now was the time. "No need for titles, Red. Sandborne's good enough. What's your question?"

"What's Halstead really like? Is he as dangerous as I've heard?"

Sandborne might not have been skilled in the art of conversation, but even he knew better than to answer such an open-ended question. "I guess that would depend on what you've heard."

Red seemed eager to tell him. "That he's as good with them Peacemakers he totes as he is with a knife. That he can kill a man with one good punch, and his mustang rides like the wind even at night."

"Listen to you talk." Buster laughed. "You're

almost forty, Red. You're a might too old to blather on about him like you're some little kid, don't you think?"

"I never said I believed it," Red told him. "I'm just saying that's what I've heard. And worse, too. Since we're riding after him, I'd say we ought to know the sort of man he is." Red asked Sandborne, "Does he really scalp them? The men he kills, I mean. I heard he has their scalps tied to his saddle horn on account of him being half a savage and all."

Sandborne remembered back to when he was growing up on the JT Ranch in Dover Station. He remembered how the old-timers used to sit outside and pass the evening telling tall stories around the fire. The gray heads spoke of encounters they'd had with Bill Cody and Hickok and various Earp brothers. They debated which towns were wildest and had the prettiest women. They argued over which outlaws were the fiercest based on the stories they had heard and sometime read.

Sandborne had not seen any gray hairs the last time he'd looked at himself in the mirror, but here he was, riding with men asking about a legend he happened to know. It was funny how life could turn a man old before his time.

"I don't know where you heard all that," Sandborne said, "but you've got three different people rolled up into one. For one thing,

Jeremiah's not a half-breed. His father was white and his mother was Mexican. He might have some Indian blood in him from her, but he's neither Apache nor Comanche as some have said."

"How about them guns?" Red asked.

"Jeremiah doesn't carry a Peacemaker, much less two of them. Aaron uses one. Jeremiah favors Colts." For Jeremiah's sake, he decided the caliber and number he carried was none of his business.

Sandborne went on. "He's handy with a blade, uses his father's Bowie knife, but I don't recall him ever scalping a man either living or dead. It was Zimmerman who used to have scalps on his saddle. They had the desired effect, as they were enough to give a man pause before tangling with him."

This time, it was Buster who asked, "What about the way he fights?"

"I've seen him knock down plenty of men," Sandborne said. "In fact, I've never seen him lose a fight. But I've never seen him knock a man cold with one punch. He grabs hold of a man until he's down. He was raised at a mission for Indian children from many tribes, so I imagine he learned how to fight from them in the schoolyard."

Langham surprised Sandborne by interrupting. "But Halstead's a stone killer, ain't he?"

Sandborne nodded. "That part is true enough."

Another silence fell over the four men after that. Sandborne was unsure if his answers satisfied their curiosity or only confirmed their worst fears. Sandborne did not care which it was. At least now they knew the sort of man they were up against.

A mile or so later, Langham rode up to join him at the head of the small group. "I thought you'd never been in this part of the state before, deputy."

"I haven't. Why?"

"Because you've chosen the same path I would've used. You ride as though you know this country like the back of your hand."

Sandborne did not think there was any trick to it. They had been riding through the lowlands and the snow was not as thick as it had been back in town. The wind had blown the snow into drifts that helped him read the ground better.

"We're two hours out of Missoula, Langham. You can quit trying to pay me compliments."

"It's less of a compliment than an observation," Langham bristled. "We're bound to be out here for quite a while. There's no reason to be unpleasant about it."

"I'm not unpleasant," Sandborne said. "Just focused. This isn't a pleasure ride."

Back before he had ridden with Halstead, he might have tried to be on friendly terms with Langham and his men. He had always deferred to age, and Langham was certainly older than him. He had probably been a law man for as long as Sandborne had been alive.

But Jeremiah always had a way of reading a man within a few moments of meeting him. He had never seen his friend treat a man poorly who did not ultimately deserve it. Sandborne's instinct told him Langham was not to be trusted. His attempt to have Vandenberg talk to him had not been an innocent mistake. It had been an early test of his resolve and leadership. If he showed the slightest weakness around him or the others, they would not hesitate to take advantage. He could not allow that, for Halstead's sake or his own.

He tried to let some air out of the tension that had settled over them. "Where does this trail lead anyway?"

"I thought you had all the answers."

He knew what Mackey would say. "I asked you a question."

"A small settlement they call Barren Pines," Langham told him. "It's as good a place for us to start looking for Halstead as any. Trappers and hunters like to spend the winter there. Miners, too, as few as there are up in the Flatheads."

Sandborne had known about such places but had not heard much about Barren Pines. "What makes it so popular?"

"It's right in the middle of a bunch of similar settlements just like it," Langham explained.

"There's a good chance that we'll find someone who may have stumbled across Halstead or have heard where he is. Someone might give us a good lead on where we might find him. Trappers are worse than old washerwomen when it comes to gossip. If anyone knows where Halstead is, we'll find them in Barren Pines."

Sandborne decided Langham was right about it being a good place to start. "Got any law there?"

Langham said, "I like to rotate my deputies in and out of there based on the seasons. It helps them know the county better and the citizens like seeing new faces. I sent Jason Fremont to Barren Pines for the winter."

Sandborne had never heard of Fremont. "What sort is he?"

"You won't like him," Langham said. "He's the friendly type."

Sandborne allowed the insult to pass. "Kind of a gloomy name for a town, isn't it? Barren Pines?"

Langham looked back at one of the men with them. "Tell him about the place, Red."

"The Salish called it that on account of a stand of dead pines that surround the place," Red said. "They say the land is cursed, but it's just a case of tree rot if you asked me. They say lightning hit the place a few years back. A lot of the pines burned but didn't fall. That didn't exactly make the natives look any kinder on the place."

Sandborne could understand why. "I'd imagine your deputy is kept pretty busy, with all those trappers holed up there for the winter."

"You'd be surprised," Langham said. "We've had to lock up a drunk now and then, but they mostly behave themselves. They don't even have a mayor, though the Armand brothers are the closest they've got to any order up there. Dave runs the general store and Moses runs the livery. Between the two of them, they're pretty good at keeping a lid on things. They even have a showgirl who's mighty popular with the men. The Glamorous Glenda. I imagine Fremont's managed to be pretty popular with her, too. Like I said, he's the friendly type."

Buster was trailing both pack horses at the back of the group. "When we get there, it might be a good idea to let the sheriff do most of the talking at first. They can be an ornery bunch when it comes to strangers. A friendly face will go a long way to easing them into the idea to talk to us."

Sandborne turned in the saddle to look at him. "You saying I don't look friendly, Buster?"

"I'm saying they don't know you," Buster answered. "And trappers tend to be a suspicious breed."

Sandborne turned back around and focused on the trail ahead. He hoped Jeremiah had not already run afoul of them as he tended to be suspicious of strangers, too.

Chapter 11

Halstead could feel the barber's hand tremble as he scraped the last remaining stubble from his face. The floor of the jail was covered with scraps of what had once been his beard.

Halstead knew why the barber was nervous and tried some conversation. "You feeling poorly, Sam?"

Sam Rivers stopped shaving. "Is it that obvious?"

Halstead ran his fingers across his skin and came away with flecks of blood. He held them up for the barber to see. "I'd say the results speak for themselves."

"Can't blame me for that," Rivers said. "I'm not used to working in these kinds of conditions. I like to be in my shop with my own chair and hot towels for my customers. This is highly irregular, mister. Highly irregular indeed."

Halstead glanced back at the cell and saw Fremont silently glaring out at them from his cot. "I didn't have anyone to watch my prisoner, and I don't trust him enough to leave him alone, so you had to come here. But since the deputy is making you anxious, I'll be glad to knock him senseless if it'll steady your hand."

"Try it, half-breed," Fremont spat from behind

his bars. "It won't be easy for you to get the jump on me a second time."

"No call for that," Rivers said as he wiped his blade on a towel. "It's just that this is highly irregular is all. First Dave gets killed. Now Fremont's locked up for it. We're not used to all this excitement around here."

Halstead imagined they were not, especially during the winter months when life tended to slow to a crawl. "You ought to see if the doctor can give you something for your nerves."

"Then we're in trouble," Sam said, "because I'm the closest thing to a doctor this town has."

"That so?" He looked at Sam's shaking hands. "Let's hope no one needs an operation anytime soon."

"The way things are going, they probably will." The barber finished wiping his razor on his towel. "You know, there was a time when barbers and doctors were the same thing. Bet you didn't know that."

"Can't say that I did." And Halstead was not sure he cared to know it now.

Rivers's hand was steadier now that he had gotten talking and resumed his shaving. "In the olden times, we barbers used to do all sorts of things. We did operations, pulled teeth, and even used leeches to bleed folks when something ailed them. That pole I've got in front of my shop ain't just red, white, and blue on account of this being

America. It's the caduceus, the staff Hermes the Healer is said to have carried back in Ancient Greece."

"Fascinating." Halstead raised his chin, hoping Rivers would take it as a sign to go back to work.

The barber continued talking. "Snakes back then represented wisdom and understanding. The Bible kind of says the same thing if you think about it the right way. Adam and Eve and all."

"Guess I'm behind on my Bible reading."

"A man in your position ought to consider taking up the Good Book once in a while." He quickly added, "No offense meant, mister."

"None taken."

Rivers continued shaving. "I called you 'mister' just now, but that don't seem right for a man like you. I don't even know what to call you. You're not the sheriff, and you're not a deputy anymore."

"Just call me Halstead." As bored as he was by the banter, he was glad the barber's hand had steadied because of it. "Jeremiah, if you're feeling friendly about it."

"I don't know how I should feel," Rivers admitted. "That's what bothers me most."

Halstead did not have an answer for him. "Well, the quicker you're done, the quicker you can get back to your shop and put it out of your mind. Can't say I understand your hurry. It's not like you've got customers lined up on the street.

149

I haven't seen a man in town yet who didn't have at least five-years-worth of beard on his face."

"Truth be told, I make most of my living by tending to women's hair. The menfolk around here tend to save their grooming until the thaw. They prefer to spend their money at the gambling tables and saloons when they first come to town for the season. I always do a fair bit of business right before the spring. You'll see."

But Halstead knew he would not. "I don't plan on being here that long."

"From what I hear, you weren't planning on being here at all," Rivers remarked. "Look how that turned out."

"You've got a point." Halstead was curious about Rivers. He had never met a barber yet that was not full of opinions. He decided to see if Sam Rivers was the exception. "You believe all those stories you've heard about me, Sam?"

"Had no reason to doubt them until last night," the barber admitted. "Now I don't know what to believe." He stopped shaving in mid stroke. "Why would Jason want to kill Dave? And why would you be willing to get yourself caught up in the middle of it all. It just doesn't make much sense for an outlaw to do such a thing."

"Fremont dragged me into it when he told people I killed Dave. As for me being an outlaw, I guess you'll have to make up your own mind on that score."

Rivers used the razor to plow through more shaving cream on his neck. "But if you're innocent, why'd you run? To my way of thinking, a man with nothing to hide has nothing to fear from a court of law."

Halstead saw it as a fair point. "You ever find yourself looking at a judge?"

"Only in the chair back at my shop," Sam said. "The circuit judge rides through here twice a year." Rivers moved his blade to begin clearing away Halstead's moustache. "But I guess that doesn't count for much."

"It counts more than you think." Halstead spoke out of the side of his mouth while the barber continued to shave. "A judge is just a man, same as any other. They have likes and dislikes and opinions like the rest of us. They have family and a life outside their courtroom. It just so happens that the judge who swore out the warrant on me has a relative who doesn't like me much. His family wants to make an example out of me over some trouble I caused them a while back."

Rivers continued to work. "Sounds like a long way to say you're guilty."

"I never said I didn't kill those men," Halstead said. "But it wasn't murder. There's a difference."

"Sounds complicated if you ask me. I like things plain. If your hair is too long, I can cut it. Want a shave? I put some soap on your face and scrape it away. I can see what I do while I'm doing it. Seems to me your line of work ought to be the same way."

Halstead could not argue with him. "The law's clear enough. It's the people who make it complicated."

Rivers finished shaving him and wiped Halstead's face clean with a fresh towel. "I'd be able to give you something to stop those nicks from bleeding if we were in my shop, but we ain't, so I can't."

Halstead ran his hands over his face. His skin felt smooth and the air felt good on it. He felt ten pounds lighter and judging by the amount of hair piled up on the jailhouse floor, he thought he might be. "You did a great job under the circumstances. What do I owe you?"

Rivers took the towel from around Halstead's neck and balled it up on the desk. "No charge. Miss Glenda's orders."

Halstead remembered her offer of a free shave when he had talked to her in her dressing room the previous afternoon but had not expected it to still be valid. "I'd have thought she'd change her mind now that I've got her beau locked up."

Sam Rivers wiped his razor clean on a dirty towel. "Miss Glenda's got lots of beaus, mister. Jason ain't the only one. He just likes to think he is."

Fremont kicked the bars of his cell. "I'll remember you said that, Sam."

The barber folded his razor and slid it into his shirt pocket as he spoke to Halstead. "If you've got a broom, I'll be glad to sweep up all this hair for you."

Halstead had not expected him to do that. "I saw one out by the back door. You can find it there if you'd like."

Sam began to rub his left arm as if it was sore. "Think you could go get it for me? This cold weather is making my rheumatism kick up something awful. Guess that's why my hands were shaking so much while I was working on you." He smiled and added, "Well, maybe not the only reason."

Halstead did not believe him but was interested in why he was lying. He nodded toward the stove in the opposite corner of the room. "If your bones are aching, stand over there for a while. I hear the warmth can be good for the pain."

"Can't hurt none." Rivers moved toward the stove. "Just old age creeping up on me, I guess. You'll find out for yourself soon enough."

"Not if Fremont has anything to say about it."

Halstead listened as he opened the back door, found the broom and pail half buried in snow, and brought them back inside.

He was surprised at how quickly Sam took the broom from him and began to sweep up. His aches seemed a distant memory. "Thanks. I'll be done here in no time. I imagine you'll be anxious to go back to keeping an eye on Jason without me being underfoot."

Halstead glanced at Fremont. And for the first time since his arrest, he looked away.

Something had happened. Something had changed.

"No need to rush," Halstead told the barber. "Unless you've got somewhere you'd rather be."

Sam swept up the hair in earnest. "Like I told you before, I'm a man who likes his routine. Why, if I'm away from my shop for any length of time, I begin to feel poorly. I guess a man can't change how he feels about things. All part of getting old."

"He can't change how he feels, only what he does." Halstead sat on the edge of the desk. "What did you do, Sam?"

The barber swept in quick strokes, making a point of keeping his back to him. "Just cleaning up the mess we made. You boys are going to be here a while. I like to leave a place as clean as I found it, if not cleaner."

Halstead had heard enough. "Stop."

Another tremor went through Sam as he stopped sweeping.

"Turn and face me."

Sam slowly obeyed.

Halstead immediately saw what was wrong. The folded razor was no longer in the barber's shirt pocket.

"Looks like you dropped something, Sam."

Sam let the broom fall as he backed up against the wall. "Don't hold it against me, mister. I didn't have a choice. Miss Glenda told me I had to do it. She owns the deed on my place and threatened to lock me out if I didn't slip him that razor like she wanted."

Halstead did not doubt him. He also saw no reason to hold it against Rivers. "But you didn't give it to him. Because if you'd given it to him, I'd have to arrest you and throw you in there with him. But if it fell out of your pocket, just like I said, it would just be an accident, wouldn't it?"

The barber was smart enough to play along. "Yes, sir. I reckon it must have happened like you say it did."

Halstead looked at Fremont. "And since I don't see it on the floor, you must've been kind enough to find it. You'd best give it back to him so he can be on his way."

Fremont slowly produced the barber's razor from his boot as he stood. "I told you it wouldn't be easy the next time you came at me and I meant it." He unfolded the blade and held it like a knife. "You come near me again, I'll slice you open for your trouble."

Against the wall, Sam Rivers began to pray.

Halstead remained leaning against the desk. "That's not going to happen."

Fremont's eyes were wide, almost wild. "Take

a step closer to this cell, and we'll see what happens."

Halstead crossed his arms. "You're going to stick that blade outside your cell, drop it, and back away from the bars. If you don't, I'll shoot you in the knee and take it from you. Ever see a man shot in the knee, Fremont? It's painful. It's even more painful considering Sam here is the closest thing we've got to a doctor in town, not that he would be able to do you much good. You'll still be a cripple the rest of your life. I don't have to tell you what happens to cripples in prison."

Fremont cursed as he raised the razor and threw it—end over end—in Halstead's direction.

Halstead moved his head to the right, easily dodging the spinning blade as it sailed past him before rattling to the floor.

Halstead kept his eyes on his prisoner as he spoke to Rivers. "Pick up your blade, Sam. Put it in your pants pocket this time. It'd be a shame if you lost it again."

The barber grabbed his razor, folded it, and stuffed it in his pants pocket. "Thank you, mister. I'm grateful to you."

Halstead watched Fremont drop onto his cot and pull the blanket over his head. "Finish sweeping up and be on your way. The prisoner needs his rest."

Rivers picked up the broom and made quick work of sweeping up the rest of his cuttings. He pulled on his hat and coat and picked up the pail of old hair. "I'll take this over to my shop and bring the bucket back later."

Halstead would not look at him. "You do that. And Sam, no more mistakes. Understand?"

The barber swallowed loudly. "Yes, sir. I appreciate your understanding."

But understanding had nothing to do with it. Halstead wanted to backhand the barber for being foolish enough to slip Fremont a weapon but decided there was little to be gained by that. He would tell everyone who would listen about what had just happened. Hitting a barber would only serve to set even more people against him.

"Leave the door open," Halstead told him as he left. "The fresh air will do us some good."

Sam Rivers was all too happy to oblige and dashed out to the boardwalk as a cold blast of air blew through the tiny jail.

Fremont cursed and flipped in his cot, facing away from the door as he pulled the blanket tightly around himself.

Halstead took his hat and coat from the hook by the desk and put them on. He reached through the bars of the cell and yanked Fremont's blanket from him. He balled it up and tossed it in the far corner, well out of the prisoner's reach.

"You can't do that!" Fremont protested as Halstead walked outside. "I'll freeze to death without it."

157

"You'll get it back when you learn how to behave yourself."

A cloud of foul language followed Halstead out onto the boardwalk.

It had snowed quite a bit since he had last been outside the previous evening. Someone had cleared the snow from the boardwalk in front of the jail and the rest of the town, too. For a place that did not have a doctor or a mayor, they certainly managed to keep themselves organized.

He looked up the street and saw Glenda's large Chinese man tending a horse in front of The Town Hall Saloon. He was only in a thin shirt and did not seem to mind the cold. He still managed to look menacing from half a town away.

Halstead watched Glenda walk out the front door in a fur coat that appeared to be mink. Her red hair was hidden by a hood she had pulled up to protect her from the cold.

The bodyguard moved the horse so she could step into the stirrup from the boardwalk. He watched her right herself in the saddle and begin to ride toward him through the snow while her guard remained behind.

She smiled when she saw Halstead but did not quicken her pace. She was a good rider and kept the horse under control as its footing slipped on the ice just beneath the snow.

He could see why so many men had fallen in love with her. She was not a raving beauty but the tintype he had found among the dead trapper's belongings had not done her justice. She had an elegant grace that no picture or painting could capture. He had only been in her company for a few moments, but there was an alluring nature to her that Halstead found difficult to describe. A feeling she inspired more than anything else.

Halstead counted himself lucky for having recognized her for what she was. He had been born with a skill for violence. Practice and trial had served to make him a killer. Glenda had a way with men she had spent years honing to her advantage to bend them to her will.

He wondered how she planned on seducing him to get what she wanted. He would enjoy finding out.

Glenda stopped her horse in front of the jail. "Good morning, deputy."

Halstead touched the brim of his hat. Despite all that had happened with the barber, there was no reason to be rude. Yet. "Miss Glenda."

"Stop sounding like a field hand. You're not some love-struck cowboy gawking up at me during a show. Only Joe calls me 'Miss' and that's because he can't say 'Glenda' properly."

"Who's Joe?"

"My manservant." She inclined her head back toward the large man now waiting in front of Town Hall. "He's from the Orient. Corea, if you must know. He was somehow brought over here with a load of Chinese workmen some years ago. He's had a rough life. Sold into slavery. Abused. One of his masters took his tongue and some other, more personal parts."

Halstead did not care. "Life is hard for everyone."

Glenda continued. "I acquired his services when I was last in San Francisco. I guess you could say I won him in a card game, but it's a far more complicated story than that. It's quite an interesting tale."

"I'm sure it is."

"I'd be happy to tell you all about it inside where it's warm." She offered her hand to him. "Help me down?"

Halstead leaned against the doorframe. "It's not that interesting a story."

She pouted. "You mean you're not enough of a gentleman to help a lady dismount?"

"No reason for you to dismount because you're not staying," Halstead told her. "Your beau has had a rough morning and isn't up to having visitors just yet."

She laughed it off. "How rough could it be in a jail so small?"

"He threatened to kill me with a razor. A razor Sam Rivers said you told him to slip him."

Glenda laughed it off. "Men are always looking to blame women for their own crazy ideas, aren't they?" She smiled down at him. "Don't tell me you believe such a ridiculous notion."

Since she was sure to deny it, he knew there was nothing to be gained by arguing. "It doesn't matter what I believe, but you're a hard woman to figure out. Yesterday you tried to hire me and today you try to have me killed. And I still haven't figured out why Fremont shot Dave, but I'm pretty sure you had something to do with it."

"You can't prove that," she shot back.

"Not right now, but when I can, you'll be in the same cell with him."

"You have such a devious mind." She demurred beneath her hood as she flattened out her skirts. "I was nothing but honest with you yesterday. I want you to help me get a show of my own. A show that could profit both of us handsomely if you're smart enough to let me help you."

"Your idea of handsome sounds mighty ugly to me. Bloody, too, or at least it could've been if I hadn't spotted that razor Sam slipped your beau."

"Stop calling him that!" Glenda's eyes flared. "He's not my beau. He's more of a convenience than anything else. He serves a purpose is all. You might say he amuses me."

"I'm sure he does," Halstead said. "And so would I if I was dumb enough to believe you. I guess we're both lucky I'm too smart for that. People get hurt for thinking I'm stupid."

"My, what a subtle threat," she said.

"Facts aren't threats except to liars," Halstead told her. "But now that you know I'm on to you,

you can quit wasting your time trying to charm me."

He watched her mouth grow thin as she sat straighter in the saddle. She was clearly not used to being refused by a man, much less spoken to like this. "Is he hurt? Jason, I mean."

"He's fine, except for a bad case of wounded pride. Don't worry. He'll get over it in time for the hanging."

She smirked. "It's a funny thing to hear a man in your position be so eager to see another man swing. You should be careful what you wish for, deputy. There's a good chance you could find yourself standing next to him on the gallows one day."

Halstead caught the change in her tone and everything began to make sense. "Now I understand what yesterday was all about. You were hoping to keep me around so you could turn me in for the reward money. You thought you could hook me just like you'd hooked Fremont. I'm glad I was a disappointment."

Her bright eyes narrowed as her jaw clenched beneath her hood. She did not have to say a word. Her expression spoke volumes.

Halstead grinned up at her. He was seeing her—the real her—for the first time. The woman beneath the powder and gowns. The woman who was sick of the endless limelight of the stage and the stench of stale beer and whiskey. She had seen her way out from beyond all that. Halstead was her ticket to a better life.

It was a sobering thought. He had never seen himself as much of a commodity. "You have yourself a good day."

She brought her horse around and faced him head on. "You haven't disappointed me yet, Halstead. You're not going anywhere now, not even if you wanted to. Your sense of nobility is too high to run. You'd never leave the rest of us to see to Jason because you know we'd let him loose when you did. He'd run you down like the miserable cur you are."

He continued to lean against the doorframe. "He might catch up to me, but he'd die trying. And so would anyone else who came after me."

"We'll see about that." Glenda snapped the reins and sent her horse into a gallop back toward The Town Hall Saloon. Joe was there to take control of the horse and help his mistress down from the saddle. He carried her over to the boardwalk, where she quickly went back inside. She was a pretty lady, even when she was angry, but Halstead counted himself lucky that he had always been more partial to brunettes. And one brunette in particular. Abigail Newman.

He watched Joe take the reins of Glenda's horse as he glared back at Halstead. He sensed a challenge in the big man's eyes. He did not look away, not even as Joe led the horse across the thoroughfare to the Armand livery. Halstead remained where he was until Joe crossed the street a final time before entering the saloon.

He hoped the big man had the sense to stay away from him, but common sense seemed in mighty short supply these days in Barren Pines.

Chapter 12

It was almost noon by the time the eastbound train unloaded Riker's men, animals, and supplies at the Missoula station. Riker had not wanted to risk spending more time in town than necessary, out of fear word of his arrival might reach Halstead if he happened to be nearby.

He was about to climb into the saddle of his horse when he heard his name being called out from a man on the platform.

"Mr. Riker," a smallish man called to him. "Please wait. I have news."

Riker remembered Mannes's description of Hy Vandenberg, the reporter, and knew this had to be him.

"Vandenberg," Riker said as he led his horse away from the others to talk to the man in private. "What's the latest?"

The reporter shuddered in the cold. "Deputy Sandborne is here. At least he was until early this morning."

Riker had been expecting that. "Does he know where Halstead is?"

"Not from what he told Sheriff Langham," Vandenberg said. "He thinks Halstead might be in the area, but he plans to check all the towns nearby. The sheriff, Red, and Buster rode out with him at first light. They rode off in the direction of Barren Pines. I think they were going to start their search there."

Riker was pleased. Glenda would be helpful to him there. "What sort of man is Sheriff Langham?"

"Ambitious," Vandenberg said. "I mean he's going places, or at least he thinks he is."

"I know what ambitious means," Riker said. "Don't talk down to me again."

Vandenberg bowed in apology. "He's got his eye on being mayor one day. Maybe even governor. He thinks bringing in Halstead will help him get there and he's probably right."

Riker knew an ambitious man could help as much as hurt his pursuit of Halstead. "Will he be a problem for us?"

"Not if you handle him right," the reporter said. "And even if you don't, I suspect you and your men will be able to handle him well enough."

"I've tangled with men like Langham before. How far is Barren Pines from here?"

He looked where Vandenberg pointed to the east. "They rode out in that direction about four hours ago, so they should be there by now."

Riker had spent much of the previous week and most of the ride east committing maps of the area to memory. He could always refer to them if he needed to, but unfolding a map was not an easy task for a one-armed man. He needed the men he had hired to see him as a leader, not an awkward cripple.

"If the maps I've seen are right, it seems like flat ground most of the way there."

"There's a ridge that overlooks the town from this direction," Vandenberg confirmed. "You'll be able to give the town a good looking over before you ride down to it."

Riker had learned all he could from the reporter. "Get back to your office and wait to hear from me."

Vandenberg began to fidget with his hands. "Of course, but about our agreement—"

"I haven't forgotten. If we find Halstead, I'll send a man ahead so you'll be ready with a photographer when we bring his body back here."

Vandenberg frowned. "I was hoping you might allow me to join you and your men, Mr. Riker. I won't be a hinderance, I assure you."

Riker did not bother to consider the idea. "No. You'll stay here and do what I told you. I'll send for you if I need you. You've done good work here today, Vandenberg."

Since there was nothing more for them to discuss, Riker grabbed the saddle horn with his left hand and hauled himself up onto his horse.

Vandenberg tried to block his way. "You'll need to be careful, Mr. Riker. Sandborne told me he'll be watching his back trail. Said anyone who follows him will get themselves shot for their trouble."

His brother Warren would have gotten a good laugh out of that had he been there. He would have enjoyed hearing Halstead's pet had grown a spine.

But Warren was not there. He was lying in a grave in a cemetery on the outskirts of Battle Brook. And Emil Riker was not in a laughing mood.

"That's what he told *you,* Mr. Vandenberg. The difference is we plan on shooting back." He looked back at Keane and the others. He was glad to see the pack horses had already been outfitted and all ten men were ready to ride. "Get a good look at this burg as we ride through, boys. It'll be your last taste of civilization for a while. We're bound for the east and a little place they call Barren Pines."

The reporter was still gaping up at them as Riker led the men toward whatever vengeance he could find among the ice and snow ahead.

When they reached the clearing on the hill, Sandborne raised his right hand to signal the others to halt. He had seen Mackey do the same thing on the trail, and it had always worked.

But the marshal must have done it better, for Langham, Red, and Buster continued until they were alongside him.

"There it is," Langham said. "Barren Pines lies just below us."

Sandborne had not known what to expect the place to look like, but the sight of it sent a chill through him. Red's description had been correct to a point, but nothing had prepared him for this.

It had stopped snowing, but a thin fog hovered above the crooked wooden buildings that sat on three streets, including a main thoroughfare. Only one building was taller than two stories and even that looked like a good wind might pitch it over at any moment.

Blackened pines rose into the sky like jagged spikes. What little snow and ice that had managed to cling to the scorched wood only served to make it look more sinister.

From beside him, Red said, "Cozy little place, ain't it? You ought to be here when the wind picks up. It comes howling through the trees and makes a sound like nothing you've ever heard."

Buster added, "Legend says the natives used to call it 'The Howls of Hell.'"

Sandborne kept looking over the town. "I doubt that since Indians don't usually believe in Hell. At least none I've ever met."

Buster laughed as Red said, "You can't blame us for trying to have a little fun at your expense, can you, deputy?"

Sandborne did not know whether he should take the teasing as a sign of disregard or that they were starting to warm up to him. He decided it was safer if he did not take it as either. "Let's ride down there and see what we can find. Langham will take the lead. And if the Devil himself jumps out at us, I'll expect you to shoot the horns right off his head."

The three men laughed as they rode their horses down the hill.

Sandborne rode into Barren Pines last, preferring to hang back as he took his time looking at the town. There wasn't much to the place, but more than he had seen from the hill. It was already well into the afternoon, and he was surprised to see every saloon was still closed. He wondered if it was from a lack of business or a town ordinance that only allowed them to open at certain times.

The buildings were not much to look at, not even now that he was up close, but each store was well kept with various goods on display in the windows. The boardwalks were cleared of snow, which he took as another good sign of the town's respectability.

Langham slowed his horse and waited for Sandborne to catch up. "We'll stop first at the jail to check on my man Fremont. If anyone has heard anything about Halstead, it'll be Jason."

"We agreed to let you do all the talking at the beginning," Sandborne reminded him. "That still goes as far as I'm concerned."

Langham offered a wink as he steered his horse to the jail. "Leave it to me."

The sheriff climbed down and wrapped the reins around the hitching rail. Red and Buster did the same, followed by Sandborne.

Langham strode up onto the boardwalk and called out, "Hope you're decent, Jason because I've brought company with me this time around."

The sheriff pushed in the jailhouse door but recoiled back into Red as if he was shot. "Stand back, boys. It's him!"

From inside the jail, Sandborne heard a familiar voice say, "Hands where I can see them."

"Jeremiah?" Sandborne called out as jumped down from the saddle and eased his way between Langham and the others. "You in there?"

"Who's asking?"

Sandborne shouldered the others aside and held his hands up as he stepped in front of Langham. "It's me. Sandborne. I'm going to stick my head in. Don't shoot."

Sandborne saw Halstead crouched behind a desk with one of his Colts trained on the door. It took a long moment for him to recognize his friend. He had never been heavy, but his face was gaunt and his collar was loose around his neck.

Halstead slowly rose. "Sandborne?"

"The one and only. Put the gun away, Jeremiah. These men are with me. They're the law. No one's here to hurt you."

Halstead lowered the Colt and slid it back into the holster on his hip. "What are you doing here?"

Langham recovered and was about to speak when Sandborne held up a finger. "Don't. Say. Anything."

The sheriff swallowed his words and remained outside with the others.

Sandborne told Halstead, "Aaron sent me to find you when the weather turned bad. He hadn't heard from you and thought you might need some help." He saw a man gripping the bars of his cell in the far corner of the jail. "I can see you haven't lost a step. Who's he?"

Sandborne kept Langham back as the sheriff looked inside for himself. "That's Jason, my deputy. What's he doing in that cell? Let him out this instant."

Halstead's hand remained on the Colt on his hip. "Who's that loudmouth?"

"Sheriff Henry Langham out of Missoula," Sandborne told him. "He and these men rode out with me this morning to look for you. If I'd have known we'd find you so soon, I'd have left them behind."

"Tell him to calm down before he gets hurt. Same goes for his friends."

Langham's face reddened as Sandborne pushed him back. "Shut your mouth or he'll kill all three of you."

On the boardwalk, Red slid his pistol from his belt. "No one's that good."

"He is." Sandborne focused on Langham. If

172

things turned bad, it would start with him. "I know you've got plenty of questions, and I'll get you plenty of answers, but I need you to stay outside while I talk to him."

Langham turned on Sandborne. "Conspire with him is more like it. I want Fremont out of that cell this instant."

Sandborne knew Halstead would not be rushed. He could not afford to allow the sheriff to rush him, either. "You boys can surround the place if it'll make you feel any better. I'll come get you in a little while."

Langham shook himself free of Sandborne's grip and backed out onto the boardwalk. "We'll do it your way for now, Sandborne, but me and my men will shoot anyone who steps outside who isn't you. And the next time I see you, you'd better have a good reason why Jason's locked up in there or there'll be trouble."

Sandborne waited for him and the others to back away on their own before quietly shutting the jailhouse door.

He leaned against it when it was closed and was glad to see Halstead sitting down. "I swear, Jeremiah, I spend half my time keeping people from trying to kill you."

"That fop out there? Let him try. He'll wind up worse than his deputy."

Sandborne had seen Jeremiah like this before. He might look relaxed but he was coiled and ready to strike at anything. "You calm enough for me to lower my hands?"

Halstead blinked. "Yeah. I'm fine."

He looked over at the man in the cell. "I was figuring I'd find you in a jail somewhere, but not on this side of the bars."

Halstead ran his hands over his face. "Fremont killed a man and tried to blame me for it. He wasn't very good at it."

Sandborne hoped Fremont remained quiet. "Who'd he kill?"

"Dave Armand," Halstead told him. "Owns the general store up the street. At least he did until Fremont put a bullet in him last night."

"Why?"

Halstead shrugged. "I don't know, and he's not talking. Maybe your friend Langham can pry it out of him. I don't even care anymore."

Sandborne saw his friend was not only gaunt. He also had dark circles under his eyes. "You look like you haven't slept in a week."

"Try several weeks. I've been up all night keeping an eye on him. I was asleep when he shot Dave. Guess I nodded off when Langham came barging in here. He's lucky I saw that star on his chest before I started shooting."

"That luck cuts both ways," Sandborne said. "You're already in enough trouble as it is."

"Thanks for reminding me. I'd almost forgotten all about it."

Sandborne knew sarcasm was a good sign that Jeremiah had calmed some. "Besides needing some sleep, are you hurt? You spent a lot of time alone up in those mountains."

"I'm fine as far as it goes. Had to kill some men when the weather forced me down to lower ground."

Sandborne had been expecting that. "How many?"

He held up five fingers.

Sandborne had expected it to be more. "And that ain't the record, either."

Halstead surprised him by laughing. "No. I guess it's not."

From his cell, Fremont said, "Well, ain't this a sweet sight. If you two lovebirds want to be alone, I'll be happy to wait outside with my friends."

Halstead told him, "The only thing I want to hear out of you is why you killed Dave Armand. Until then, keep your mouth shut."

Sandborne could see Jeremiah was more ragged than he could ever remember seeing him. He needed to get him out of there, maybe get a good meal into him. But he knew Jeremiah would not leave until he got some answers.

And he had an idea of how he just might get them. "Let me bring Langham in here to talk to him. Just Langham, not the other boys. He's a good man, Jeremiah, and I think you can trust him."

"Trust is a funny notion," Halstead said. "You used to trust me once and look at where it got you."

"I still trust you," Sandborne said. "That's why I came all the way out here. Now I'm asking you to trust me. If Langham pulls anything, it'll be you and me against him. We've gone up against worse odds than that. What do you say?"

Halstead rested his elbows on the arms of his chair. "I'm in another man's jail with its deputy in a cell and a five-thousand-dollar price on my head. I don't think I've got much to say about anything at all. Let him in if you think it'll do any good. And as long as he behaves himself, he'll get no trouble from me."

Sandborne rested his hand on the door handle. "You won't regret this, Jeremiah."

"That's good because I already regret plenty."

Chapter 13

"Absolutely not!" Langham exclaimed. "I refuse to have that man in here while I question my deputy. He's a wanted criminal, Sandborne. He's not even a law man anymore."

Halstead remained quiet while Sandborne continued to try to negotiate a peace. "He might be a wanted man, but he's still a deputy marshal, same as me. The marshal didn't take his star. Jeremiah says Fremont killed a man last night, and there's not a man in town who says different. Even the dead man's brother agrees. You told me that very thing outside just a little while ago."

Langham placed his hands on his hips. "Which only makes me even more insulted that you think I might let Jason go free. Halstead might have his star, but mine still means something."

Halstead had heard enough, but for Sandborne's sake, he remained seated when he said, "I'm not leaving him alone with you. He's my prisoner, and I plan on taking him to your jail in Missoula, assuming you've still got enough sand to lock him away for murder."

Sandborne moved between them as Langham glared down at Halstead. "I'm just as liable to lock you in the cell right next to him."

Halstead tented his hands on the arms of his

chair, less than an inch away from the Colt on his belly. "You're welcome to try."

Sandborne remained between the two men. "We've got more important things than fighting between us, boys. Your man's locked up and you want to know why. So do we. Bickering like this won't get us the answers we all need."

Halstead was quietly proud of his former partner. The kid had grown up a lot since Battle Brook. He supposed coming close to death had a way of aging a man beyond his years.

Langham leaned against the bars of Fremont's cell. "Well? What do you have to say for yourself, Jason? I might not like Halstead, but it sure sounds like he's got you dead to rights."

The prisoner had been watching the three men argue about him and seemed to have enjoyed the show. "I should've gunned Halstead down as soon as I saw him. If I had, I wouldn't be in this mess."

"But you didn't," Langham said, "so here we are. Out with it, son. Why did you kill Dave Armand? We've known each other too long for you to lie to me."

Fremont sat back in the bunk. "A confession's as good as putting the noose around my own neck."

"Not necessarily," Langham said. "You know I have some influence with the judge. If you talk now, we might be able to work out a deal.

A lesser charge, perhaps, where execution is not even a consideration."

"Just life in prison." Fremont shut his eyes. "Life in prison's no life at all."

"You know how it works as well as I do," Langham reminded him. "You've seen men get out much earlier than they thought due to good behavior. But I can't promise you anything unless you talk to me. Give me something that can help you, Jason. Something that will help me save your life. Why would you want to kill poor old Dave?"

Fremont's eyes snapped open. "Because he got stupid and greedy, that's why."

Langham blanched as he backed away from the bars.

Sandborne stepped forward and took his place. "What do you mean? How was he stupid and greedy?"

Fremont looked at the wall. "I don't have to talk to you."

Sandborne said, "You don't have to live, either. You already took a step toward the truth. At least be man enough to see it through."

A vein in Fremont's neck bulged. "I was man enough to do what needed to be done last night when that old fool sent for me. I thought Dave wanted to talk over some gossip he'd heard about that butcher sitting in my chair over there, but it wasn't that innocent. Dave told me he'd been looking out his shop window that morning when Lance McAlister brought Halstead to see Glenda. She'd told me she was going to feed him some story about him coming into business with us for a show she wanted to do. Said if he agreed, she could make all his troubles go away by writing a letter to the governor for him."

"Jeremiah?" Sandborne made no attempt to hide his surprise. "In a show?" He looked back at Halstead. "That true?"

"That's what she told me," Halstead said. "But I didn't believe her."

Fremont said, "I told her it was a dumb idea. I'd had a chance to look him over in Millie's that morning and knew he'd never fall for it. But she wouldn't listen to me. She thought she could get him to fall in love with her just by batting her eyes and showing some skin. She thought she could get him to just ride into Missoula with us to pick up the governor's answer. I was going to ride ahead of them so I could get Langham and some others ready to grab him before he knew what was happening. She'd collect the reward on Halstead and everything would be fine. Or so she thought."

Halstead was disappointed the scheme was not more complicated. "Doesn't sound like much of a plan to me."

"Because it wasn't," Fremont went on. "She was plenty angry when you turned her down flat.

I was planning on shooting you the next time you went to Millie's for a meal, but you never left Moses's loft after you left Glenda's place. I figured I'd have to wait until the morning for my chance. That's when Dave sent word that he wanted to see me. I went to his store, and that's when he told me he'd figured out why Glenda wanted to see you. That he knew she had her eyes on that reward money. He said he'd be happy to help set you up if he got a piece of the reward. He said if I didn't agree, he'd walk over to the livery and tell his brother what I was planning to do. He said he'd tell Langham how I'd been scheming with Glenda for the reward, even though I wasn't supposed to get it. The thought of being under any man's thumb boiled my blood. The old snake thought he had me backed into a corner, so I shot the fool right where he stood."

Langham walked over to one of the chairs near Halstead's desk and dropped into it. "My God, Jason. My God."

Halstead finished the story for him. "When you realized what you'd done, you made it look like someone busted in and shot him. You gathered up those men and torches to come get me. Guess you weren't counting on Moses to stand in your way."

"Or him bringing you over to the store with him," Fremont said. "I saw how you were putting things together and went for my gun, but you hit me before I could get it. If Glenda had stayed out of it, Dave would've still been alive and you'd be dead."

Halstead shook his head. "It wouldn't have been that simple. Men have been trying to kill me my whole life. You couldn't even get the jump on me while I was eating breakfast. The only dead man would've been you, and we'd all be better for it."

Langham took off his hat and ran his hands through his thinning brown hair. "I can't understand it. You threw your whole life away and for what? The dreams of a red-headed whore and a loudmouthed shopkeeper? I wouldn't have fired you over the money."

Fremont folded his arms across his chest. "I wasn't thinking that far ahead. My temper got the better of me."

But Langham did not seem to have been listening. "We could've been famous, you and me. We could've gotten money by selling our stories to the newspapers. I would've become mayor and you would've gotten my job. But now?" The sheriff hung his head. "Now we're both ruined."

"No, we're not." Fremont leapt off his cot and gripped the bars of his cell. "It's still not too late, Henry. We can still pull it off. We can still be famous. I saw you've got Red and Buster out there with you. They've always been steady boys, and they'll back us up now. Gun these boys down and we'll all ride into Missoula as heroes. We can have Glenda give Moses a piece of the reward money. I know he's sore about me killing his brother, but there's a lot of money on the table. We can have everything you want and more if we take it."

Halstead and Sandborne eyed the sheriff carefully as the tall man slowly stood. Halstead thought he might burst into tears.

Langham kept his head low as he said, "You were the best man I had, Jason, but that's all over now. I suppose all of this is my fault for putting you here. I knew you were sweet on Glenda. What man in his right mind wouldn't? But I never thought you'd be capable of anything like this. I'm ashamed of you. Ashamed I ever knew you."

The sheriff turned to Halstead but could not look at him. "Did you take his star from him? If you did, I'd like it back."

Halstead took it from the drawer and handed it to him. He watched Langham slip it into his coat pocket and shuffle to the door. He looked twenty years older than when he had first come in.

"Henry!" Fremont called after him. "Think it over. You know I'm right. Tell the others what I said. They'll agree with me. I just know they will. They'll follow you anywhere, just like I always have."

Langham opened the door. "I'm going to the hotel and getting a room if they have one, and a bottle. I'm going to get stinking drunk and hope I won't have to think about this until the morning. We'll bring him back to Missoula in the morning if the weather holds."

"We?" Halstead asked. "Who's we?"

Langham said, "I need you to tell me, Halstead. Are those murder charges against you true?"

"I killed them," Halstead admitted, "but it wasn't murder."

Langham nodded slowly. "God help me, but I believe you. If you ride with us, I promise I won't lock you up. Sandborne can wire Mackey about what he wants done with you and I'll abide by whatever he says. I hope you will, too, even if it means a cell. Can you agree to that?"

Halstead thought that was more than fair. "I agree to it."

Langham stepped outside and began walking toward the hotel. Red and Buster glanced inside the jail, then at Fremont. They stood in the doorway, unsure of what they should do.

Fremont told them, "Go with him, boys. Make him listen to reason. Things aren't nearly as bad as they seem."

The two deputies looked at Sandborne, who said, "Go on, fellas. The sheriff will be needing some company."

They withdrew and followed Langham.

Fremont clapped his hands as he sat on the edge of his cot. "Don't worry about old Henry. Red and Buster will win him over once he gets over the shock of it. You boys best be making your peace with your maker, because the next time you see them, they'll be gunning for you."

"Shut your mouth," Sandborne told him. "You've had enough disappointments for one day." He came over to Halstead. "You ought to get some rest, Jeremiah. Get something to eat if you can. I'll stay here and keep an eye on Fremont for you."

Halstead wanted to stay with his prisoner, but the prospect of food and sleep were too much for him to resist. He took his hat and coat down from the hook and put them on.

But as tired as he was, he could not resist the temptation of teasing his old partner. "I'll go if you promise not to get yourself shot this time. The closest thing this town's got to a doctor is a barber with shaky hands."

Sandborne smiled. "It's a deal, as long as you promise not to go riding out into the hills looking for trouble again."

As he began to leave, Halstead paused to shake Sandborne's hand. "It's good to see you, Joshua."

"Good to be seen, Jeremiah. And speaking of stars, do you still have yours?"

Halstead touched it through the fabric of his coat. He had slipped it into his pocket when

185

Mackey had refused to take it back in Helena. He had not been able to bring himself to look at it since. He had not even put his hand in the pocket, but constantly patted his coat to make sure it was still there. "I still have it. Why?"

"Good. Might as well go ahead and put it on."

Halstead felt his legs grow numb. Sandborne could be a bit dense at times, but he knew how important being a law man was to him. He would never make such a statement lightly. "Why would I do a thing like that?"

"Just do it," Sandborne encouraged. "It's all fine and proper, or at least it will be real soon. I'll explain why later."

From his cot in his cell, Fremont said, "Do what he told you, Halstead. Go ahead and put it on. It'll give Red and Buster something to aim for when they come for you."

Halstead ignored him as he took the star out of his pocket and held it. He could still remember the day Aaron Mackey had handed it to him.

It had always been more than just a job to him. It was more than just the authority that came with it. It had meant his wandering had finally come to an end and that he finally had a place in the world. A purpose. It had almost been enough to scrub away the three years he had spent rotting in an El Paso prison for a crime he had not committed.

He hoped putting it on again would mark an

end to the charges against him now. "You're sure about this?"

"As sure as I can be of anything."

Halstead felt his hand begin to shake as bad as Sam Rivers's had as he pinned the star to the lapel of his coat. His breath caught. He finally felt whole again. Almost like he was back home.

Sandborne sent him on his way. "Rest up and take your time getting back. Me and Fremont here are going to get acquainted with each other."

Halstead closed the jailhouse door behind him, blocking out the sound of Fremont's mocking laughter from his cell. And as he walked back to the livery, he felt a little taller than he had in months. Lighter, too, and not just because he no longer had a beard.

Chapter 14

Riker stopped at the edge of the hill that overlooked Barren Pines. Sandborne and his companions had left a trail through the snow that even a boy could follow. He could see that they had stopped at this very spot before heading down into the town. It was as though they had stopped here by accident, for the view was not particularly pretty, and the town was not all that admirable.

Beside him, Keane said, "This place looks abandoned to me."

"But it isn't." Riker pointed down at the town. "You can just make out smoke rising from some of the chimneys."

Keane said, "Not the prettiest town, is it? Those dead pines over yonder look mean. I've seen cemeteries that were more inviting."

But Riker was interested in more than just how the place looked. "Remember that woman you asked me about on the train? The one I said I was writing to."

Keane adjusted himself in the saddle. "I remember you didn't want to talk about her much."

"It wasn't the right time then, but it is now, because the woman I've been writing is waiting for us down there."

Keane remained still. "But you didn't know Halstead would be here. Nobody did."

"She was one of those many telegrams and letters I've been sending out for the past few weeks," Riker told him. "She's traveled to Missoula once a week to give me regular reports on what she had heard."

Keane put it together. "Mannes had Vandenberg, but you had her. A woman of your own. That was smart, Mr. Riker."

Riker did not care about compliments. "Glenda runs the shows at The Town Hall Saloon. She hears everything that goes on in these parts. I'm only telling you this because I want you to ride down there right now and talk to her."

"Why me? You're the one she's been writing to all this time."

Riker hated having to explain himself, but it was necessary. "It has to be you because if Halstead's down there, it won't be long before he gets word of a one-armed man being in town. You blend in better than I do because he doesn't know you. You came to Valhalla after he left town."

"That makes sense." Keane looked at the sky as he thought it over. "Why don't we all ride down there together? There'll be less chance of trouble if there's a bunch of us."

Riker was beginning to lose patience. "Twelve men riding into town will feel like an army. People will remember it. Even if Halstead isn't there, he might hear about it, and I don't want anyone to know we're here until we know more. One man having a quiet conversation with a lady isn't as memorable. If she tells you he's down there, come back here and we'll go get him together."

Keane considered it. "And what if I find myself in trouble?"

"Don't get in trouble," Riker said. "But if you do, give us a sign and we'll come riding in guns blazing."

Keane smoothed down his beard. "Let's hope it doesn't come to that. I might wind up getting shot in all the confusion. You said this woman is at The Town Hall Saloon?"

"Her name is Glenda." He looked up at the darkening gray sky. They had only a couple of hours at most before dusk or a storm descended on them. "Get moving."

Keane rode back and spoke to his men. "Rest the horses, unload the supplies, and get ready to make camp here." He spoke over the chorus of complaints that rose from them. "Quit your whining. I said get ready, not to make camp. We might be staying indoors tonight, but there's a chance we won't. I'll be back as soon as I can."

The men continued to complain as Riker watched Keane ride down the hill and toward town. Riker remained where he was, preferring to see whatever happened next for himself. He hoped Halstead was down there. He hoped he had a warm place to sleep and good food to fill his belly. Perhaps even some female companionship to help him pass the long, cold nights at the base of the mountain. Riker wanted him to be as comfortable and as content as possible.

For the more Halstead had, the more Riker could take from him, just as Halstead had taken his arm and his brother from him.

He took a pair of field glasses from his saddle bag and watched as Keane rode through the snow and into Barren Pines. The prospect of revenge warmed him against the cold wind as he sat and waited to see what happened next.

He brought the image into focus in time to see a large bald man walking across the thoroughfare and wondered where he was going. Barren Pines might prove to be an interesting place after all.

Halstead was glad that Moses had agreed to see him when he got back to the livery. As much as he needed food and sleep, he felt a greater need to tell him why his brother had been killed.

Moses listened to him as he sat by the stove, nursing a cup of coffee as Halstead finished his sad tale.

And when Halstead was done, the liveryman sat quietly as the words and reasoning sank in. "As much as it pains me to admit it, I can see it happening like you said."

Halstead set his mug on the floor beside his chair. "You can?"

Moses nodded. "I can see Dave pushing Fremont to that point. He always said I was the disagreeable one, but my brother had a way of getting under a man's skin like no one I've ever known. He was always smarter than me when it came to learning and figures and such, but he could never see when a man was riled up. And by the time he did, it was usually too late. I always knew that mouth of his would get him killed one day and now it has. Sometimes I hate being right."

Moses got up and walked over to the stove to refill his coffee. "You weren't fooled by Glenda's charms, were you?"

"No."

"Asking you to join her show was a pretty flimsy proposition on her part." Moses poured himself more coffee and filled Halstead's cup, too. "She's always been a clever one, that Glenda. Can't see her taking no for an answer. She was probably just sizing you up to see how you worked so she could sharpen her blade to take another stab at you."

Halstead had not spent much time thinking about it. "Wouldn't have made a difference. According to what Fremont said, he was planning to gun me down the next time I went to Millie's."

Moses set the pot back on the stove. "Can't see you being fooled by that, either."

"True."

Moses retook his seat next to the stove. "I know you can handle yourself, Jeremiah, but you ought to do your best to stay out of Glenda's way if you can. She's got a talent for twisting men into knots when she sets her mind to it. If she can't get you one way, she'll try another. I've seen her do that to Fremont and to plenty of men before him since she's been here. She's not likely to give up on that reward money so easily."

"Five thousand is a lot of money." Halstead remembered something Fremont had said to Langham. "Jason was thinking of cutting you in for some of it if Langham and his men turned on me and Sandborne."

"And give up all this?" Moses smiled as he swept his hand over his humble room. "Money's never been important to me, but it is to most people. You'll find no shortage of men here in town who might try their hand at collecting it. They like you for what you did for me and Dave, but greed is more powerful than gratitude. You should—"

The door splintered open as Glenda's body-guard Joe barreled inside.

Halstead reached for the Colt on his belly but a massive right hand from the giant slammed into his temple, knocking him off his seat.

Moses threw his cup of coffee at the man, but Joe easily knocked him to the floor and delivered three swift kicks to the ribs for his trouble.

The tiny room tilted as Halstead tried to shake off the fog from the heavy blow. Joe snatched him by the back of the neck and threw him out into the livery.

Horses screamed and kicked at the walls of their stalls as Halstead landed hard on his stomach. The impact of the Colt still holstered on his belly knocked the wind out of him in a great rush of air. A swift kick to the shoulder from the large Corean flipped Halstead onto his back before his attacker ripped the Colt from him and tossed it aside. The big man hauled him up by the lapels of his coat and pinned him against the wall.

Halstead was still desperately trying to draw in a decent breath when Joe clenched him by the throat and put his weight behind it, using only his right hand.

Halstead felt his boots scrape on the hay as he brought up a knee into Joe's groin. He knew he had connected, but not enough to break the larger man's grip. He kicked him again and a third time but the vice on his throat only grew tighter before he felt himself lifted off the ground.

He managed to draw in a half breath as the tips of his boots dangled in the air. The bald man's face was a blank mask devoid of any emotion or strain as he slowly choked the life out of him.

Halstead's vision began to blur, but in his dizzying confusion, he remembered the gun still on his hip. His hand shot down to it. Joe's left hand closed around his as he grabbed the butt of the Colt. Halstead easily wrenched his arm aside and away from Joe.

The giant's face tilted and faded before Halstead, but he felt the pistol in his hand. As his strength began to fail, he willed his fingers to squeeze off a shot. Maybe Sandborne or someone else would hear the shot and come to investigate.

But Joe's hold on his wrist was tighter than the one he had on his throat, and the pistol fell to the hay below.

A thin stream of bile rose in Halstead's throat as he felt his life beginning to leave him. He used whatever breath he still had to spit it in his attacker's face.

The big man shut his eyes and tried to shake the acid away. His grip on his right hand relented and Halstead quickly slipped it behind himself, desperately searching for the handle of the Bowie knife he prayed was still there.

His fingers found the handle as he felt the hold on his neck falter ever so slightly. The relief caused a surge of renewed energy to pump through his body and he brought up his left knee into the monster's stomach.

Joe flinched from the blow, and Halstead slid farther down the wall. He planted his feet and delivered another knee to the same spot as his fingers once again found the handle of his father's knife.

The big man dropped to a knee and Halstead pulled the blade free and plunged it down at the fallen man.

But the blade only sliced into his left shoulder before Joe managed to knock him off his feet with a flailing arm.

The horses continued to scream and batter the walls of their stalls as Halstead landed on the floor. His stomach seized up on him, causing him to retch the rest of its contents onto the floor.

He tried to get his knees under him, but the livery tilted again, causing him to fall onto his side. He still had the Bowie knife in his hand, and he tightened his grip on it. He knew he still had a chance if he could just manage to hold on to it.

He swayed as he rose and saw Joe was beginning to recover. The larger man's face was slack and his mouth hung open. Halstead knew one of his blind knee strikes must have connected with his liver, which was known to take the fight out of a man.

Halstead knew he would not survive if he allowed that fight to return.

But the livery tilted as his vision blurred once more. His empty stomach lurched, and he saw Joe was beginning to recover.

Halstead cut loose with a guttural yell as he blindly launched himself at the giant. He fell against his bulk and the two of them tumbled over together. He could not tell if he was on top of his attacker or beneath him; only that he was still there and his knife hand was still free.

He plunged the knife deep into Joe and held it there with all his remaining strength. He put all his weight into it and ducked his head against wild blows battering his arms and shoulders.

Halstead kept his eyes closed, fearing he might grow dizzy as he felt the tips of his boots scrape against the hay strewn all over the floor. He found some traction and used it to give him leverage as he felt the blade sink even farther.

Halstead felt his legs begin to tremble from the effort as what he hoped was a death rattle rose from the giant beneath him. The frantic blows grew slowly weaker before his arms dropped to the floor.

But Halstead would not move. He had to be sure Joe was dead. He had to hold on for as long as did. He was still alive. He needed to live. He had just gotten his star back. He had to get back to Abby. He could not die now. Not here. Not that day.

He laid on the handle as he heard someone calling out his name. He continued to press down on the knife as they grabbed at his shoulders and tried to pull him away. The handle slipped from his hands as faces and straw and wood blurred and spun out of view.

He was on the floor again and drew his knees beneath him as his empty stomach clenched. His fingers curled as strength and weakness coursed through his body at the same time.

"It's gonna be all right, Halstead," a man told him. "You're gonna be just fine."

Halstead shook as he panted for breath. He never thought cold air could feel so good. He heard his own voice sharp and ragged as he managed to say, "Is he dead?"

"As dead as he can be, partner. That much is for certain."

Halstead rolled onto his back and saw Red, Buster, and Langham looking down at him.

Langham knelt beside him. "You sure are a hard man to kill, Jeremiah Halstead."

Halstead turned his head and spat out the remaining poison from his mouth. "And don't you forget it."

Chapter 15

As he rode into Barren Pines, Keane looked around to get a sense for the kind of place it was. He took the lack of saloons open as a bad sign. Although there were other saloons in town, The Town Hall Saloon appeared to be the only one that was open for business. The sign tacked up out front promised "Good Gambling, Good Drink and Good Company." He hoped Glenda was as friendly as Riker had claimed.

Keane got off his horse and tied the reins to the hitching rail out front. He heard a loud crash come from the livery across the thoroughfare but paid it little mind. Liveries tended to be noisy places.

Keane clutched his coat tightly against his throat as an icy wind cut through town. He pushed in the door to The Town Hall Saloon. There was an awkward mood in the place. It was too late for lunch and too early for dinner. Half the gambling tables were empty, but the craps and roulette wheels were still spinning, dashing dreams, and making fortunes until the next spin of the wheel.

Keane decided the bar would be the best place to ask for Glenda. After he had a drink, of course. He headed for an opening next to a group of rough-hewn men he took to be trappers.

A fancy man in a gray suit that matched his moustache and Van Dyke beard was standing by himself. His hair was long enough to curl away from his collar.

A bartender with sad eyes and heavy jowls that reminded Keane of a basset hound asked him, "What'll you have?"

Keane blew into his hands to warm them. "How about a whiskey?"

The bartender produced a glass and a bottle and poured him a drink. Keane placed a dollar coin on the bar and the bartender took it before walking away.

Keane decided he might as well try to chat up the dandy standing next to him. He looked like a regular, so he might be talkative. "The barman's not much for conversation, is he?"

The older man kept his eyes on his whiskey. "What's he need to talk about? You ordered whiskey and he served it to you."

Keane shrugged it off. "Guess where I come from, the bartenders tend to be a bit more hospitable."

The old man sipped his drink. "Barren Pines isn't known for its hospitality, mister. Men come here to wait out the winter until the thaw. It's a friendly enough place if you've got money in your pocket."

"I've got plenty of that." Keane had said it loud enough that the other men standing around them could hear. He hoped it might generate some interest from curious patrons.

Now that he had broken the ice with the older man, he offered his hand to him. "My name's Lester Keane. Les to my friends. What's your name?"

"Lance McAlister." The man looked at the hand before shaking it. "Can't say it's a pleasure to make your acquaintance because that remains to be seen."

Keane decided to butter him up some. "You look like the type who can handle himself well enough. Let me guess. You were an Indian fighter in your day."

"I always found it better to run away from them whenever I could. I do my fighting with a deck of cards. Those tables you see over there are the closest I get to a battleground. I try to steer clear of folks looking to kill me. I'd suggest you do the same."

"I'll keep that in mind." Now that he'd gotten McAlister to start talking, he decided to keep it up. "What brought you to Barren Pines, Mr. McAlister?"

"Same thing that brought you and the rest of these men here. Shelter. A warm bed. And the chance to win a little money at cards."

"Can't argue with you there," Keane said. The old goat did not leave much room for conversation, but he worked with what he had. "I suppose you don't get many visitors around here this time of year."

"You'd be surprised," McAlister said. "This old town's turning into quite a holiday destination. If this keeps up, I might give up cards and start giving tours. Sell sandwiches and sarsaparilla on the side."

"Sounds like a promising enterprise," Keane said. "Though I'd think a place this out of the way wouldn't have much trade after the snow started. I hear Miss Glenda is quite a draw. What kind of gal is she, anyway?"

Keane had just reached for his whiskey when he was shoved from behind. He turned to face the man but found himself staring at a wall of bear hide. He had to crane his neck to see the man who had shoved him was a good head taller. His eyes looked in two directions at once.

Keane had met many men with this condition before. He found it best to pick one eye and keep looking at it for the duration of the conversation. "Sorry, friend. I guess I wasn't paying attention to my movements."

"Too busy running your mouth," the trapper said. "We don't like strangers around here. We like questions even less, especially about Glenda."

Keane held up his hands. "No offense meant, friend. Just trying to make conversation with Mr. McAlister here." He looked back, hoping

McAlister would back him up, but the gambler was gone.

The trapper said, "That your horse I saw hitched to the rail out there?"

"If you're talking about the bay," Keane said, "then yeah, he's mine. A good animal."

"Not toting much. Not even a bedroll." The trapper looked him over. "You don't look like a man who's been sleeping outside much."

Keane had not counted on having an answer for that. He decided the truth would serve him best. "I just got off the train in Missoula and came straight here. Figured I'd stock up on supplies before I headed out."

"Nobody does that," the trapper said. "No one makes the trip all the way out here without provisions. And no one comes in here asking that many questions just out of conversation. Why are you here?"

Keane could not tell if the man was armed, but assumed he at least had a knife somewhere on him. He backed away from the trapper and lowered his left hand to the pistol on his hip. "I came in to get out of the cold and enjoy some company. Don't make it out to be anything more than that. I didn't come in here looking for trouble, just Miss Glenda. I'd be obliged if you told me where she was."

The trapper grabbed Keane's left arm and pulled him away from the bar. He had not been manhandled so easily since childhood. "Maybe you're telling the truth and maybe you're lying, but I can smell trouble off you. That'll be up to the law to decide."

Another man pulled the pistol from Keane's holster and handed it to the trapper. It looked like a toy in the bigger man's hand.

Keane tried to pull away but cried out when the grip only grew tighter as he forced him out of the saloon and into the street.

Keane almost lost his footing in the thick snow of the thoroughfare, but the trapper did not miss a step. His grip on his arm kept him upright. Keane knew if he slipped, his arm would break. The trapper did not break his stride as he pushed him up onto the boardwalk and toward the town jail.

The trapper pounded at the jail door. "Open up. It's Petite. I've got a troublemaker here."

As soon as the door opened, Petite shoved Keane inside the jail. A young, sandy-haired man with a deputy marshal's star pinned to his shirt closed the door and accepted the pistol the trapper handed to him.

Keane saw a man in the cell but did not know who he was. He recognized the deputy, though. By descriptions he had heard of the man, anyway. It was Joshua Sandborne. And there was no sign of Halstead.

Sandborne set the pistol on his desk. "What makes you say he's trouble?"

"Found him over at Town Hall talking to McAlister and asking all sorts of fool questions. He was asking about Glenda, too. Came into town only a few minutes ago with nary a can of beans or a bedroll on his horse. He said he was fixing to buy supplies here in town, but I think he's lying. I think he was working up to asking about Halstead. He smells like a lousy bounty hunter to me. And I hate bounty hunters. They're nothing but trouble."

"What makes you say that?"

Petite crossed his arms. "I'm big, not stupid."

Sandborne picked up Keane's pistol, opened the cylinder, and dumped the bullets into his hand. "What's your name, mister?"

"Keane. Lester Keane."

He placed the bullets on his desk. "What are you doing in Barren Pines, Mr. Keane? And if you lie to me, I'll know it."

Keane knew he was already in trouble, so he went as close to the truth as he dared. "This big fella is right. I am a bounty hunter, and I'm looking for Halstead. I was hoping Miss Glenda might know where he is. Five thousand is a lot of money to a man like me."

"It's a lot of money to anyone, I'd imagine." He looked up at the trapper. "Thanks for bringing him in, Mr. Petite. I'll take it from here."

But Petite stayed put. "I'll help you lock him up. I've seen Fremont in action. He's liable to try something when you open the cell door. He won't do anything if I'm here with you."

"Petite," Fremont spat from his cell. "A dumb name for an oaf like you."

The trapper shoved Keane toward the cell. The momentum carried him more than halfway across the floor and he had to hold onto the bars to avoid falling.

Sandborne took the keys and opened the cell as Petite pushed him inside.

"Sounds like you've got a history with the sheriff," Sandborne said as he locked the door.

"You could say that. With Langham, too. I don't trust either of them. Neither should you. If you need me, I'll be minding things over at Town Hall. Joe took off a while ago and I don't know where he is."

Keane felt Fremont staring at him as Keane waited until the trapper left before he began to work on Sandborne. "Now that he's gone, you and I can speak like civilized men. This is all just one great big misunderstanding, Sandborne."

"Sandborne?" the deputy repeated. "You know my name?"

Keane tried to cover his mistake. "I saw you once or twice in Helena. People pointed you out to me. You've got quite the reputation."

Sandborne did not seem interested in that. "How many men you bring with you? And remember, don't lie to me."

"Nobody," Keane lied. "That big man wasn't too far off. I took the train here from Helena to try my hand at that reward money they've got out on Halstead. Figured I'd get outfitted while I'm in town. Maybe buy a pack horse from the livery if one is available. No sense in lugging all those goods any longer than I had to."

"I came in on the train from Helena yesterday," Sandborne told him. "I didn't see you on it. But the train from Wellspring would've come in today. You're from Battle Brook, aren't you? Or is it Valhalla?"

Riker had told Keane that Sandborne was just another young idiot with a star pinned to him. He was proving to be smart for an idiot. "Like I said, it's just me."

"I'll bet." Sandborne surprised him by drawing his pistol and holding it on Keane. "I didn't have time to search you proper before I locked you up, so take off your coat and drop it on this side of the bars. Take off your gun belt and do the same. Then turn around real slow."

"Better do as he says," Fremont chided. "He's a dangerous one, this Sandborne. Been living off Halstead's reputation for so long, he's eager to make one of his own."

"Don't listen to him," Sandborne told him. "Do as I say and you won't get hurt."

Keane shrugged out of his coat and tossed

it outside the cell. He took off his gun belt and dropped it on top of the coat. He kept his hands in the air as he slowly turned around. He even untucked his shirt to show he was not hiding anything.

Sandborne rested his foot on the coat and pulled the bundle toward him. "Now your boots. Pry them off and dump them out."

Keane had a five-shot Remington repeater tucked in his left boot and a knife in his right. They were his only way out of this mess.

He tried to stall. "My feet are all swollen up something fierce, deputy. If I pull them off, I might not be able to get them back on."

"You won't be needing them in your cell." He thumbed back the hammer of his pistol. "Do like I told you."

Fremont grinned as he watched Keane lean against the bars while he awkwardly pulled off his right boot first. A thin blade dropped to the floor.

"Kick it out here."

Keane did so.

"Now the other one," Sandborne ordered. "And do it real slow."

Keane made a show of tugging on the boot and acting like it was tight. "I told you it's swollen up. It won't come off."

Sandborne kept the pistol trained on him. "It better."

"I can't get it off hopping around like this," Keane strained. "I'll have to sit down and try it that way."

Sandborne told him to stop as Keane dropped to a knee before sitting on the floor. "That's better. It's starting to—"

He pulled the small repeater from his boot and fired. His bullet ricocheted off the bar of his cell.

Sandborne's shot struck him in the center of the chest.

Keane looked down at the hole as it began to bleed. The small pistol became heavy in his hand as he tried to lift it for a second shot.

"Don't do it, Keane!" Sandborne shouted.

Keane had just managed to lift it as another bullet struck him just below the first, causing the pistol to drop from his hand.

He watched Fremont quickly snatch it up and begin to raise it as Sandborne fired three more shots. Keane did not know how many times he had been struck, but watched the prisoner fall to his cot before sliding onto the floor. He uttered a final gasp, perhaps even a curse, before his eyes grew vacant.

As vacant as Keane knew his would soon become.

Sandborne remained where he had been. A thin trail of smoke rising from the barrel of his Colt.

And as Keane felt his life begin to slip away, he could not go without some measure of revenge.

"You're a dead man, Sandborne. You and every man with you."

He wanted to say more. He wanted to make one last stab at the fear in the younger man's eyes, but his body grew numb and his chin fell to his chest as his eyes lowered to the two holes in his shirt.

A final breath escaped him and he was gone.

Chapter 16

The sound of his pistol firing still rang in his ears when Sandborne heard the jailhouse door burst open. He saw Sheriff Langham and Petite, the trapper, in the doorway.

Langham held his pistol low as he stepped into the jail, looking down at the two bodies in the cell. "What happened?"

Sandborne slowly lowered his pistol. "A new prisoner named Keane snuck a gun into his cell. I shot him when he tried to kill me. Fremont grabbed for it, so I had to shoot him, too."

Petite punched the open door. "I didn't think to check him before I brought him to you. Sorry about that. Guess I'm stupid after all."

"There wasn't time for that," Sandborne said. "It wasn't your fault."

Langham slowly knelt beside the cell as he looked over Fremont's body. He reached through the bars, picked up the small Remington on the floor, and began to examine it. "A hideout gun. This is one of those five-shot numbers. You're lucky they didn't kill you, Sandborne."

The deputy opened his pistol and removed the spent bullets from the cylinder. "Luck had nothing to do with it." He pulled two new bullets from the loops on his belt and fed them into the cylinder. "Guess I don't have to worry about you letting Fremont go free anymore, do I?"

Langham stood up and pocketed the gun. "You never did, but you've got bigger things to worry about than that, deputy. Halstead almost got himself beaten to death just now."

Sandborne knew that had to be an exaggeration. He had never seen anyone come close to getting over on Jeremiah. "How?"

"Glenda's man Joe went after him at the livery. He knocked out Moses and rang Halstead's bell pretty hard from the looks of it. He's alive, but he's in a bad way. You'd better go look him over for yourself. Red and Buster are with him now. I came running as soon as I heard the shots in here."

Sandborne flicked the cylinder shut and slid his Colt back into his holster as he pushed past Petite to run along the boardwalk to the livery. He saw townspeople had already begun to form a knot around the entrance as Sandborne cut through them and dashed inside.

Buster was standing over a large Chinese man splayed on the floor near a bale of hay. The handle of Halstead's Bowie knife still protruded from his chest.

Buster said, "We heard the shots. You hurt?"

Sandborne shook his head. "The same can't be said for Fremont. He tried to kill me. Looks like you had some action of your own here."

"Not us." Buster gestured down toward the

dead man. "Halstead had already killed this fella before we got here. Red's inside with him now. He doesn't look too good."

Knowing how much the blade meant to his partner, Sandborne went over to the corpse to retrieve it. It was sunk deep into the big man's heart to the hilt. It took him three good tugs before he managed to pry it free. He wiped the blade clean on the dead man's shirt as Red stepped out of the livery office.

"You'd better get in here, Sandborne. He's been asking for you."

Sandborne moved inside and found Halstead slumped on a stool in the corner of the room. He had a blanket around his shoulders and the left side of his face was beginning to swell. An older man was holding a tin of beans against Halstead's face despite a nasty cut on his own head that had bled onto his collar.

"I'm Moses Armand," the man said as he beckoned Sandborne to take his place. "You'd better come over here and hold this for him. The cold will help keep the swelling down. He can't hold it himself on account of his hands aren't working too good right now."

Sandborne took hold of the tin as Moses stepped outside.

Halstead's fingers were curled as his body began to shake. "Sorry for all the bother, boys. I just can't seem to get warm."

Sandborne held the tin in place as he used his free hand to pull the blanket tighter around his friend's shoulders. "What happened?"

"Glenda sent her man over here to kill me." Halstead's words were slurred as if he was drunk. "He would've killed me if I hadn't gotten hold of my knife when I did." He winced and stifled a groan. "I think my head's busted. I felt like this when a horse threw me once, but this feels worse."

Sandborne had seen plenty of men suffer like this when he was growing up on the JT Ranch in Dover Station. "Are you dizzy?"

"Only when I open my eyes," Halstead told him. "But I'm fine if I keep them closed."

He felt around Halstead's skull while he kept the cold tin of beans against his cheek. "I've seen plenty of men with cracked skulls. You would've yelped just now if your head was broken, but it sounds like that big fella out there scrambled your eggs some. That's why you're cold. I've seen it happen to other men in your condition."

Halstead arched his neck, causing some of the bones to crack and pop. "Everything sounds like I've got my head in a bucket of water."

Sandborne knew that would pass in time. "How many times did he hit you?"

"A lot," Halstead admitted. "The first shot knocked me clean off my chair. He tried to choke me, too. It hurts when I swallow. The whole thing is just a blur to me."

Sandborne imagined it was. He had not seen the big man in life, but even in death, he looked like he could kick like a mule. "That fella's just about the biggest Chinaman I've ever seen."

"That's because he's Corean," Halstead corrected him. "I didn't know the difference before, but I sure do now." He patted at the empty holster on his belly. "He took my guns off me in the struggle. Go find them, will you?"

Sandborne saw them on a table next to the stove. "They're right over there, but you won't have any need for them now. Just sit here nice and still until the dizziness passes." The curled fingers concerned him, but he saw no reason to trouble Halstead with his suspicions.

Halstead opened his eyes for a moment, then quickly closed them again. "I thought I heard shooting as they were carrying me in here, or was that just my imagination?"

"You heard right," Sandborne told him. "A trapper named Petite found a bounty hunter named Keane asking questions over at The Town Hall. He thought he was looking for you, so he brought him over to the jail. Keane snuck a gun in his boot and took a shot at me."

Halstead opened his eyes again. "You hit?"

"No, but after I shot him, Fremont grabbed the gun and gave it a go. He's dead."

"Fremont was never as good as he thought he was." Halstead closed his eyes. "A big fella named Petite? Barren Pines is one mighty strange town."

"I'm beginning to think you're right." Sandborne held the cold tin against Halstead's face. "Keane said he was from Helena, but when he said he'd just gotten off the train, I knew he was lying. He was really from Battle Brook or Valhalla. Does that name mean anything to you?"

Halstead winced from the effort of sitting up straighter. He balled his fingers into fists and began to work them straight. "Never heard of him. What did he look like?"

"About our height. Brown curly hair. Flat nose that looked like it had been broken a couple of times."

"That describes half the men in both towns. Did he come alone?"

Sandborne did not want to add to his troubles. "We'll talk about it later when you're feeling better."

"I'm feeling good enough to hear the truth." Halstead took the tin from him and held it against his swollen face. "Was he alone?"

Sandborne took his friend's stubbornness as a good sign. "He rode in alone, but he didn't have supplies with him. He said he'd planned on buying some while he was here looking for you, but Petite didn't believe him and neither did I. I'd wager he's got friends waiting for him outside of town. Since he's from Valhalla or Battle Brook,

I figure he learned that trick from Zimmerman."

"Yeah." Halstead bent forward as a loud sound came from his stomach. "But Battle Brook means Valhalla and that means Riker."

Sandborne was not so sure. "I guess you were already on the run by the time word reached us in Helena. Riker lost an arm after we left town. His right one. His shooting arm."

"That doesn't mean anything," Halstead said. "His father taught him how to shoot with his left hand, too. Riker hates me enough to come after me with both arms and a leg missing. He's probably sitting out there on the ridge right now and he's not alone. I'd bet he's got at least five men with him. Maybe more."

Sandborne knew Halstead was probably right, but there was nothing either of them could do about that now. "You'd best worry about yourself for the moment, Jeremiah. If Riker's out there, he won't risk coming into town. Not after what happened to Keane. This town won't just roll over for his kind."

He watched Halstead struggle to open his eyes. First at a squint, then slowly wider. "That's a relief. At least the room stopped spinning." He worked his jaw from side to side. "Don't think my jaw's busted, but my left eye is a bit cloudy. How does it look?"

Sandborne crouched in front of him and examined it. "It's awfully red but seems to be working fine. It'll take time, though. In the meantime, we ought to get as much coffee into you as you can stand. If you fall asleep, there's a good chance you won't wake up again. Don't laugh me off because I've seen it happen."

Halstead groaned as he pushed himself off the stool and slowly rose. "In case you haven't noticed, I'm in no condition to laugh at anyone."

Sandborne stood ready to catch him if he fell over, but after a shaky start, Halstead righted himself. "Help me get walking, Joshua. Sitting in here like a foal won't help me get better. Might give those folks ideas about taking a shot at that reward money. And I plan on walking over to the saloon and arresting Glenda for sending her man after me."

"I don't think that's a good idea, Jeremiah. You can hardly stand, much less arrest anyone."

"I'm not sure it's a good idea myself," Halstead admitted, "but it's necessary. Tuck my guns in my holsters for me, will you? I don't want anyone to think I'm an easy mark."

Reluctantly, Sandborne followed Halstead's orders and slid the guns into their proper places and hovered around him as Halstead took his first tentative step, followed by another.

"Don't worry, Jeremiah. I won't let you fall."

Halstead grinned, then winced from the effort. "No. You never have."

· · ·

From atop his horse on the ledge overlooking the town, Riker worked the dial of his binoculars to bring two men in front of the livery into focus.

He had seen the flurry of activity in the small town over the past several minutes, and he watched now as the group of townspeople in front of the livery backed away as two men stepped outside. Riker did not need the glasses to confirm who one of them was. He would know this man on a pitch-black night. His hands shook as he tried to keep the field glasses steady as he watched Sandborne lead Halstead along the boardwalk.

Weeks in exile had clearly taken a toll on Halstead. His face was drawn, and his clothes hung loose on him. He was limping as he held something against the left side of his face. And although his enemy moved on his own power, Sandborne looked ready to grab him if he stumbled.

Halstead appeared to be in a poor way, but he still had his guns on him. And as long as there was a breath of life in the man, Riker knew he was still dangerous.

He kept his binoculars on Halstead's and Sandborne's trek toward the jail as one of Keane's men approached him. Riker remembered his name was Gains or something like that.

"Sorry to bother you, Mr. Riker," Gains began,

"but me and the others were wondering what's going on down there. We heard those shots earlier, and we're worried about Keane."

Riker did not lower his glasses. "You don't have to worry about him anymore. I think Keane is dead."

"Dead?" Gains repeated. "You mean Halstead got him?"

"No. I think Sandborne shot him over at the jail."

"Why would Keane be in the jail?" Gains asked. "Did you send him there?"

Riker let out a long breath. Dealing with hired guns always tested his patience. "No. I sent him to talk to someone at the saloon. A bouncer grabbed him and brought him to the jail, probably for asking too many questions. Halstead was in the livery. Sandborne was alone in the jail when the shots happened."

"How can you know all that from up here?" Gains asked. "Did you see Keane dead?"

Riker passed the glasses down to him. "Sandborne ran out of the jail after the shots. He's bringing Halstead back from the livery. Take a look for yourself."

Gains worked the dial to bring the image into focus. "There's no way Sandborne could've killed the boss. He never would've let that mangy pup get the jump on him like that. Not even if he was drunk."

But Riker remembered how the bounty hunter

had often boasted that he always kept a small Derringer in his boot for emergencies. Riker figured he must have made a play for the pistol when Sandborne had undoubtedly killed him. He did not think much of the young deputy, but he was more than a match for a desperate prisoner with a gun.

The other men began to draw closer now as Gains worked the lenses to bring the image into focus. Riker told him what he was looking at. "Look at the two men on the boardwalk. The one with the sandy hair is Sandborne, one of the men we followed here from Missoula. The dark, limping one with him is Halstead. I think there was a fight in the livery and Halstead got hurt, but Sandborne was in the jail when we heard the shots. From what I've seen, I'm pretty sure he was alone when it happened."

He watched Gains track Halstead and Sandborne with the binoculars. "I don't see anything that proves Keane is dead."

"Sandborne usually hits what he aims at, boys. You'd better get used to the idea that Keane is gone."

Gains passed the glasses to another man as he said, "We won't know anything for sure until we ride down there and see it for ourselves. Halstead doesn't look too good, so now's our chance. Get to your horses, boys. We've wasted enough time waiting around up here."

Riker quickly moved his horse between them and their mounts. "Hold on, boys. Let's talk about this."

"There's nothing to talk about," Gains said. "You told us Keane's down in that jail. He's either hurt or dead. Either way, we're not leaving him with the likes of them. And we're not letting Sandborne or Halstead get away with killing our friend."

Riker and his horse moved with them as the men began to go for their horses. "Riding down there right now is nothing short of suicide."

Gains stopped and the others stopped with him.

"Suicide? You saw the shape Halstead's in as clear as I did. He can barely stand much less put up a fight. You can stay up here where it's safe if you want to. We're going down there to make him and Sandborne pay for Keane."

Riker brought his horse into a tight spin, forcing the men to back away. "Use your head, Gains. You've never seen Halstead in action. I have. Plenty of times. He might look hurt now, but if he's up and breathing, he's dangerous. And any man who goes against him angry is already dead." He turned so they could see his missing right arm. "I learned that lesson the hard way."

Riker sensed a change in the men, just like he had sensed a change in the men that night in the bar back in Valhalla. The night he had led them to Battle Brook to attack Halstead. The same night

Halstead had killed his brother and taken his arm.

Riker kept talking. "Sandborne didn't catch Keane and bring him into the jail. A bouncer from the saloon grabbed him and brought him over. That means there's bound to be more like him in town. If we go charging in there right now, there's a good chance they'll put up a fight."

"So what?" one of the men said. "Any one of us is worth ten flea-bitten trappers."

Riker spoke over their grumbles. "All of you heard what happened to me in Battle Brook, didn't you? How more than twenty of us had Halstead dead to rights and he still managed to wipe us out. I didn't think he had a chance then, but by the time it was over, I'd lost a brother and, a few weeks later, an arm. You want to go up against him now, I won't be able to stop you, but don't be surprised when you come back here with your tails between your legs."

Gains stepped forward and stood looking up at Riker. "Sounds like you lost more than your arm in Battle Brook. Sounds like you lost your nerve, too."

Riker spun his horse again and knocked Gains to the ground. He drew his pistol as he came out of the turn and held it down at the others as they helped Gains get back on his feet.

"I'm paying you boys good money to be here, but I know I'm not your leader. Keane ran your outfit and now he's dead. The men who killed him will pay for that, but only if we're still alive to make them suffer. You don't have to take my word for it. Pick up those field glasses and look the town over for yourselves. It's a turkey shoot down there. Closed buildings on either side of the jail. No cover to speak of. Keane went in there alone because he didn't think we should ride in there and make easy targets of ourselves. He was right then, and he's still right now."

Gains got to his feet and pushed the snow from his pants and backside. "What do you expect us to do? Just sit out here in the cold and wait?"

The others agreed with him.

Riker gestured up to the darkening sky. "We've only got an hour or so of daylight left, but we've got enough provisions for a week. I say we play it smart. We camp out here tonight while I head down into town after dark and find out what happened. I'll know where Halstead and Sandborne are, too. Come first light tomorrow, we'll make our move. They're not going anywhere, and neither are we."

Gains shook the rest of the snow off his coat. "You expect us to sit up here eating beans while you're down there sipping champagne and eating steak?"

Riker nodded toward his shoulder. "I lost my drinking arm, boys. And steak's not my favorite meal these days."

The dark humor caused the men to laugh, which

broke the tension that had settled over the group.

Gains was the only one who had not laughed. "You really think Halstead's as dangerous as all that? Even now?"

"I don't think," Riker said. "I know."

Gains looked at the others, gauging their mood before looking back at Riker. "You want a night, Mr. Riker? Fine. We'll give you a night, but only one. But come first light, me and these boys do things our way."

Riker tucked his pistol away. "Just make sure you get plenty of rest because you're going to need it."

Chapter 17

Billy Sunday had just finished building a cigarette when he heard the whistle of the eastbound train echo through Helena. It was a cool night, but not as cold or as windy as it had been. It was warm enough that some of the snow on the station roof had begun to melt, striking a comforting rhythm as it dripped to the ground.

He thumbed a match alive and lit his cigarette as the train slid into view. He waved the match dead and tossed it on the tracks as the train slowed to approach the station. He allowed smoke to escape through his nostrils as a great blast of steam rose from the engine.

Billy stood as the train braked to a halt. He watched as porters, baggage handlers, and people waiting for passengers began to swarm to the iron beast like flies to a fallen steer.

Whistles sounded as conductors stepped down from the train and placed stools on the platform to help passengers who were about to disembark.

Billy got to his feet and watched as ladies and children began to descend the narrow steps of the cars. He had chosen his spot with purpose. His man on the train had already wired ahead to tell him where to wait.

He spotted the thin, bald man with wire-rimmed

spectacles struggle to lug his heavy bag down the stairs. Billy watched him stop at a clear patch on the platform to put his hat on and clean his foggy glasses on his scarf.

Billy stepped forward and picked up the bag.

Mark Mannes squinted up at him blindly as he continued to clean his glasses. "Put that down, boy. I didn't call for a porter."

"That's good because I'm no porter," Billy said. "I saw you struggling and thought I might lend a hand."

Mannes quickly put his glasses back on and continued to squint at him. "Wait a moment. I know you, don't I?"

"Lots of men who look like me on the train," Billy said. "I'll bet you can't tell one of us from the other."

Mannes's beady eyes drew narrow. "Not you. You're different. You're Billy Sunday, aren't you? You're one of Mackey's men."

"Right you are." Billy hefted the bag. "Now, come on. This thing isn't getting any lighter. What did you pack in here, anyway? A scrawny fella like you doesn't need this many clothes."

"You can set it down right where you are, thank you." Mannes began to look around for a porter. "I know what this is and I won't stand for it." He snapped his fingers at a black man passing with a luggage cart. "Here, boy! I need you to take my bag."

The porter glanced at Billy and continued without stopping.

"Guess he's busy," Billy said. "Good thing for you I'm here to lend a hand."

Mannes raised his weak chin at him. "You're here to lend a hand, all right. A hand for your friend Halstead."

Billy made a show of looking around at the passengers beginning to crowd the platform. "Jeremiah's here, too? Why didn't he tell me? Folks are looking for him."

Mannes pointed a thin finger at Billy. "I know you're here to try to intimidate me, deputy, and I can assure you that it won't work. Halstead is a—"

Billy took a step forward, forcing the lawyer to back away. "It's not polite to point, Mr. Mannes. Some folks take that as an insult. You wouldn't want to insult me, would you?"

Mannes lowered his hand. "I suppose Mackey sent you here to try to get me or my cousin to withdraw the warrant for Halstead's arrest. Well, you've wasted your time because that's never going to happen. Jeremiah Halstead is a fugitive from justice, and he's going to remain that way until he's either captured or killed. And if you so much as lay another finger on me, you'll find yourself in even more trouble than he is."

Billy set the heavy case on the ground. "Here I am trying to welcome a leading citizen to Helena, and this is the thanks I get."

Mannes grabbed his bag, but Billy set a boot on it, pinning it to the platform as he took another drag on his cigarette. "You're lucky I knew what car you were on, considering how we've never met until tonight. Not formally, anyway." He gestured at him with the cigarette. "We sort of met each other back in Valhalla, remember? I was up in the rocks while Zimmerman and his men were talking to Aaron. You were hiding behind your office at the time, but I saw you just the same."

Mannes swallowed again. "I remember seeing you butcher a man."

Billy smiled at the memory. "A fifty-caliber slug can do a lot of damage to a man's head. It's a shame a delicate man like you had to see that. I thought you might've learned from it, a smart fella such as yourself."

"Learn what exactly? That you and Mackey and Halstead are nothing more than killers with stars on their chests? I knew that already."

"We're more than just killers," Billy told him. "Killing's part of the job, but it's not all of it. We're flesh and bone, just like you. Aaron has a wife. Jeremiah's got a sweetheart."

"And what do you have?"

"A good eye and a steady hand."

Mannes swallowed again.

Billy went on. "Some folks think the army taught me how to shoot, but that's not true. I was already a good shot before I enlisted. Got plenty of practice with a rifle back when I was a boy. My daddy taught me how to hunt small game as soon as I was old enough to hold a rifle. I developed a real skill that way."

He tapped Mannes in the chest with his cigarette hand. Some ash flaked on the lawyer's coat. "Want to know what I used to like hunting the most? Weasels." He cocked his head to the side. "Anyone ever tell you how much you look like a weasel, Mr. Mannes?"

Mannes tried to keep the fear out of his voice. "Of all the gall."

"Doesn't take much gall to kill a weasel," Billy continued, "though I'll admit they sure are crafty critters in their own way. Just when you think you've got one lined up in your sights, it cuts the other way and spoils your shot. It'll go jump in a hole or duck behind a rock. It can be mighty tough to track them again after that. Some men give up and go after another one, but not me. Want to know what my trick is?"

Billy leaned in close. "I hold the shot until I know I've got him dead to rights. Wait until he's far away from any rocks or holes before I squeeze the trigger. That's all there is to hunting, Mr. Mannes. It's not about being ready to kill something. Anyone can do that, especially a hungry man looking for a meal. It's not even about being a good shot. Most folks can get the knack of it if they practice long enough. The real secret is knowing what that weasel is going to do. That makes the difference between a full belly and an empty one."

Mannes kept his hands at his sides. Billy knew he wanted to look away, maybe even run, but did not. He did not because he could not. He was too scared to move.

The lawyer cleared his throat. "Concealment also plays a part in the hunt, deputy, and you've overplayed your hand tonight. Dozens of people have seen us here together on this platform. They're witnesses. If something happens to me, you'll be held responsible."

"Nothing wrong with two men talking at a train station," Billy said. "And that's all we're doing, isn't it. Talking about hunting. Talking about how you let Zimmerman and Hubbard talk you into hunting a critter you didn't understand. You figured all you had to do was scribble some words on a piece of paper and have your cousin swear out a warrant on Halstead. You figured that would be the end of it. That the law and your family would be the rocks you could hide behind. That they'd be enough to keep you safe."

Billy slowly shook his head. "But any weasel, assuming he could talk, would tell you there's no such thing as safe in this world, Mr. Mannes. He'd tell you a good hunter can hit his mark from any direction no matter the weather or the terrain because he knows where that old weasel's gonna be. Just like I knew where you would be tonight."

Billy flicked the ash from his cigarette. "Yes, sir. When I look at it that way, I'd say weasel hunting's just about the most rewarding kind of hunting there is."

Mannes slowly shook his head. "As soon as I leave here, and I *will* be leaving here as healthy as the moment I arrived, I'm going to tell my cousin, Judge Owen, about this ham-fisted threat of yours. I'm going to enjoy watching him ruin you and Aaron Mackey because of it."

"No, you won't." Billy finished his cigarette and flicked it away. "Instead, you'll remember this conversation. You'll come to understand the error of your ways and realize the mistake you made by going after Jeremiah. You're going to have your cousin rescind his warrant first thing in the morning."

"Rescind?" Mannes repeated. "That's quite a technical term for a man who, as I understand it, can't read."

"A man doesn't need to know how to read to know the law," Billy responded. "You're going to rescind it because it's the right thing to do and because it'll make your life a whole lot easier."

Mannes's fingers began to tap at his sides. Billy's message had finally struck a chord. "How easy?"

"That depends on what you want."

Mannes looked around the crowded platform as he thought it over. "I might be able to talk my cousin into rescinding Halstead's warrant if Mackey agrees to turn his attention away from Battle Brook and Valhalla. Brunet's not Zimmerman and he's happy to grow old in the town he started. Cal Hubbard is only interested in making money, not enemies. If you agree to give us a wide berth—within obvious limits, of course—I may be able to help Halstead get his good name back."

Since Billy knew Mackey had made a similar agreement with Zimmerman, he felt reasonably sure the marshal would agree to it. "Then I'll expect to hear some good news from the judge first thing in the morning."

The lawyer hesitated. "And if that's not possible."

"You're a crafty man, Mr. Mannes. You'll find a way to make sure it is."

Mannes's sloping shoulders sagged even further. "Agreed."

Billy slid his foot off the bag. "I'll be looking forward to getting that notice in the morning."

He watched the lawyer pick up his heavy bag and thread his way through the crowd as quickly as he could manage.

Billy was proud of himself. He had resisted the urge to punch the man in the face.

He waited until the crowd thinned out a bit

before he joined them in leaving the station for the hotels and wagons that waited to greet them after a long journey.

And Billy was not surprised to find Aaron Mackey waiting for him beneath one of the new gas lamps the city had just installed all over town.

He smiled at the marshal. "Funny running into you here. I thought Katherine was having a roast for dinner."

"The roast can wait," Mackey said. "What were you talking to Mannes about?"

Billy stalled as they began to walk back to town. "How'd you know I was coming here?"

"That look in your eye when you heard Mannes was on the train tipped me off. I wanted to make sure you didn't kill him."

"The thought never crossed my mind."

As they reached the thoroughfare outside the station, Mackey asked, "What did you two talk about?"

"Hunting weasels."

"Subtle," Mackey said. "Real subtle."

Billy laughed. "Got the job done, though."

Chapter 18

Glenda stood alone in the dark corner at the end of the bar, eyeing the front door as she downed a whiskey before quickly pouring herself another.

In her life, trouble had always come in threes, and she had already had two items of bad news that day. Joe had been killed instead of Halstead, and Sandborne had shot her lover to death.

She did not count Jason Fremont as a loss. He had forgotten his place in their plans and had begun to think of himself as her equal. He had been foolish enough to kill Dave Armand before talking to her about his demands for more money and had paid the price for it. Her life was much simpler with him dead.

But Joe's death had been a terrible blow. The mute had been her only protector and now he was gone. She had known of Halstead's reputation, but Joe had never failed her before. All of her troubles would have been gone with both Halstead and Fremont out of the way. But now that Joe was gone, she was alone. And whatever third bit of trouble that came next would barrel straight at her like a stampede. She was the only link between Fremont and Joe. Two dead men that threatened to pull her into the grave with them.

She had thought about making a run for it, but she had never been a skilled rider, even in the best of conditions, and the road to Missoula was bound to be slick with snow and ice. With night fast approaching, the trip could prove even more dangerous than remaining in Barren Pines. At least here she had admirers. She had Petite to look after her. The big oaf was not as capable as Joe had been, but he was better than nothing.

Keane's visit was the only notion that gave her hope. Petite had said the man had come to town without any provisions. She hoped that meant he had not come alone. If Sandborne and Langham had come in search of Halstead, perhaps Emil Riker was close by. It was not much of a hope, but it was all she had for the moment.

She felt the liquor begin to affect her as she reached for her glass. She flinched when she heard the saloon door open but was relieved when it was only a couple of regulars coming in from the cold. She decided to slow down her drinking. She would need a clear mind for whatever lay ahead.

She had heard that Joe had given Halstead quite a beating, but she had also heard he had managed to walk out of the livery on his own. He was a brute, but he was not a fool. He would know Joe and Fremont had been working under her orders. It was only a matter of time before he kicked in the saloon door and dragged her off to jail. She only hoped one of her customers rushed to her aid when the time came.

The saloon door squealed on its hinges as she saw Sheriff Henry Langham walk inside. Tall and bearded, his arrogance was only rivaled by Fremont's. His two deputies, Red and Buster, remained at the entrance as the three of them looked over the crowd.

She held her breath as she waited for Halstead or Sandborne to follow behind him but began to breathe again when the door remained shut. Perhaps Halstead was hurt worse than she had heard?

Langham peered through the haze of smoke that had settled over the card tables and looked in her direction. She beckoned Stumpy, the night bartender, and handed the bottle of rotgut whiskey to him. "Put this away and get me a bottle of the good stuff. Two fresh glasses, too. The fancy ones we keep behind the bar."

Stumpy quickly did as he had been told as Langham made his way to her part of the bar. Ever the actress, she managed a forlorn look as she peered down into an empty glass.

None of the men standing at the bar moved to stop Langham, but they all watched him as he approached her. He stopped at a respectable distance as he said, "Miss Glenda, we have to talk."

Glenda kept her eyes on the empty glass.

"You'll have to do all the talking, sheriff. I'm afraid I don't have the words."

Langham slipped his hands into his pockets and looked down at his boots. "I guess you've heard about what happened earlier. Your man Joe is dead and so is Deputy Fremont."

She blinked hard and hoped he saw the tear she worked free for his benefit. "I heard, but still can't believe it. My two great protectors gone within a moment of each other. Life can be so terribly cruel sometimes. How is Deputy Halstead doing?"

"Better than he should. Joe got hold of him pretty good in that livery. It's a miracle he's still alive."

One man's miracle was often a woman's curse. "I don't know what could've gotten into him. Into Joe, I mean. I guess he must've seen the way Halstead treated me earlier today in front of the jail."

Langham grew still. "Treated you how?"

She could tell by his tone that she almost had him on her hook. "He was so gruff with me. So very angry when I tried to visit Jason this morning. I suppose I can't blame him for it. Jason had tried to pin Dave's murder on him, so I understand why he was cross. But Joe obviously couldn't. He never could see things clearly, not when I was involved. I suppose he must've taken Halstead's mood toward me as a threat. I don't

238

know how he could've gotten it into his head to hurt the deputy. He was never one to act so rashly before." She looked up at the sheriff. "You knew how he was. A gentle giant except when it came to defending me. If only he had told me what he was planning to do, I would've talked him out of it." She looked back down at her empty glass. She did not want to oversell Langham on her grief. "That's foolish I know, especially because he couldn't talk, but he could feel. He was so very human in that way."

Langham scratched his chin. "You mean you didn't send him over to the livery after Halstead?"

She kept her eyes on the glass, afraid she might accidentally tell the truth. "How could I have known where Halstead was? I was back in my room, quietly weeping after our unpleasant meeting on the boardwalk in front of the jail. I suppose Joe got it into his head that Halstead had hurt me somehow. He was very perceptive in that way, sheriff. Those from the Orient may not speak our language, but not every emotion can be conveyed in words."

Langham took a step toward her, and she slowly lifted her head to look at him.

"You're saying Joe went after Halstead on his own. Without any prodding from you?"

She had to keep herself from laughing in his face. The fool was looking for any excuse to believe her. Most men were a sucker for a woman

239

in distress, and Langham was no exception. "How could I have told him to do anything? I was back in my room from the time I got back from the jail right up until Petite came to tell me what had happened. Losing Joe was horrible, but when he told me what Sandborne had done to Jason, well, I don't remember what happened after that. I suppose I came out here. I must have, considering I'm here now."

She grabbed the lapel of his coat and forced another tear from her eyes. "Tell me the truth, sheriff. Did he suffer?" She let go of his coat and looked away. "No, please don't tell me. I don't want to know. I don't think I have the strength for it."

"I was there right after it happened," Langham said. "He went as peaceful as any man could hope under the circumstances."

She had thought that had been the case. He deserved to suffer for all the trouble he had caused her. For all the trouble he might still cause her. "He was so full of life, I can't bring myself to believe he's dead."

"Yeah." Langham's voice was thick with emotion. "Kind of hard for me to believe it myself."

She gestured toward the full bottle of fine whiskey on the bar. Grief had made him pliable. Liquor would make him even more so. "Would you join me in drinking to Jason's memory, sheriff? Not to what he did, but to who he was. To the man he used to be."

Langham rested his hand on the bottle. "We can drink to him tonight, Miss Glenda, but tomorrow, Deputy Sandborne's going to have some questions for you. He's a gruff young pup, but he's a federal marshal and I can only put him off for so long."

Perhaps a night might be all the time she needed. Since Keane had not been traveling alone, there was a chance that his riding partners might come looking for him. She might be able to manipulate them as she had Joe and Fremont and now, Langham.

She inched her glass toward him. "The deputy can ask me all the questions he wants, but tonight is about the friends we've lost."

She hid her smile as Langham pulled the cork out of the bottle and began to pour.

Riker waited until after dark before he rode down into Barren Pines. He was careful not to ride through the main throughfare. He took the side street to the north of it instead. Most of the dwellings along the stretch were small, modest structures, and the people who lived in them were not the curious type.

Riker stopped his horse at the back door of the Town Hall Saloon, wrapped the reins around a post of the back porch, and found the side door

241

Glenda had mentioned in her letters. Finding the side door open, he slipped inside the narrow hallway, and followed her instructions by turning right. Through the wall, he could hear someone out in the saloon doing a decent job of playing "Old Dan Tucker" on a piano. A sheet of paper with "Glenda" written on it was tacked to a door.

He knocked and heard a woman answer, "Damn it, Mac. I already told you I ain't doing an encore. I'm tuckered out and my feet are killing me."

"This isn't Mac. It's Emil Riker."

He heard a flurry of activity from inside the dressing room. Bottles clinked and fabric rustled as the showgirl answered in a more refined tone, "Just a minute while I powder my face."

Riker looked down the other end of the hallway and saw that it led to an area behind the stage. There was a large canvas with crudely painted snowcapped mountains and one that looked like it was supposed to be the inside of a barn.

The dressing room door swung in and Glenda smiled up at him. She held a white silk gown closed at the waist. Her face sported fresh powder, and the thick red hair he remembered from the photo she had sent him was piled high on her head, secured by a pin. He caught the scent of rosewater as she offered him her hand. "It's nice to finally meet you, Sheriff Riker. I'm Glenda."

Riker ignored her hand as he stepped inside.

"Save it for your customers. I'm here with a purpose."

"So much for pleasantries." She pushed the door shut. "I see you're as charming in person as you were in our correspondence."

Riker sat in the first chair he saw. "I've spent most of the day watching the town from a distance." He would not trust her with more details than that. "What happened to the man I sent here? Keane?"

Glenda swept past him on her way to her dressing table. She held her smile as she lowered herself onto her seat and crossed one long leg over the other, revealing more thigh than her patrons saw onstage. "Your timing couldn't be better. Sheriff Langham just left after asking me a similar question. I even gave him a bottle to take back to his room for company. Would you like something to drink while we talk, sheriff? It's an awfully long story."

Riker imagined she was used to men allowing her to steer a conversation in a direction of her choosing. "Answer my question about Keane. Did you talk to him before your bouncer brought him to the jail?"

Glenda scratched her knee with a long, painted nail. "If I had, he wouldn't have been brought to the jail. He'd still be alive and so would Fremont."

"Fremont?" He remembered the name from

Glenda's letters. Hy Vandenberg had also mentioned him back at the train station in Missoula. "The deputy? I thought Sandborne and Keane were alone in the jail."

Glenda's smile faded. "If only he had been. Fremont got himself locked up for killing Dave Armand, a shop owner who demanded a piece of our reward money on Halstead. He's in town, you know. Halstead, I mean."

Riker began to piece together all that he had seen from the ridge. "I saw Halstead, but how did this shopkeeper know you and Fremont were in on the reward?"

"He was also the postman," she said. "He must've seen the return address on all those letters we've been sending each other for the past few weeks. A man can hardly think of Battle Brook without thinking of Halstead these days. Dave also knew I'd asked Halstead here to my dressing room to see me. Dave knew Fremont and I were close, figured we were up to something, and threatened to tell Halstead about it. Jason lost his temper and shot him for his trouble."

Riker tried to hold onto his temper as he ran his hand over his mouth. He did not know why Glenda had decided to interfere, but he had to get something else straight first. "Since Fremont was in jail, you sent that Chinaman after Halstead, didn't you? Figured you could still collect that reward."

244

"The man was from Corea, not China, and now he's dead. I don't know how Halstead got the better of him, but he did." Glenda's thin eyebrows lowered. "You saw quite a bit, didn't you?"

"I saw everything except the reason why you wanted to talk to Halstead in the first place. I told you to send me a message if you heard about him. That's all."

"And just how was I supposed to do that?" she asked. "We don't have a telegraph office in town and the road to Missoula was snowed in. We haven't had a regular mail delivery in a week. Halstead told Fremont he was planning on leaving town as soon as the snow stopped. I wanted to find a way of keeping him here until I could get a message off to you." She looked down at her slippers. "Obviously, things didn't go as I'd hoped."

Riker watched her pout. She was awfully convincing, but not as good an actress as she thought. "A shopkeeper's dead. So is my mercenary, your boyfriend the deputy, and your Chinaman."

"Keane got himself killed all on his own, and Fremont got shot when he went for Keane's gun. I told you Joe was Corean."

"Quiet," he snapped. "That's four men dead in the past day on account of you."

"Not because of me," she said. "Because of Halstead."

Riker was not interested in a debate. "If you'd done what I told you, they'd still be alive, Halstead would be dead, and you'd have that reward money. Now that his guard is up—"

"His guard is always up." Glenda gestured at his missing arm. "You found that out the hard way. I found out for myself, and here I am without a scratch."

"For now." Riker lowered his hand. "You're not as smart as you think you are, Glenda. In fact, you've become a downright problem for me. I could be forgiven for thinking you've outlived your usefulness."

Riker and Glenda stood at the same time.

But it was Glenda who had the tip of a blade to his throat before he could grab his pistol.

"Mind your tone in here, Riker," Glenda whispered. "Men don't talk to me like that, especially when there's no reason to be angry."

There was a time when Riker would have made her regret pulling a knife on him. But that time had long passed. A one-armed man had to tread carefully. Glenda had proven to be more dangerous than he had thought. "What do you mean there's no reason? Halstead's still alive and we'll never be able to get to him now that Langham and his men are here in town."

Glenda grinned up at him. "Everything can still work just like you wanted if you'll just sit back down and listen like a good boy." She took some of the pressure off the knife tip. "Nothing is lost and there's still everything to be gained. You can have your pound of flesh, and I can still get my money. You're not the only one around here with a plan."

Riker touched the tiny wound on his neck and his fingers came away red. "You cut deep, Glenda."

The showgirl stepped back but kept the knife ready. "A tough man like you won't fret about a little old flesh wound, will you? I'll fix you up good as new if you'll just sit down and listen to what I have to say."

Riker saw no harm in hearing her out, so he sat back down.

She set the stiletto on her dressing table, picked up a bottle, and poured some into a ball of cotton. "This'll sting a little, but you can take it. How much do you know about Sheriff Langham?"

Riker noticed her robe had fallen open down the middle and she was not wearing anything beneath it. He had not seen a naked woman in a long time and was in no hurry to look away. "I've heard he's the ambitious type."

"Just like Jason Fremont was." She came to him and placed the cotton against the cut on his neck. He refused to yelp from the sting. "But Langham's much smarter than Jason ever was. Cunning, you might say. He's got a sentimental side to him, too."

She told him to hold the cotton in place, which he did. "What's that got to do with Halstead?"

Glenda sat at her dressing table and closed her robe. "I was entertaining Langham about an hour ago before my show. He came over here to ask me why I'd sent Joe after Halstead. I just batted my eyes and told him I had no earthly idea why he'd do something like that." That grin again. "I didn't think he believed me at first, but he did. Men are so easy to fool. A quivering voice and a few tears at the right time make them melt faster than snow on a hot stove."

Riker pressed the cotton harder against his wound. "Not me."

"No," Glenda said. "I can see that. Fortunately, Langham's a different sort. He knew Jason and I were more than just friends, so I made him forget about his questions and got him to commiserate on losing Jason. He thought of Fremont as the son he never had."

"Touching," Riker said. "So what?"

"It's more than touching. It's useful. He told me all about how he'd planned on sharing the glory of bringing in Halstead with him. He wanted to see his name right next to his in all the papers. He told me he and those idiots he calls deputies are riding back to Missoula tomorrow to bring Fremont back home where he belongs." She giggled. "The sentimental fool. He told me he's leaving Halstead behind in Sandborne's care because Halstead's too hurt to travel. Seems Joe scrambled his eggs some." She tapped her temple. "He can't see straight and isn't too steady on his feet."

Riker was encouraged by the news. His ten men against Sandborne and a weakened Halstead. It just might work this time. "You sure he meant it?"

"Ever heard the expression 'in vino veritas'?" She giggled again. "By the time Langham went back to his room with that bottle I gave him, he was in no condition to lie. And I think he just might be useful to us."

Riker forgot about the cut on his neck. "How?"

Glenda reached over to pull the cotton from the wound and reapply it. "Because he came here looking for glory but thinks he's leaving with a dead, disgraced friend. If you and I work together, we can make him see this can still have a happy ending. He can still have the glory he came for, which he'll want now more than ever because it's all he's got left. And we can even make Jason Fremont into a hero."

Riker had not expected to think much of any plan of Glenda's devising. But now that he had heard her out, he thought it might have some promise. "You think you can bring him around to our way of thinking? After all this?"

"I got you to listen to me, didn't I?" Glenda winked. "And you're not drunk and awash in grief like Langham is. We'll give him a couple of hours. Let the liquor take hold of him and, when he's as soaked as that cotton you've got on your neck, we'll talk to him together. Like my mama always told me, a drowning man will grab any branch."

Riker decided to hear her out. He had nothing to lose but time, and he had plenty of that until sunrise. "You're a devious woman, Glenda. Tell me more."

She went behind her dressing screen, brought out a bucket with a bottle of champagne in it, and set it on her dressing table. "I had it packed with snow when I heard about Keane. I was expecting you."

Yes, Riker would enjoy hearing what she had to say. "We'll need glasses."

She produced two from a drawer in her table. "Now, let's talk about how we're going to corrupt the good sheriff of Missoula and get rich in the bargain."

Riker watched her work the cork of the champagne bottle. Something a man in his condition could not do. "I didn't come here for money. I came here for Halstead."

"Wealth comes in all types of currency." She worked the cork free with a quiet pop. "Now, listen to what I have to say."

Chapter 19

Halstead sat on the edge of the boardwalk holding a handful of packed snow against his aching left cheek.

Sandborne stood against the wall of the jail. His hands dug deep into the pockets of his coat. "Don't know why we're standing out here when we've got a perfectly warm jail waiting for us."

The icy cold of the snow numbed the pain in his face better than the tin can had. "It smells like death in there, even with the bodies gone. Go inside if you want. No one asked you to watch me."

"Not with you seeing double and with Riker liable to be out there on the loose," Sandborne said. "Besides, I need to ask you something."

Halstead braced to add a headache to his list of ailments. Once Sandborne got to asking questions, there was no telling how long it would last. "What is it?"

"How come you didn't kick that big fella where it hurts? I've never seen a man of any size be able to hold a grip after that."

"I tried, but it didn't work. He was a eunuch."

"A eunuch? I thought he was Chinese."

"Corean," Halstead corrected him. "A eunuch is different." He thought of a term a cowboy like

Sandborne could understand. "He was gelded."

Sandborne shuddered and not just from the cold. "Mercy."

"Yeah." Halstead was glad the dizziness had stopped and his vision had returned. It still hurt to swallow, but the cold night air kept his throat from aching. He had tried not to think about the attack, but the constant pain made it impossible to forget. The Corean giant had thrown him the beating of his life and taught him a lesson he would not soon forget. He could not lower his guard for a second.

Sandborne stomped his feet. "I was glad you listened to me about staying here instead of talking to Glenda. Shows that gelded fella didn't beat all the sense out of you."

Halstead hated the idea of having another man do his job for him, much less Langham. But with the prospect of Riker being nearby, he knew he needed as much rest as he could get. Glenda was not going anywhere.

Halstead remembered something from their earlier conversation in the jail. "Why'd you tell me to put my star back on earlier?"

"Because it's my understanding that an opportunity might be coming your way as soon as we get back to Missoula."

Halstead turned to look up at him, but a web of pain from his neck to his temple made him regret it. "What kind of opportunity."

Sandborne rubbed his gloved hands together for warmth. "An opportunity I think you'll like. The circus is coming to Helena. Folks started putting up flyers all over town the day I got on the train to come here."

Halstead gathered more snow from the thoroughfare and packed it against his face. "Don't do this, Joshua."

Sandborne continued. "Seeing as how you were thinking of a career in show business with Glenda, I figured you'd jump at the chance."

"You are traveling a dangerous path."

"I could put in a good word for you with the man who runs it. Maybe get you a job as a juggler. Or balancing a sword on your nose."

Halstead kept his head still as the cold from the packed snow seeped in. "I'll never hear the end of this, will I?"

"This?" Sandborne shook his head. "This is nothing. Wait until Billy finds out. It'll just about make his year."

Halstead had made a point of not thinking about his old life when he was up in the mountains. About Aaron and Billy. About Abby waiting for him back in Helena. Life up there had been easier to take when it was one meal at a time.

"I'd like to see Billy. And Aaron, too." He was not sure he could ask the next question, but he did. "How's Abby?"

"She misses you, though I can't see why,"

Sandborne said. "She's working with Miss Katherine at the hotel. Teaches school, too. I hear she's popular with the kids."

Halstead was not surprised. She always had a knack for teaching. She had taught him much in the short time they had enjoyed with each other. "Maybe I'll be seeing her someday. Probably through a set of bars."

"I don't think that'll happen, Jeremiah. I ran into an admirer of yours back in Missoula. Mr. Frazer Rice."

Halstead ignored the spike of pain in his head as he turned around again. "The railroad man?"

"The very same," Sandborne said. "He told me he's heard a lot of good things about you. Wants to hire you on as a detective with the railroad. He said he knows all about your troubles and wants to help you get clear of them. Seemed to mean it, too."

Halstead was glad to hear it, though he could not understand why. "He could get anyone he wants. Why would he go through all that trouble to hire me?"

"I guess your reputation has left a mark with him. There's lots of gunmen out there, but only one Jeremiah Halstead. Maybe he wants to get in good with Aaron? Maybe he wants to do a good deed in his old age? Who cares about his reasons? If he can get the governor to make your warrant go away, you'll have your life back."

Halstead knew he should have welcomed the prospect of it. It was the first bit of good news he'd had since Mackey had told him about the warrant right after Zimmerman had been hung back in Helena.

But Halstead had made the mistake of trusting powerful men before and had paid dearly for it. "The last time I had an important man offer me something, it cost me three years of my life."

"That was a long time ago, and Montana's a long way from El Paso. If he—" Sandborne stopped talking and nodded toward the street. "Here comes Sheriff Langham, Buster, and Red, too. Guess they want to tell us what Miss Glenda told them."

Halstead watched Langham walk through the snow with the deliberate gait of a drunken man trying to look sober. Red and Buster were on either side of him.

Langham stopped several feet away in the middle of the thoroughfare. "How's the head, Halstead?"

"Still attached." He noticed Langham was doing his best not to sway in the snow. "I see you boys have been keeping warm."

"We availed ourselves of a bottle of whiskey offered to us by a concerned citizen," Langham slurred. "Given the circumstances, I was in no condition to decline it."

"Given your current condition, you ought to

recline, Langham. You're drunk. Go back to your room and sleep it off. A hangover will only make the ride back to Missoula even longer."

Langham slid his hands into the pockets of his coat and peered down at him. Halstead had not seen the sheriff's approach as a threat at first but caught a dark gleam in the drunken man's eye.

Halstead was glad he had left his coat unbuttoned. The Colt on his belly was easily within reach.

Langham swayed a bit as he said, "When the four of us rode in here this morning, I was counting on riding out with more than I'd come with. You, for instance. Fremont, too."

Sandborne moved next to Halstead. His coat was now open, too. "I didn't have the chance to tell you how sorry I am about Fremont, sheriff. I truly am. I know you two were friends, but he didn't leave me any choice when he grabbed that gun off Keane."

The sheriff looked at Sandborne for a beat longer than Halstead liked. Maybe it was the whiskey. Maybe it was something deeper.

Red tapped Langham on the shoulder. "Let's go inside for that nightcap, Henry. It's been a long day for everyone."

But Langham remained where he was. "Thought I'd be riding into Missoula to a hero's welcome, not with my best deputy draped over the saddle. Thought I'd be getting headlines, not ordering headstones."

Buster stepped in front of Langham. "Red's right, boss. It's been a real long day. Let's get some rest. Maybe something to eat, too."

Langham moved away from him and looked at Halstead and Sandborne. "I've heard what they say about you boys. How trouble follows you wherever you go. Dover Station. Silver Cloud. Battle Brook and Valhalla, too. That's why I tried to reason with you at the hotel last night, Sandborne. Tried to get you to do things a different way. But you wouldn't listen. We had to do things your way." He glared down at Halstead. "His way. The bloody way."

Halstead could feel the conversation had taken a nasty turn. He allowed the packed snow to fall away from his face and ignored the pain in his ribs as he stood up. "Listen to your friends, Langham. Go to bed."

Buster took Langham by the shoulders and forced him to turn around before leading him away.

Red hung back, hands in clear view. "I'm sorry about that, boys. He gets like that when he gets a belly full of whiskey."

Halstead asked, "Where'd he get the bottle?"

"He had it with him when he left Town Hall. I guess Miss Glenda gave it to him."

Halstead looked at the saloon up the street. "He

left with a bottle, but not her. Guess that tells me how their conversation went."

Red said, "He's torn up on the inside about what happened to Fremont. He'll regret what he said to you boys in the morning, I promise you. The words and the whiskey."

Halstead saw Buster had gotten Langham across the street. Whatever threat he had posed was over. He was glad to retake his seat on the edge of the boardwalk. "No harm done. It's too cold to fight anyhow."

"Get him to bed," Sandborne told Red. "He's apt to start trouble like he is."

Red touched the brim of his hat and backed away to join the others.

Sandborne sat down next to Halstead. "Don't pay Langham any mind. He's just drunk."

Halstead began to pack together more snow from the thoroughfare. "Drunk or not, he wouldn't have said it if he didn't think it. You think he'll still ride back to Missoula tomorrow?"

"Probably, if he's in any condition to ride a horse. Why?"

"Might be a good idea if you rode with them. Make sure Langham doesn't let his temper get the better of him on the way. Maybe wire Aaron and let him know you found me. See if there's any word about that warrant going away."

But Sandborne would not hear of it. "You can barely stand and your left eye is almost swollen shut and there's a good chance Riker's out there looking to take you. We'll worry about that warrant and wiring Aaron when you're fit to travel. You stayed with me when I was hurt back in Battle Brook. I'm not leaving you now."

Halstead pressed the packed snow against his face. He would be glad to have Sandborne with him while he healed. "Maybe you can help me practice my juggling?"

Sandborne dug his hands back into his coat pockets. "Maybe I can."

Henry Langham pulled free of Buster's grip and moved up the boardwalk on his own. "Quit grabbing at me. I'm not drunk."

"You'd have woken up dead if I hadn't gotten you out of there," Buster said. "You were going at those boys pretty hard back there, Henry. No good would've come of it."

Langham turned up the collar of his coat against the biting cold air. "You and Red were singing a different tune on the ride out here this morning."

"That was before I saw Halstead kill that big Chinaman in the livery," Buster said. "You would've been smart enough to leave him alone if you were sober."

Langham felt the warmth of drunken indignation rise within him. "I reckon if I'm sober enough to put one foot in front of the other, which I am, I'm sober enough to cut a half-dead outlaw down to size."

Red jogged to catch up to them. "The only thing you're going to be cutting is some wood in your sleep. We're putting you straight to bed and that's all there is to it."

But Langham was in no mood for sleep for he knew it would not bring him any rest. Every time he closed his eyes, even to blink, he saw the horrible sight of Jason Fremont's body sagged beside the cot in that cell. In only a few short hours, a man he had come to think of as a son had not only admitted to being a murderer but had been shot to death by an upstart like Sandborne.

Langham had hoped this Halstead mess would help him make his name in Montana. He had thought he would have his picture in the paper as he led the famous outlaw into Missoula to face the justice he had evaded for so long. Instead, he would be returning with Fremont over a saddle and his career in ruins. One of his deputies had gunned down a man in cold blood and no amount of printer's ink would be enough to wash it away.

As Langham continued walking ahead of Buster and Red, his mind filled with questions and regrets. How everything could have crashed down in such a short amount of time? What had driven Jason to the point of murder? A woman's schemes? Greed?

Not what. Who?

Langham stopped short when he saw a large man in a bearskin coat blocking his path. The same man who had run back to the jail earlier when Fremont had been killed.

He was as good a target for his rising anger as anyone. "Get off the street, Petite, or I'll lock you up for loitering. I'm in just the right mood to do it, too."

"Ain't loitering if I've got a reason for being here," the big trapper said. "Miss Glenda told me to look for you. She wants to see you."

"Is that so?" Bits of their earlier conversation flashed through Langham's drunken mind. He had finished most of the bottle she had given him but had found little comfort in it. Only more questions for the beautiful young woman. "Well, it just so happens that I want to see her, too. I've got some more questions that need answers. Where is she?"

Petite stepped back and gestured toward The Town Hall Saloon.

Langham wheeled inside before Red or Buster could stop him.

The sheriff found Glenda chatting up a table of gamblers just inside the entrance. She was wearing a low-cut red gown with carefully arranged feathers that hinted at an attempt at modesty.

She turned away from her customers when she saw Langham and the others come in. She rested a hand on his arm as she brought her hand to her mouth. "Oh, thank goodness Petite found you. I'm so glad you're here."

Langham scowled at the men she had been talking to. "You sure don't act like a woman who's supposed to be mourning."

"Oh, but I am, sheriff." She kept her voice low. "I can't keep acting like I'm happy in front of all these men when my heart is simply drowning in grief."

It was the quiver in her hushed voice that caught him. "You are?"

Buster tried to move between them. "This isn't a good idea, Henry. Let's get you back to the hotel where you belong."

Glenda gently pulled Langham toward her. "Please stay with me, sheriff, even if it's only for a little while. We've both suffered a terrible loss today. We both loved Jason, didn't we? In our own ways."

Red took hold of Langham's other arm and began to pull him back to the entrance. "Let's go, boss."

Langham had walked into the saloon with a head full of questions, but none of them seemed important in the dark pall of the young woman's sadness.

Langham pulled himself free from Red. "Leave me alone, boys. This has nothing to do with you."

Glenda's hand slid up to Langham's shoulder.

"Thank you, sheriff. Jason always looked up to you. He was always talking about how brave you were. How strong. I need some of that strength now if I have any hope of getting through this awful night."

Red made no attempt to whisper when he said to Buster, "Can you believe this nonsense?"

Langham felt a duty to defend the poor young woman. "No one's asking you to stay, Red. Get back to your room and leave us alone. You never even liked Jason anyway."

The deputies remained behind as Glenda slipped her arm through Langham's. He could feel her sadness mingle with her soft warmth.

She said, "Jason tried to be so much like you, Henry. May I call you Henry?"

He was honored she had thought enough to ask. "Of course."

"He wanted to be so much like you, I'm sure that's why he killed poor old Dave. He would never let any man stand between him and making you proud of him. Proud for bringing in a horrible, desperate man like Jeremiah Halstead." She pulled herself closer to him as she began to lead him past the tables and farther into the saloon. "Barren Pines used to be such a nice and peaceful town. To think that, only yesterday, we were all so happy and warm together, but today, there's so much death and misery. And all of it caused by one man."

263

Langham felt ashamed that he had not been able to put his feelings into words as well as Glenda could. The young woman was wise beyond her tender years. "It's like you said earlier. Evil has a way of following some men wherever they go."

"Did I really say that?" She demurred. "I can't remember now. Except for the kindness you showed me, this entire day is like a bad dream I keep hoping I can wake from."

Langham patted her hand as they walked together now, past the murmurs and the groans of the gambling tables. "Nobody knew Jason's qualities as well as we did."

"We're not the only ones who mourn him," Glenda said. "One of our dear friends and I were talking about that very thing just now. Right before you came in here."

Langham felt like he had found something floating just out of reach in the sea of liquor flooding his mind. It was washing over his resolve, his anger, and beginning to melt it away. Being here with Glenda in the saloon felt right. No, it felt more than right. As if it was meant to be. "You were? Back there with those men?"

Her gloved hand moved to stroke his arm. "No. Another man who knew Jason, too. They were friends, as if any man could ever really call Jason a friend. You know how reserved he could be. So firm and stoic. Friendly, but distant, kind of like the way he always described you."

Langham was glad Fremont had found Glenda. He had worried about her influence on him. He had heard stories about the many men she had twisted and used over the years, but now that he had gotten to know her, he could see she was not like that at all. "I'd like to meet this friend of yours if he was truly a friend of Jason's."

"He'll be just as happy to meet you, too, Henry." She went on the tips of her toes and spoke gently in his ear. "Like us, he's not happy about what happened here. And he has a way we can do something about it."

Langham wondered how that might be possible as he allowed her to lead him to her table.

And to the one-armed man who sat there.

Chapter 20

Halstead woke with a start when he heard someone pounding on the door. He pulled the Colt from beneath his blanket and aimed it at the noise.

It took him a moment to remember he was in Moses's office, not the jail and not in the room up in the loft. Moses had insisted on giving up his bed so Halstead would not have to negotiate the stairs in his condition. Moses had taken the room instead, while Sandborne insisted on sleeping in the livery to keep watch.

Another knock was followed by "Wake up, Jeremiah." It was Sandborne. "The sheriff and the others are leaving."

"I'll be right there." Every muscle ached as Halstead swung his legs out from under the blankets and reached for his boots. He was not sure if the pain was from the beating he had suffered or from a night spent on the rock-hard mattress Moses called a bed. He holstered the Colt, pulled on his boots, and trudged over to the door. He ran his hand over the left side of his face. It was swollen, but not as bad as he had been expecting. His eyelid was not quite shut.

Halstead opened the office door and smelled Langham before he saw him. The stench of liquor seeped through his pores. He looked like he had only slept for a couple of hours, if that, and his eyes were bloodshot.

Halstead asked Sandborne, "Is he still drunk?"

Langham had heard that. "I'm sober enough to give you a stern warning, Halstead. You're still a wanted man and nothing that happened yesterday changes that. I'm inclined to bring you back to Missoula with us, but Sandborne here tells me you're too sick to make the trip. He's agreed to stay here with you while Red, Buster, and I go back to town. We're bringing Fremont's body with us. After we drop him off with the undertaker, I'm going to wire Aaron Mackey in Helena to let him know we've found you. As soon as he gives me an answer, I'll be coming back here to fetch you. Sandborne has given me his word you'll abide by whatever Mackey says, but I want to hear it from you."

Halstead had not forgotten what Langham had said on the street the previous night, but some of the starch had gone out of Langham since. He imagined a sore head and an aching belly had something to do with it. "You have my word."

He watched Red lead a horse out of one of the stalls. Fremont's body, wrapped in burlap, was draped over the saddle.

Halstead felt a pang of compassion for the sheriff. "I'm sorry about Fremont. Not for his sake, but for yours. I know you two were close.

It's not always easy when the men we admire disappoint us."

The words did not change Langham's dour demeanor. "I'll be back in a day or so with news." Buster brought out his horse, and the sheriff got into the saddle. He took the lead line Red handed him for Fremont's horse before riding out into the street.

Red inched his horse toward him and offered his hand down to Halstead. "No hard feelings, Jeremiah. I hope things go your way. I truly mean that."

Halstead shook his hand. "So do I."

Buster touched the brim of his hat as he rode past them, pulling a horse laden down with the supplies they had brought for the trip. "Take care not to get beaten up by any more Chinamen, Halstead. Red and me won't be around to patch you up if you do."

"He was a Corean," Halstead reminded him, "but I'll be sure to keep it in mind. Don't get lost on the way back to Missoula. If you do, send up a couple of shots so Sandborne can set you straight."

"Then you can go back to bed and sleep soundly," Buster said. "We won't get lost."

He and Sandborne walked into the thoroughfare and watched Langham and the others set an easy pace as they began their ride back to Missoula.

Sandborne crossed his arms. "From the sight

and smell of him, I'd say Langham had himself a bad night."

Halstead felt a bit dizzy and leaned against the wall of the livery. "I guess he's entitled."

Sandborne continued to watch the small party ride away. "I wonder what Aaron will tell Langham to do."

"I don't expect it'll matter much. Langham's going to do whatever he wants, and he'll want someone to pay for Fremont's death. It stands to reason he'll blame me."

"But you didn't kill him," Sandborne said. "I did."

"Grief doesn't always make sense, Joshua." The cold air felt good on his face. "That's why I've got a feeling I'm going to have to kill that man before all this is over."

Sandborne scraped away the snow and toed the icy ground with his boot. "I hope it doesn't come to that."

"So do I." Halstead blinked away another wave of dizziness. "It would be nice to go a day without shooting someone."

A light snow had fallen earlier that morning as Riker and Gains rode back to the ridge overlooking Barren Pines. Riker's missing arm ached more than usual, which he took as a sign for a promising day to come.

Riker was about to raise his field glasses to

look over the town when Gains stopped him. "We've got company, boss. Looks like a lady."

Riker saw Glenda ride out from among the tall pines to his right. The collar of her fur coat was pulled high and the hood covered her fur hat, but there was no mistaking her deep green eyes. He noticed a large traveling bag was tied to the back of her saddle.

Riker moved his horse to block her path. "I didn't tell you to come up here."

"You don't get to tell me anything anymore, remember?" Glenda looked past him and smiled at Gains, who was all too glad to smile back. "We're partners after that number we did on Langham last night, remember?"

"Partners?" Gains forgot about the flirtation. "What's that supposed to mean? You didn't tell me about her. You just told me you smoothed things over with Langham."

Riker ignored him and focused on Glenda. "I told you I'd come back with the money after we turn in Halstead."

"Forgive me if I don't believe a man's promises," she said. "A woman in my line of work has heard so many over the years. Besides, you and Langham seemed quite pleased with yourselves last night. Judging by what you two decided, Halstead's as good as caught already. You don't have to worry about me getting in the way. I know how to take care of myself."

"Knowing how to get a man killed is more like it," Riker said under his breath. "Get back in those pines if you plan on staying around here. Langham and his men are bound to be along any minute. He was drunk when he agreed to throw in with us last night. He might back out if he sees you here. He could think we talked him into something."

She looked as though she might argue, but quickly decided against it as Riker moved his horse to face the town and looked through his field glasses.

"You said you had more men with you," she said. "Where are they?"

Gains answered for Riker. "They're camped about a mile down this trail. If you hurry, you might get them before they break camp. Might as well get some coffee in you while you wait. It could be a while before we reach Missoula."

Glenda gathered up the reins of her horse. "Thank you. Glad to see there's at least one gentleman around here."

She dug her heels into her horse and rode down the trail.

Riker worked the focus wheel on his binoculars as Gains turned to watch Glenda ride away. "She sure is a pretty lady."

"Pretty dangerous, too," Riker said. "You'd best keep your eyes and your mind on what we're doing. She's got a nasty habit of getting good men killed."

Riker could hear the grin in Gains' voice. "Guess it's a good thing I'm not a good man."

Riker looked through his field glasses and saw Langham leading a horse with a body wrapped in burlap tied across its back. That would be the dearly departed Fremont. He saw Red and Buster trailing behind him, with Buster pulling a pack horse weighed down with their supplies.

Riker handed the field glasses over to Gains. "Langham's the one out front. Looks like he's bringing Fremont back to Missoula just like he said he would. The other two are his deputies. Buster and Red. You can figure out which one is which just by looking at them."

"I certainly can." Gains brought the image into focus. "That fella's moustache is almost the same color as your lady friend's hair. Think they'll be a problem?"

Riker doubted it. "Langham said they usually do what he tells them. We won't know for sure until they get up here, but I wouldn't expect any trouble. Be ready for it all the same, but only if one of them pulls first. I want to avoid any shooting this close to town."

"I'll be sure to keep that in mind." Gains continued to look through the field glasses. "I can see Halstead and Sandborne down at the livery. He looks like his wanted poster, even though the left side of Halstead's face is all swollen up." He handed the binoculars back to Riker. "Standing kind of crooked, too. Looks like he's busted up as bad as you said."

Riker smiled as he looked down at the livery. "That big fella gave him a pretty bad beating yesterday. Don't let his condition fool you. If he's breathing, he's trouble."

Gains looked ready for some action. "Guess we'll have to stop him from breathing. Him and that pup Sandborne both."

Riker decided now was the time to let Gains in on the rest of his plan. "Once Langham gets here, he'll send his deputies back to Missoula with Fremont's body. That'll mean two fewer guns in Halstead's favor. We'll get the others to ride up here and grab Halstead while he's still in the livery. Sandborne will be a problem, but we can handle him, especially when he's cornered."

He hoped Halstead and Sandborne put up a fight. All that hay in the livery would make for a fine bonfire.

Gains asked, "If we're just gonna ride down there after Halstead, why didn't we bring the rest of the men with us?"

Riker did not like explaining himself but made an exception in this case. "More men would've looked like an ambush. It might've made Red or Buster go for their guns. I didn't want Halstead knowing we were up here until it was too late. One shot would put him even more on his guard, and we don't want that. He might not be able to see straight but he can still shoot better than most." Bitter experience had taught him that underestimating Halstead could prove deadly.

When Riker saw Langham and his men approach the path up to the ridge, he led Gains a bit farther back on the trail. "Make sure you keep your hands where everyone can see them and let me do all the talking. Langham's liable to have changed his mind some since last night, so he might need a bit of convincing."

Riker and Gains had just stepped down from their horses when the sheriff crested the hill. Langham's eyes were bloodshot and rimmed with dark circles. If Riker had not personally walked the sheriff back to his hotel the night before, he might have thought he had been in a fight.

Riker held up his left hand to show he was unarmed. "Morning, sheriff."

Langham drew his horse to a stop and pulled the animal hauling Fremont's body to the side of the trail, giving his deputies room to pass. He turned in the saddle and spoke to the men who followed right behind him. "Come on up here, boys. We've got company, but you can stand easy. They don't mean us any harm."

Red's horse scrambled to the top of the ridge, and the deputy rode in front of Langham. He glared down at Riker. "You look familiar."

Riker gestured toward his empty right sleeve. "You see many one-armed men in town, deputy?"

Red's eyes drew narrow in recognition. "You were in the saloon last night with Glenda, weren't you?"

"You've got a good memory."

Buster brought up the rear as the supply horse stumbled under the burden of the supplies it carried. "What are you doing up here?" He nodded at Gains. "And who's your friend?"

Riker held up his hand to silence Gains. "He's a friend. He can be your friend, too, if you'd like."

Langham told his deputies, "This man is Emil Riker. You boys like to read the papers, especially you, Buster, so I imagine you might've heard of him."

"Riker?" Buster thought it over. "I've read about you. You're from Battle Brook. Halstead killed your brother, didn't he?"

Riker bristled at the memory. "He did. Killed my daddy, too. Cost me a good arm, as well. I tracked him all the way here to Barren Pines, and I plan on bringing him to justice for what he did."

Red inched his horse between Langham and Riker. "The warrant on Halstead is for what he did in Wellspring, not in Battle Brook."

"My warrant is written in blood," Riker said. "But I'll be glad to take him in for that charge, too, if it makes you feel any better."

Buster said to Langham, "I don't care who they are, boss. They're just a couple of bounty hunters no better than the fella Sandborne killed yesterday."

"His name was Keane," Gains said. "And he happened to be a good friend of mine."

Red eased his horse away from Langham. "These two aren't up to any good, sheriff. Let me and Buster run them off before they start trouble down there."

But Langham remained where he was. "I spoke to Mr. Riker last night. He and his men aren't here for the reward. They're here for justice, same as us. Isn't that right, Mr. Riker."

Riker was glad Langham's mind had not changed now that the liquor had begun to wear off. "The debt Halstead owes me can't be paid in gold. Everybody who's ever had the misfortune of crossing paths with that man has lost something. I lost my arm. My brother. My father down in El Paso. Gains lost Keane." He glanced at the body on the back of the horse Langham had brought with him. "Even you boys lost a friend. Jason Fremont was his name, wasn't it? I heard Sandborne shot him in his own jail."

"Sure," Buster said, "after he killed an old shopkeeper."

Langham said, "Boys, I've decided I'm going to be staying here with Mr. Riker and his men. The longer we let Halstead run around loose, the greater the chances of him heading back up into those mountains. Only this time he won't be alone. He'll have Sandborne with him and he'll be twice as hard to find. He'll be even harder to stop. That's my decision. You don't have to like it, but you will abide by it."

Red said, "You mean you're throwing in with them over us? You know Halstead's no murderer, Henry. You said as much yourself."

Buster moved his horse next to Langham. "Red was right about these men, sheriff. They'll kill Halstead and you know it. I say we throw a rope around them and bring them back to Missoula with us."

Langham glared at them. "I've said a lot of things since coming to town. I've said goodbye to a young man I once knew and admired. I said the same prayers over him that he should've said over me when my time came. I promised to bring him back to Missoula to be buried and I intend on doing that. But I made another promise long before that one. A promise to uphold the law, and I don't plan on letting anyone stop me. Not you, and not Sandborne, either."

Langham held out the reins of Fremont's horse to Red. "I want you to take this horse and bring Jason back to Missoula where he belongs. Run those supplies back to Dubois's store, too. He ought to give most of the money back, if not all of it. You can wait for us there. You can expect us back in Missoula around noon."

Red took the reins of Fremont's horse. "Don't

do this, Henry. Maybe Halstead should be brought in, but Sandborne didn't do anything wrong. These men will kill them both."

Langham held firm. "If Sandborne interferes, he's breaking the law, too, and deserves the same fate as Halstead. It'll be legal."

Riker encouraged him. "That's the style, sheriff. Justice will be done, and we're the men to do it."

Red said, "Just because it's legal doesn't mean it's right."

Buster rested his hand on the stock of the rifle poking up from his saddle. "You talk awfully big for a one-armed man, Riker."

"Maybe." Riker gestured back to Gains. "But my friend here has two perfectly good arms. And so do the nine men we left camped just up the road from here. And, in case you're wondering, the reward money was supposed to be split between them and Keane. My only reward will be to see Halstead swing for his crimes. If Sandborne gets in the way of that, no one will shed a tear."

Gains drew his pistol before Red pulled his.

Buster grabbed for his rifle, but Langham took hold of the stock, keeping the Winchester in its scabbard. "Stand easy, boys. That's an order."

Buster pushed Langham's hand away. "Red and me have ridden with you for a long time, Henry. We didn't always agree with you, but we've always done what you said. This time is different. If you want to ride back here tomorrow and take him in, we'll do that and we'll do it legal. But throwing in with scavengers is always bad business. You know I'm right."

Riker watched Langham's internal struggle play out on his face. It was clear that he liked Halstead. Most people did. Tough men were easy to admire, especially when that toughness was witnessed firsthand.

But loss left a mark as well, especially when the person you lost dies in your arms as Warren had died in his. Or when they're blinded and left to roam the El Paso wilderness as Halstead had done to Riker's father.

Or how Langham had been forced to watch his deputy die on the floor of the cell in his own jail.

Langham said, "All I know is there's a warrant out for Halstead's arrest, and he's got a price on his head. I don't know if he's innocent or guilty, but I've seen the trouble he's caused just by being in a place. I'm paid to enforce the law around here, and that's exactly what I'm going to do. Since you two don't have the stomach for this, it's best if you're on your way. Get moving before I lose my temper."

Langham crossed his hands on his saddle horn, his decision final as Red pulled Fremont's horse behind him as he rode down the road back to Missoula.

Buster got his horses moving again. "I'll be sure to tell Hy Vandenberg you're coming. I know you'll want a camera when you get there."

Riker stood in the middle of the road as he watched the two deputies ride away. He had doubted they would go along with his plan. He was glad they were out of the way, but saw Langham was not.

"I'm sorry about that, sheriff. I truly am. I didn't mean to cause so much trouble between you and your men."

Langham took no comfort in his words. "Don't hold it against them. They grew mighty fond of Halstead and Sandborne in a short amount of time. Don't ask me how, but Halstead's got a way of winning people over."

"That's the trouble with the devil. He's always charming, isn't he? Any idea how long they plan on remaining at the livery? They talk about going anywhere else?"

"They were still there when I left," Langham said. "The jail's empty, so there's no reason for them to be there. There's only one way in or out of the livery, so when we block the entrance, there'll be nowhere for Halstead or Sandborne to go."

Riker winced from the intense pain in his missing arm. It had to mean good news was at hand. He told Gains, "Give those boys a chance to ride ahead, then bring the others back. Tell them to leave the camp as it is. We can finish packing later."

Gains went to his horse immediately. "Want me to leave the lady behind or bring her with us?"

Langham perked up. "Lady? What lady?"

Riker closed his eyes. The woman was nowhere in sight, but even the idea of her was already causing trouble. "Tell her to ride on to Missoula, but don't force her. She'll just do whatever she wants anyway."

Gains got in the saddle and rode off as Langham repeated his question. "What lady was he talking about? Nobody said there was a woman involved in this."

Riker did not know how much the sheriff remembered of their drunken conversation the previous evening. But Riker remembered he was fond of the showgirl and used what Langham had said against him. "I asked Miss Glenda to join us. With her bodyguard dead, she was afraid she might get hurt in town. She said she felt safer up here with us. I figured you'd probably agree."

"Of course," Langham said. "That poor girl has been through a terrible ordeal. It's much better if she's far away from the fray."

Riker hid a smile as he climbed back up into the saddle. Langham was almost as much of a fool sober as he when he was drunk. "Glad you agree."

Chapter 21

Red slowed his horses to a trot to allow Buster to catch up to him. He had been angry when he had taken off but did not want to take his anger out on the animals. He was riding into a stiff headwind that had made the cold air feel even colder.

Buster pulled up next to him. "Can you believe that nonsense?"

Red did not have to believe it. He had seen it happen with his own two eyes. "I knew we should've pulled him out of that saloon last night. That showgirl really sunk her claws into him."

"We can't let Henry go up against Halstead and Sandborne," Buster said. "I don't care if they have a whole regiment with them. Langham wouldn't stand a chance against either of them on his best day. He'll fare even worse now given how hungover he is."

Red had lived through many of Langham's mornings that followed a long night of whiskey. He was sure getting the sheriff drunk had been part of Riker's plan. He wanted Halstead dead and would not care if Langham got killed as a result. Langham had a star on his coat, and the legal weight that came with it was all that mattered to Riker.

"What can we do?" Red asked. "We can't fight

off nine men. Even if we get the jump on them at their camp, they're bound to shoot us before we can get away. And we can't double back to tell Halstead they're coming. That incline back there is the quickest way and it'd take us half an hour or more if we rode around it. By then, we'll probably be too late."

"Maybe we don't have to do either." Buster rose in the saddle and looked farther up the trail before looking behind him. "How far would you say we've ridden out of town?"

Red normally prided himself on being a good judge of distance, but he had been too distracted by anger to pay attention that morning. "I'd say about a quarter of a mile, I guess. At most. Why?"

"I'd say you're just about right, partner." Buster slid out his Winchester. "And with the wind blowing the way it is, I'd say that might not be too far."

"What are you doing?" Red asked.

"What Halstead told us to do when he teased us about getting lost, remember?" Buster raised his rifle and fired three shots into the air.

Red heard the last of the shots echo among the pine trees. He figured anyone within a mile of where they were stood a good chance of hearing the shots. He hoped Sandborne or Halstead were still awake back at the livery.

Buster tucked the rifle back in its holster as he

turned his horse around. "Let's keep the horses to a trot until we see Riker's men. We can get off the trail or ride straight through them if they come at us."

Sometimes Red liked the way his big friend thought. He pulled the horse bearing Fremont's body with him as he rode. "We can drop these horses and take off if we have to make a run for it. We can always come back for them later."

Buster followed close behind. "We will, if we're able."

Halstead almost had his first boot off when the three rifle shots echoed through town. He stomped his foot back into his boot and bolted off the bed. He had forgotten about his concussion until the floor tilted and his stomach lurched, causing him to stumble against the door. He shut his eyes and shook his head in an attempt to clear it. When the dizziness subsided, he ran out into the livery.

Sandborne and Moses were already outside, facing the same direction Langham and his men had ridden only a few minutes before.

"Where'd those shots come from?" Halstead asked when he joined them.

Sandborne kept looking toward the ridge at the end of town. "Out there somewhere. Not in town, but from beyond it."

Moses rubbed his hands on the front of his shirt. "I remember hearing one of you boys telling Buster to send up three shots if they got lost, didn't you?"

"I did," Halstead said, "but I imagine they must've ridden the road back to Missoula a dozen times or more. They're not lost. Those shots were a signal."

"I was thinking the same thing." Sandborne scowled. "Think Riker ambushed them?"

But Halstead did not think so. "We would've heard more shots if they were in a fight. That shot was from Buster, and it's a warning. We've got trouble headed this way. Riker leading some of Keane's men would be my guess."

Sandborne ran for the stalls. "I'll ride out and take a look."

"You're staying here," Halstead said. "If Langham and the others couldn't stop them together, you won't be able to stop them alone."

Moses said, "You boys get back inside. The loft will give you clear fire up and down the street. I'll go spread the word to get everyone in town ready for a fight. Those fools will ride into a wall of lead when they get here."

"Stay here, Moses." Halstead ignored the cold sweat that ran down his back as another wave of dizziness threatened to claim him. "That isn't just a posse full of hot heads headed our way. They've probably been up there since before Keane rode in and they've been waiting all night to make their move."

Sandborne said, "Then why didn't they come in before now?"

Halstead did not know, but he suspected. "Because they're careful. Because I think Emil Riker's out there with them, and he likes to take his time. He rushed me back in Battle Brook, and it cost him. He probably waited until Langham and his deputies were gone so he'd have fewer guns to face." He said to Moses, "He'll be expecting your people to fight back, which is why you won't. Not until they're already in town."

Moses wiped his hands again on the front of his shirt. "Is this Riker really that smart?"

"Cunning would be a better word for it," Halstead said. "I'd bet they've had a man up on that ridge watching us this whole time. They probably know I'm busted up, too. Probably think they can roll me up without any bother."

Sandborne grew impatient. "We can't just stand here and let them ride into us, and we can't run because you're in no shape to ride."

Halstead leaned against the entrance to the livery. His entire body was bathed in sweat. The cold air only made it worse. It was a gray morning, but the light was sharp enough to sting his eyes. What little food he had managed to keep down roiled in his stomach.

Sandborne was right. He might not be in any shape to ride, but he did not have a choice. "We have to run because a lot of people will get

286

killed if we stay here. And since Riker won't be expecting it, that's what we're going to do." He did not give Sandborne a chance to argue. "Get our horses ready to ride and fill our saddlebags with as much ammunition as you can. Don't bother with provisions. We can come back here for them if we need them."

Sandborne ran to the stalls to carry out his task while Moses remained with Halstead. "I know you're putting on a brave face for that kid back there, but any fool can see you can barely stand up. You'll be dead in five miles. Quit being stubborn and let me get the men ready. They'll fight for you and this town if I ask them to."

But Halstead had been in towns under siege before and had seen bravado dry up and blow away once the shooting started. Citizens had not fought in Dover Station, and the town burned to the ground. They had not fought beside him in Battle Brook, and he would not expect them to fight now. The trappers were tough, maybe even tougher than Keane's men, but they weren't killers. Not killers of men and he would not ask them to be. He had chosen to run from the law. He would live with the consequences. Or die because of them.

Halstead pushed himself off the wall and stood on his own two feet. "In case you haven't noticed, I'm pretty tough to kill."

Moses looked him over, just as he had when

they had first met. "You've got a busted head, busted ribs, and can't see straight. When you get killed out there, your soul better not come back here to haunt me because I'll have no pity for you."

Halstead might have laughed if he had not been afraid of throwing up.

Chapter 22

Riker and Langham rode out to meet Gains and the nine other mercenaries with him.

Riker asked Gains, "Any sign of those traitors who shot off that rifle?"

"No," Gains said, "and I didn't waste time looking for them, either. I had the men move fast because I figured you'd be mighty anxious to get into town in case Halstead heard them."

Riker had been watching the town through his field glasses since he'd sent Gains back to get the others. He saw Sandborne and an old man lingering in front of the livery, but the street had been empty, except for a few people heading for early breakfasts.

But the quiet had given Riker little comfort. Halstead had always been a sneaky one. He could have found a way to get the town ready for a fight without him knowing it.

Gains looked past him toward the town. "What do you want to do next? My boys are just spoiling for a fight."

So was Riker, but he had learned a great deal about Halstead from the debacle at Battle Brook all those months before. Anyone who went straight on at Halstead was a fool. He would not make the same mistake again. Those three rifle shots may have taken away his element of surprise. His only hope lay in doing the unexpected.

"We're going to split up into two groups. Gains, you take six men down the back street on my left. That'll take you behind the livery at the end of the street. Langham and I will lead the rest down the back street on the right side of town. No one is to ride down the middle of the thoroughfare, no matter what happens. They'll be expecting us to do that if they're expecting us at all. Circle the livery and wait for us to meet you there. If you see Halstead or Sandborne first, kill them. No need to wait for me."

Gains tipped the brim of his hat and rode to his men gathered by the path down the ridge. He ordered three to wait for Riker and had the rest follow him down the hill into town.

Riker almost laughed at Langham's expression. He was paler than he had been earlier. "Don't worry, sheriff. We won't kill any voters we don't have to." He turned his horse to face the three remaining mercenaries. "Gains is taking the back way to the livery. We'll be circling around from the other side of town and will meet them at the livery. No one is to ride down the middle of the thoroughfare. If shooting starts, just follow my lead."

He glanced at Langham and saw his hands were shaking badly. He was not sure it was entirely from the whiskey. He did not care, either. He only cared about the star pinned to the lapel of his coat. That made whatever happened next legal. He had wanted to use the law to ruin Jeremiah Halstead, and now his chance was finally at hand.

Riker led the men down the hill at a fast trot toward Barren Pines. Langham brought up the rear.

Sheriff Henry Langham kept pace with the others as they rode down the incline. The notion of going up against Halstead had sounded simple enough the previous evening while drinking at Glenda's table in The Town Hall Saloon. His courage had been bolstered by drink and deep mourning over the loss of Fremont.

But now that the moment was here, the bolstering effects of liquor and grief had been replaced by a dreadful hangover. The prospect of facing a cornered Halstead was less appealing. He could hardly avenge his deputy if he was dead.

As he trailed Riker and the mercenaries through the edge of town, Langham had never thought of himself as a particularly brave man. He was not skilled with a pistol or a rifle. His size and his authority were usually enough to calm any problems in Missoula. He did his best work in his office; content to allow his deputies tend to the more dangerous aspects of the job.

It was a strategy that had allowed him to spend most of his time glad-handing the populace and feathering his nest for a future run for mayor. He had developed keen instincts about when a situation was untenable.

Which was why he was fearful now. He had believed Riker the previous night when he had assured him that his men could grab Halstead in a rush. They had numbers and the element of surprise on their side.

But just like his political career in Missoula, the element of surprise in Barren Pines was gone, thanks to Red or Buster's warning shots when they left. Langham knew his fate was in the hands of a one-armed lunatic bent on revenge and a passel of hired guns with blood on their minds. He dared not ride away but hoped to stay out of the fray long enough to save his skin.

As Riker led him and the others to the far side of town, Langham saw a lone figure standing alone in the middle of the street. He slowed his horse and peered through the icy fog to see who it was. *Could it be Halstead? Could he be making it this easy?*

But he quickly realized it was Moses Armand. The old fool was standing alone and looked to be sipping from a coffee mug.

Langham remembered Riker's order about avoiding the thoroughfare at all costs, but Langham was not one of his men. He was still the law in this county and knew Moses was not standing in the middle of town just to pass the time.

Langham steered his horse down the street and rode toward Moses. The old man took another sip from his coffee mug as he watched the sheriff approach.

"Morning, sheriff." Moses greeted him. "Wasn't expecting you back so soon. You forget something?" He looked down the side streets. "I see you brought plenty of friends to help you find it if you did."

Langham nervously eyed the buildings on either side of the street for rifles. "What are you doing out here, Moses? Don't you know what's about to happen? You don't even have a gun."

"Don't need a gun on account of there won't be any shooting. There's no call for it. You can tell your friends they can keep their guns on their hips. Halstead's gone. Took Sandborne with him."

Langham felt a rush of relief and fear wash over him. "They heard those shots, didn't they? They knew we were coming."

"Good thing for you they did," Moses said. "Good thing for you they told me not to call out the militia, too. He did give me a message before he left, though. Deputy Halstead, I mean."

Langham looked past Moses and watched the first of Gains' men circle around from the side

293

street to the front of the livery. Each man had a rifle in hand while Gains climbed down from his horse. The mercenary drew his pistol while he approached the livery at an angle.

"Message?" the sheriff asked. "What message?"

"Halstead says he knows it was you who led these men here. He figured there would've been more than three shots if you and the others had put up a fight. He says there's no hard feelings between you and him on account of him being an outlaw at present. He understands your grief over Fremont and that you're just doing your duty as you see fit."

Langham watched as Riker led the rest of the men from the right side of town and joined Gains's men in front of the livery. Riker began barking orders at them to get off their horses and search inside for Halstead.

"He said all that?" the sheriff asked Moses.

"He did. He also said that he'll let you all live if you ride back to Missoula right now. If you don't, he and Halstead will pick you boys off one by one, though he promised he'd save you for last. The way he sees it, he's already wanted for murder and they can only hang him once."

A shudder went through Langham strong enough to make his horse flinch. He brought the animal under control just as Gains came out from the livery and walked over to Riker. Given the one-armed man's reaction, it looked like

Moses had been telling the truth. Halstead and Sandborne were gone.

Langham felt like his chest was being squeezed between two boulders. One of them was Emil Riker. The other was Jeremiah Halstead. "He said all that, did he?"

Moses sipped his coffee. "Word for word, just like I told you. Seemed to mean it, too."

Langham watched Riker's horse buck as he jerked the reins and rode toward him and Moses.

The livery owner told Langham, "You ought to tell your friend he'd better stay right where he is."

Langham did not have the chance as Riker yelled, "I told you to stay out of the thoroughfare, sheriff. Who are you talking to?"

"This is Moses," Langham said. "That's his livery you're searching." He moved his horse around the liveryman toward Riker. "Did you find Halstead or Sandborne?"

"No." Riker kept riding closer. "Where did they go, Moses? You won't be parting any seas today, but I'll part your hair with lead if you sass me."

The door of The Town Hall Saloon opened and a crooked line of trappers bearing rifles filed into the street. Langham rode toward Riker as the one-armed man skidded his horse to a halt in the icy thoroughfare.

Langham saw the large trapper, Petit, in the middle of the line of men that spanned the width of the thoroughfare. None of them had raised their rifles but looked eager enough to do so.

Petit said, "You'll go that far and no further. Any man who tries will die for his trouble."

The sheriff counted twenty men in total. He knew most of them by name but could not recall them at the moment. "Do what he says, Riker. He's not bluffing."

Riker tightened his grip on the reins of his horse. "I asked you a question, old man. Tell me where Halstead and Sandborne went, and I'll leave this town in peace."

Moses stepped through the line of trappers and stood in front of Petit. "Can't recall which way they rode as I hadn't had my coffee yet." He toasted him with his mug. "I'm remedying that now. Doesn't matter which way they went because I know which way you're going. Out of town and back to Missoula along with the good sheriff here. You'd best get moving while Mr. Petit and his friends are in a forgiving mood."

Riker held his ground as he called back to Gains. "Your boys ready?"

"On your order, boss," Gains replied.

Langham watched Riker grind his teeth before saying, "Get on your horse and see if you can track them. They were still here when those shots went up. They can't have gotten far."

Langham saw a whisp of smoke rise into the

sky above the ridgeline that grew thicker and darker.

"Riker." The sheriff pointed at the rising smoke. "Look up there."

Riker's mouth opened but it took him a moment longer to manage to say a single word. "No."

Moses looked back in the same direction that Langham and Riker were looking. "I'd say that's your camp with all your supplies going up in smoke. And here I was thinking Sandborne was just kidding me when he said he could find your hiding spot." Moses shrugged with a smile. "Shows you what I know."

Langham knew it was a bad sign. It not only proved that Halstead and Sandborne had gotten away, but they had destroyed Riker's supplies, too. And he could feel the familiar chill of snow in the air.

Gains cursed as he ran back for his horse. "Those idiots just cut their own throats. I'll take some men and run them down. We'll be able to track them from there."

"Stay where you are," Riker barked. "We've got bigger concerns right now. Like keeping our men warm and fed." He looked over at the general store, then back at Moses. "That place belonged to your brother, didn't it? The one Fremont killed."

Moses's smile faded. "The only brother I had."

"Yeah," Riker sneered. "I know how it feels to

lose a brother. And since he's not using it, there's no sense in allowing all those fine supplies to go to waste." He looked back at Gains. "Get some men to help you take as much as we need. Be quick about it. I want to be riding down Halstead within the hour."

Langham and his horse flinched when the trappers took a few steps forward as they raised their rifles.

Moses moved ahead of them. "Any man who sets one foot on that boardwalk gets himself shot. Right after you, Riker. You, too, sheriff."

Riker's horse fretted, forcing him to ride it in a tight circle to bring it back under control as the trappers closed in. "I'll set this town to the torch, old man. Don't test me!"

"You won't have the chance to light a cigarette, much less a torch." Moses continued walking forward and the trappers followed. "You can ride back to Missoula or straight on to Hell for all I care, but you're not staying here. Get moving."

Langham backed up his horse and silently willed Riker to do the same. The trappers grew more wide-eyed with each step they took. They were working themselves up for a fight, and it would not be long before one of them fired.

Riker turned his horse around and trotted back toward Gains. "Get your men mounted and moving. Head out front and try to pick up their trail. We've still got a whole day in front of us. The sooner we run down Halstead and Sandborne, the sooner we can be back to Missoula and shelter."

Langham brought up the rear behind Riker and the others as they rode to the end of the street. They broke to the left and took the back street toward the ridge at the edge of town. He expected Moses and the trappers to throw up a cheer for running off Riker and his men.

But they were too grim for celebrations. Half of them began moving toward the far end of town to ensure the mercenaries did not double back.

Langham thought about staying in town but knew the men of Barren Pines would have no welcome for him now. He followed Riker and the others, for he had nowhere else to go.

He thought he saw the silhouette of a man up on the ridge but knew that had to be his imagination. Halstead would not be that careless.

Chapter 23

As soon as they had ridden around the far edge of town, Halstead rode off to find where Keane's men had made their camp. Halstead rode Col to the ridge so he could see what unfolded down in town.

He needed to catch his breath. He had only ridden half a mile or so but was already exhausted. His sore ribs ached, and his head was pounding. He knew this had to be more than just a concussion. It felt like he had a fever, and he feared that meant an infection somewhere in his body. Maybe from his broken ribs.

Sandborne and Moses had been right. He had no business on a horse. But he had no intention of surrendering to a gang of gunmen, either. He needed this time to gather his strength for the fight that was sure to come once the bounty hunters found the livery empty.

His face was drenched in sweat, and the salt stung his eyes, but he wiped them clear with his sleeve to see Moses and Langham talking in the middle of the thoroughfare. He was not surprised to see the sheriff there. He thought Langham had been acting peculiar back at the livery but had written it off as a hangover. Now it was clear there was much more to it than that. At least Red and Buster were not with him. It restored his faith in his own judgement.

But as he watched the men approach the livery, there was one figure who caught Halstead's attention.

No one else sat a horse like him. He remembered the stories about how his father had taught him to ride before he could walk. The empty right sleeve that hung at his side only confirmed what he already knew.

Emil Riker was hunting him.

That was why Keane had ridden into town alone. He was scouting for Riker and the others. Riker had done the same thing back in Battle Brook. He snuck into town, got familiar with the place and its people before making his move. But knowing a one-armed man would draw attention, he sent Keane instead.

Halstead rocked in the saddle and realized he had nodded off. He woke in time to see Riker and Langham were facing a line of angry trappers spread across the thoroughfare. Moses had spread the word after all. Good old Moses.

He smelled the beginning of a fire and knew Sandborne must have found Riker's camp. He watched the trappers begin to close in on Langham and Riker before Riker turned heel and led his men out of town. He waited until they had rounded onto the back street behind the livery before riding off to join Sandborne.

It was time to get ready, and there was still much to do.

Sandborne had waited until the fire caught before he went back for his horse. He had hastily piled all the goods he could find in the camp, emptied an oil lamp on everything, and lit a match. The smoke grew thick in a hurry and billowed high above the pines as the wind carried it upward. He did not know if they could see it back in town, but the damage had been done.

He rode into the middle of the trail, hoping Halstead was on his way, when he heard a woman's voice call out to him from the forest. "Help me! I think my leg is broken."

Sandborne did not know why anyone would be way out here all by themselves, much less a woman, but he looked through the trees to try to spot her.

"Help!" the woman called out again. "I'm over here. I'm looking right at you."

He looked in the direction of the voice and spotted a lump of brown atop the snow. At first, he thought it was a rock, but a waving arm proved him wrong.

Sandborne drew his pistol and slowly rode toward the woman. He eyed the trees carefully as he went, aware that one of Keane's men might be waiting for him.

It was only when he got closer that he noticed

the red hair poking out from beneath the woman's fur hat.

Sandborne brought his horse to a halt. "You're Miss Glenda, aren't you? That showgirl from Barren Pines."

"Tell that to him." Glenda pointed at a horse who nosed the snow several feet away, then clutched her right leg. "He threw me as soon as he saw that campfire you're starting over there. Well, don't just stand there, silly. Help me up."

Sandborne kept his pistol ready as he took a closer look at Glenda's horse. And at the ground around it. "He didn't run very far for a spooked animal. Didn't kick up a lot of snow, either. What are you doing out here all by yourself?"

"Those men snuck into town and kidnapped me last night." She held onto her right knee. "But what difference does that make now? I think I broke my leg in the fall. You've got to check and see. I can hardly stand the pain."

Sandborne heard a rider coming up the road at a good clip, but when he saw it was Halstead, he kept questioning Glenda. "Those men kidnapped you, but didn't tie you up? They just left you all alone?"

"I got out of the rope they used," she whimpered. "And all this talking won't help my leg any. Help me get on my horse before they come back and kill us both. I think I hear one of them heading this way right now."

Sandborne watched Halstead steer Col through the pines to where they were standing. His friend's face was slick with sweat, but he looked better than he had earlier that morning.

Upon seeing Halstead, the woman stopped gripping her knee and cursed.

Halstead ignored her and told Sandborne, "We'd best get moving. Riker and Langham are leading them back here."

Sandborne holstered his pistol. "So, Riker is with them just like we thought. That's bad news." He gestured down at Glenda. "The lady here says she was kidnapped. Said her horse threw her when I lit the fire. Says her leg's busted."

Halstead hardly glanced at her. "You believe anything she said?"

"Not a word," Sandborne said. "But I don't doubt she'd shoot or stab me if I gave her half a chance."

"Then let's make sure we don't give her one." Halstead slapped Glenda's horse on the rump and sent it off at a hard run into the woods.

Glenda sprang to her feet, knife in her hand, and lunged at Sandborne, who easily moved his horse out of the way.

Halstead beckoned Sandborne to follow him as they rode through the trees. "Good thing you stayed mounted, Joshua. She'd have buried that in your belly if you'd gotten close enough."

A stream of Glenda's curses followed them into

the forest. "Maybe we should've shot her. If she keeps hollering like that, Riker will find us in no time."

"We can't spare the bullet. Besides, he already knows where we are." Halstead leaned forward in the saddle as he ducked beneath sagging pine branches. "But he doesn't know where we're going to be."

"That makes two of us," Sandborne said. "Where are we going anyhow?"

"Following Glenda's horse for a while to blend our tracks," Halstead called back. "We'll swing around after a while and hit them somewhere between here and Missoula."

Sandborne saw Glenda's frightened gelding had stopped about thirty yards ahead of them and had taken to loping through the trees.

He saw Halstead slow Col to a walk as Glenda's frightened horse loped off in the opposite direction. Despite the cold wind blowing through the trees, a bead of sweat dripped off Halstead's nose.

"You don't look so good, Jeremiah. Tell me what's wrong and don't lie."

Halstead's eyes flickered, but he managed to remain upright without help. "Everything hurts, and I think I've got a fever. My ribs ache, and all this pounding on horseback doesn't help it any."

Sandborne had been afraid of that. "You still dizzy?"

"No, but I can't keep my eyes open. I feel awake one minute and nod off the next. The last time happened back on the ridge after you went to find the camp."

Sandborne knew Halstead would not survive a run-in with Riker and the others. They had managed to stay ahead of them so far and would have to keep it that way. There was only one chance to save themselves from the men hunting them. "If I remember the map from Aaron's office right, Fort Missoula is only a couple of hours ahead in this direction. There's bound to be a doctor there who can look you over and fix you up."

"And a captain or a major who'll be all too glad to throw me in the stockade," Halstead said. "I'm still a fugitive, and those wanted posters are all over the state by now. They'd slap me in leg irons and lock me up before I knew what was happening."

"Maybe." Sandborne checked their back trail but saw no sign of anyone behind them. "But being locked up and safe is better than passing out while Riker is trying to kill us."

Halstead used his sleeve to wipe away the sweat. "I spent half my childhood on a fort, so I know how the army works. After Riker and Langham track us there, Langham will talk the commander into handing me over to him and we're right back where we started."

Sandborne had not thought of that. "He wouldn't dare. You're my prisoner."

"You're also my old partner and my friend," Halstead said. "The army doesn't like problems and are apt to split the difference by handing me over to Langham. It's the nearest civilian jail and the army would be glad to be rid of me. Both of us will be as good as dead then."

Sandborne hated the lack of choices. "We can't go to the fort. We can't go to Missoula, and we can't stay here. We don't have many options, Jeremiah."

"There's another way." Halstead grunted as he shifted in his saddle to relieve whatever pain ailed him. "The Apache way. We can hit them at a distance and run. Thin out their numbers a bit at a time if we can." He looked past Sandborne and in the direction of Riker's camp. "They must've made it back to the camp by now, but they haven't sent anyone after us. They're probably trying to see what they can save. We know where they are and that they'll be there for a while. That's where we'll hit them."

Sandborne looked around at the pines that stretched in all directions as the fog began to rise above the snow. It was peaceful country. Too peaceful for the ugly work they had to do.

"They won't stop coming after us, will they? Riker will want to avenge Warren, and those bounty hunters want me for killing Keane."

Halstead said, "The bounty hunters might give up eventually, but Riker never will. He wants me dead, and since Langham must've told him I'm in sorry shape, he'll think now is the time." He winced from another spike of pain. "He might be right."

But Sandborne did not agree. "Until we run out of bullets, my money's still on us."

"You always were a sucker for long shots." Halstead brought Col around. "Let's get moving. It's time to make Riker's day a little bit worse."

Chapter 24

Aaron Mackey looked up from his paperwork when he heard a man yell somewhere out in the hallway. He came out from behind his desk and went to see what the fuss was about.

Billy was running up the stairs two at a time, waving a piece of paper. It had been years since he had seen his old friend so animated.

"We got it, Aaron!" Billy proclaimed. "Judge Owen just rescinded Jeremiah's warrant."

Mackey had not expected it to happen so fast. "How do you know?"

"Got it right here." He thrust the paper at him. "The clerk had it brought to me over at the boarding house first thing this morning. He even told my landlady what it said."

Mackey knew his friend had never gotten the knack of reading, so he read it for himself. He was glad to see the landlady had heard right. "Says here a witness recanted his statement. I wonder who that could've been."

Aware that his celebration had drawn people into the hallway, Billy put a lid on his enthusiasm. "I don't know, but it's good news. It means Jeremiah . . . I mean, Deputy Halstead, can come home now. Free and clear."

Governor Joseph K. Toole barged out of his

office, clutching papers in his hand. "What in the world is all this ruckus about?" His bearing and an iron-gray moustache gave him a formidable appearance. His vest was open and his shirt sleeves had been rolled up. "This is a government building, not a saloon, Deputy Sunday."

Mackey said, "Sorry about the noise, governor, but we just received this from Judge Owen." He handed him the paper. "Looks like he's just dropped the warrant against Deputy Halstead."

An attorney by trade, the governor read the document quickly. "Says here a witness has withdrawn their statement. That seems mighty convenient to me, Aaron. I know you and Halstead are friends. I know your fathers were friends, too. Did you have a hand in this?"

The new governor of Montana had a reputation for being a fair but firm man. He had played an important role in Montana becoming a state and deserved respect. If Mackey lied to him, the governor would know it, so Mackey answered carefully. "I didn't have anything to do with it."

Governor Toole searched his face for the truth. "I'm not going to ask my next question because I don't want to put you in an awkward position. But one of your men was seen speaking to Judge Owen's cousin at the train station last night. A tall negro gentleman some believe might have been Deputy Sunday."

Mackey knew better than to try to defend it, so he said nothing.

The governor continued. "I might be new to this office, but I want both of you to understand one important fact. I will not tolerate any interference with the laws of this state. Not from you or county sheriffs or town marshals or even the constables on the Indian reservations. Montana is a place of law and order, gentlemen. That goes for its citizens and for the men who enforce the law." He handed the paper back to Mackey. "You and your men might be federal law men, but you're not beyond my reach. Have I made myself abundantly clear?"

Mackey and Billy answered together. "Yes, sir."

"Good." His stern expression softened. "And congratulations about Halstead. For what it's worth, I'm happy for him. Just make sure he makes the most of his second chance. He got lucky once, but the next time might not turn out so well for him."

Mackey waited until Governor Toole went back to his office to tell Billy, "Get over to the telegraph office and have them send a wire straight to Missoula. Have them send a rider out to Barren Pines right away. I don't care if they're in the middle of a blizzard. Even if Halstead and Sandborne aren't there, word will spread through the trapper camps and mining towns and, hopefully, to Jeremiah, too."

Billy looked at the paper as proudly as if he had just been handed his own freedom. "It's a happy day, isn't it, Aaron?"

It was. The first happy day he'd had in a long while. "It will be once you send that telegram. Let's just hope it reaches them in time."

"In time for what?"

"In time to stop whatever trouble Jeremiah and Sandborne are bound to have found themselves in by now."

Hy Vandenberg was writing the second part of his article about Sheriff Henry Langham's intrepid quest to bring the dangerous outlaw Jeremiah Halstead to justice, when a knock sounded. Annoyed, he pulled the shade aside and saw it was Ben, his clerk from the telegraph office. Vandenberg had bribed the clerk to let him know if anything came over the wire about Halstead. Given his level of excitement, he knew it must be important.

Ben beckoned the reporter to come outside and held up a telegram as an enticement.

Vandenberg dashed out from behind his desk and did not bother putting on his hat or coat despite the freezing temperatures outside. He ignored the biting wind as the clerk gave him the telegram.

"I figured you'd want to be seeing this right away, Mr. Vandenberg. It's about Halstead. He's free."

Vandenberg read the telegram three times to make sure Ben had gotten it right. There was not much room for doubt.

JEREMIAH HALSTEAD WARRANT RESCINDED BY ORDER OF JUDGE OWEN. STOP. DO NOT ARREST. STOP. OFFICIAL DOCUMENT TO FOLLOW. SIGNED A. MACKEY — U.S. MARSHAL. END.

Vandenberg could not believe his luck. The biggest story in the state and he was the first reporter in town to have it. It would mean scrapping his second article on Langham's efforts, of course, but it was worth it. The only thing readers loved more than a good justice story was a redemption story.

He asked the clerk, "Who else knows about this?"

"My boss told me to bring it to the sheriff and the town marshal's office," Ben said, "then share it with all the papers in town. But I came to you first, seeing as how you and me . . ."

"Yes, yes, I know." The less said about their arrangement, especially on the street, the better. "But the telegraph doesn't run to the other trapper towns like Barren Pines. How will they learn of it?"

"My boss was given orders to send a rider out

to Barren Pines since they're in the middle of the towns. He wants me to go, but you know how bad my back is."

Vandenberg spoke without thinking. "I'll take it out there for you. Don't worry about that. How long before your boss will expect you back at the office? How long can you keep this from the rest of the papers in town?"

"An hour," Ben offered. "Maybe two if I had a reason. Everyone knows how bad my back is in this weather. I suppose I could get it done a lot sooner, unless I had a good reason to take my time."

Vandenberg dug some coins out of his pocket and handed them to the clerk, who gladly accepted them. "Delay it as long as possible. Longer, if you can manage it without being fired."

Vandenberg ran back to his desk and did some quick calculations in his head. Thirty minutes to write up the exclusive. Another hour to get a special edition printed and sold on every street corner in Missoula. He could still ride out to Barren Pines and get there before noon, with plenty of time to come back to town and write a follow-up story for the morning paper. The look on Langham's face once he learned about his lost chance at glory would be worthy of a special edition all its own.

And he was sure Mr. Riker—and his wealthy

friends back in Valhalla—would be grateful to be among the first who heard the news. Perhaps grateful enough to use their influence to get him a spot on a larger, more prestigious paper in Denver or Chicago.

Riker stood alone among the smoldering ruin of their camp.

The fire had already consumed almost everything by the time he and the others had reached the site. Food and canvas tents and bedrolls were burned beyond any use. Even the oil for their lamps was gone up in smoke. Only the snow and ice had kept the trees from catching fire.

And out there, somewhere among the icy mist, he knew Halstead must be watching. He could practically feel the man's eyes on him as he stood among the ruins of his embarrassment.

He kept a tight grip on his rising temper for the sake of Gains and the men. Emotion was weakness and he could not afford to look weak to them now. Their desire to avenge Keane may begin to dry up now that all their food and shelter were gone. They were, after all, only mercenaries. They were not as committed as he was to seeing Halstead dead.

Langham had chosen to remain and watch over the horses, alone with his hangover and his regret. Glenda was quietly sitting on some blankets beside his horse. She said Halstead had run off her own.

Gains finished an assessment of the camp and reported what Riker already knew. "It's a total loss, boss. Tents, bedrolls, everything we didn't bring with us when we rode out this morning went up. Sandborne worked fast and knew what he was doing."

"Sandborne." The boy was proving to be as much of a menace as Halstead. "I should have killed him when I had the chance."

Gains continued to deliver bad news. "All of the food is gone, except for a couple of cans we were able to salvage. We lost most of our coffee, too."

Riker had deeper concerns than a lack of coffee. "What about the ammunition?"

"That's the only good thing about all this. We brought most of the ammunition with us, so we've got plenty of bullets left. What do you want us to do now?"

Riker had been giving that plenty of thought since the ride from Barren Pines. "What do the men want to do?"

"I didn't think you'd care what they thought."

Riker did not, but he was still making up his mind about their next steps. "I asked you a question, Gains."

"They heard what that old fella said back in town about Halstead letting us go back to Missoula."

Riker had expected as much. "And they want to take him up on his generous offer."

"If it was any other man, no," Gains said. "But like I told you before, they've heard about Halstead. They've heard what he can do when he has time and he's had plenty of time to figure out a way to come after us. We can't just stand around here breathing smoke, and we don't have enough food to last us more than a day. The lack of cover will make for a long night on the cold ground. We can feel snow in the air, and that'll only make it colder. That's bad for the horses and bad for the men. Now, they all had breakfast, which will last them until tomorrow. The horses were fed this morning, too. We've got plenty of branches around to build fires and structures, but that'll take time we don't have."

Riker had already considered that. "Time we could spend hunting Halstead. He doesn't even have to kill us. He can just wait us out."

"Which is why some of the boys think it would be a good idea to head back to Missoula, resupply, and hit him again in the morning. Halstead had to leave Barren Pines in a hurry and probably isn't better outfitted than we are. The men can push on until tomorrow, but I won't make any promises on their loyalty after that. Cold has a way of draining a man of spirit."

Riker knew how extremes could sap the soul. Blistering heat could make a man see water that was not there. Cold and hunger could bleed a man of courage. Fear could freeze him where he stood, and rage could envelop him in a fire all its own.

Riker had left Valhalla with enough men and supplies to hunt Halstead in the open for a week. Now, he would be lucky to last until dark before the mercenaries began to turn on him. So much for careful planning.

If Riker still had his right arm, he would've sent the men back to town and continued the hunt for Halstead and Sandborne on his own. But going against Halstead with only one arm would be nothing short of suicide.

There was only one decision he could make. "Take whatever you can find and have the men mount up. The woman over there said they rode east. We'll spread wide and follow their trail. It should be easy to track them in the snow. If we don't find them by this afternoon, we'll head back to Missoula, resupply, and try again in the morning, just like you said."

Gains looked relieved. "That's a good idea, boss. You can count on my boys to give you their best."

Yes, Riker thought. *Until their grumbling bellies start gnawing at them.*

As Gains went to spread word of his decision to the men, Riker walked over to where Langham and Glenda were minding the horses. The sheriff was sulking near a tree while the showgirl stood among the animals for warmth.

"We're going to be moving soon," Riker told them. "You two will have to share a horse. Make sure you try to keep up. We'll be hunting Halstead and won't have time to wait if you fall behind."

"Talk," Glenda sneered. "All we ever hear from you is talk."

He was about to show her more than talk when the crack of rifle shots began to cut through the air.

Riker pulled Glenda out from between the horses and shoved her to the ground beside a tree.

Langham crouched behind the same tree, revolver in hand. "It's coming from behind us. That's the west, not the east like this fool woman told us."

Glenda shouted above the shots. "I told you what I saw."

Riker ducked as a bullet struck the tree. "They must've ridden ahead and worked their way around us." *Smart.* Misdirection had given him an element of surprise. It was something he might done if he had been in Halstead's shoes.

He counted two men up front lying face down in the snow. The others had found cover at the nearest trees. Gains was behind an old log that had fallen over.

"Hold your ground," Riker called out to the mercenaries. "Shoot anything that moves."

Gains and some of the others began to return fire, shooting blindly as bullets from Halstead and Sandborne continued to slam into trees.

A man one tree over from Riker cried out as splinters of bark struck him in the face, causing him to recoil and stagger back. Riker yelled for the fool to get down, but the wounded man was rocked by two bullets in the back. He dropped to the snow, dead, causing Glenda to shriek.

Gains and his men stopped firing as more rounds continued to pepper the snow and trees.

Another man up front yelped and fell, clutching his knee. Gains managed to pull him back to relative safety behind the log.

The shooting stopped as suddenly as it had started.

Halstead's voice called out to him from among the trees. "Take your men and head back to Missoula, Riker. No one else needs to die today. You and me can settle up later."

Riker felt the remaining mercenaries looking back at him. He knew what they were thinking. This could end right now if he only gave the word. One man was dead and one was wounded badly. How many more of them would have to die because of him? He could spare more lives if he just agreed to give in.

They wanted him to be reasonable. To negotiate. They only knew the legend of Halstead, not the man himself. They did not know Halstead never gave up that easily. He had them pinned down and would never give up that advantage. He would shoot them down as soon as they broke cover, even if Riker agreed to his terms.

They were long past the time for reason. Halstead may have them pinned down, but he had given away his position in the process. Riker would make him pay for it.

Riker got to his feet and leapt into the saddle of one of the horses picketed beside him. He had not moved this quickly since he had lost his arm. He had not thought it was even possible, but rage was a powerful emotion.

Langham reached up to undo the tether from the picket rope just as Riker pulled the horse backward from the others and heeled it forward in a desperate charge. Gains and the men cheered as he sped by and began firing into the trees to provide their leader cover until he rode in front of their guns.

Riker held onto the reins tightly, leaning forward as he brought the horse to a gallop. He could not hold the reins and a pistol with only one hand, but he could send the animal charging into Halstead when he found him.

He sped past a clearing and brought the horse to a skidding stop on the icy snow. He had found the spot from where Halstead and Sandborne had opened fire. The horse droppings were still fresh, but men and horses were gone. Their tracks headed in the direction of Missoula, though he doubted they were moving in a straight line. They would veer off soon, maybe even cross the road and wait to strike them later. They would pick them apart on the long road back to town. Hit-and-run tactics. Just like an Apache or a Comanche. Halstead was neither but had learned how to fight like they did.

Halstead's tactic was about more than just thinning his numbers. It was about breaking their spirit.

Riker heard Gains call out to him from behind a tree. "You find them, boss?"

"Found where they were," Riker said. "Get the others mounted. We'll run these devils down yet."

The remaining mercenaries slowly stepped out from behind their trees but began to check their dead, not get to their horses. Even Gains took his time.

Riker could see he had already begun to lose them. He rode back to them as he shouted, "You boys too afraid to move? Have you already forgotten why you're out here? Have you forgotten about what they did to Keane? Don't you have the same guts as a one-armed man?"

Riker felt his right boot slip from the stirrup just before he spilled from the saddle. He crashed to the snow on his back and wondered if he had been shot.

But he knew he had been thrown off his horse as Gains placed his boot on his chest.

"We just lost some good men because of you, Riker. Beetner's got a hole in his leg and all you care about is killing Halstead. You do what you want, but we're not taking orders from you anymore. We're gonna collect our dead and head back to Missoula where a doctor can tend to Beetner's leg. Once he's taken care of, we can talk about what to do about Halstead and Sandborne."

Gains put more weight on Riker's chest. "I'm gonna take my boot away now. Don't do something stupid, like reaching for your pistol. One of these boys are liable to kill you if you do."

Gains removed his boot and walked over to the men treating Beetner's wound.

When Riker pushed himself upright, he saw two mercenaries watching him. Their pistols were at their sides.

Riker shouted after Gains. "You think Halstead will make it that easy? Don't tell me you're stupid enough to believe he'll just let you boys ride back to Missoula."

Gains kept walking. "Maybe he'll shoot at us, maybe he won't. But he'll shoot at us for sure if we're riding with you."

As Riker struggled to get his knee under him, Langham stepped forward to help him up. "Don't push them anymore, Riker. They're all a bit raw right now. They've lost men."

"They've lost nothing compared to what I've lost." Riker swatted the snow from his coat. "I figure you'll be taking their part in all of this."

"Can't see any other part to take," Langham said. "There's nothing but trees all around us, and Halstead can hit us any time he wants and from any direction. Given how him and Sandborne can shoot, we'll run out of men long before they run out of bullets. I know you don't like the idea of heading back to Missoula, but it's the only way. Sometimes, a man has to take a step or two back before he can keep going."

The advice almost turned his stomach. "Get away from me, you idiot."

He led the horse he had taken for his charge and walked it over to the where the others were still picketed. He found Glenda still hiding behind a tree. Her usual sassiness was gone. Her eyes now wide and wild with fear as she stared at the dead man one tree over who continued to stare back.

Riker had no comfort to offer her. "Cheer up, darling. At least you won't have to ride double with Langham on the way back to town. We've got some horses to spare."

Chapter 25

Halstead slowed Col to a trot when he decided they had ridden far enough from Riker and the others. He wanted to give his mustang a rest. The harsh cold air was hard on her lungs.

Halstead needed to rest, too. His body was even more sore than before the ambush. His head ached from the constant pounding of the ride. At least his stomach had settled, and his vision had cleared a bit. He had not seen double since he had watched the town from the ridge.

Halstead pulled his Winchester and began to reload it with the bullets he had dumped into his coat pocket. An empty rifle was useless, and he knew he might need it again and soon.

Sandborne caught up to him and began to do the same. "Looks like your plan worked back there, Jeremiah."

Halstead quickly fed bullets into the rifle. He had been keeping count of the men they had hit throughout the attack. Their survival would depend on having an accurate number of the enemy. "We only killed one. I just clipped that last one in the leg before he got dragged behind the log. At least he's out of the fighting, and we've got one less gun to face."

"It certainly does," Sandborne said, "though

I've been wondering about why we took off before we got Riker."

Halstead had wrestled with the idea of getting his enemy since the moment they had circled around behind the ruined camp and got into position. "I shot at him the whole time we were there, but he had good cover behind that tree. You and I had a plan to fire fifteen rounds each and take off. It was a good plan, and it worked because we're still alive. Getting greedy tends to get a man killed."

Sandborne continued to reload. "Maybe this time should've been the exception. This won't end until Riker is dead."

"Or we are." Halstead finished reloading and slid the rifle back in its scabbard under his left leg. "We'll let them track us to the opposite side of the road and hit them again. They'll be less sure of themselves now, especially with a wounded man to slow them down."

Sandborne finished reloading, too. "You see Langham back there? He had his gun out, but I don't think he even fired a shot."

Halstead had seen him. "He's got no stomach for this. He and Glenda will probably break off from the others and go off on their own back to town."

"I hope you're right." Sandborne tucked away his rifle. "It's bad luck to shoot a lady, even a lady like Miss Glenda. I had a chance to look over this country pretty well when I rode out here from Missoula with Langham. There are a couple of places off the road where we could hit Riker and his men."

Halstead fought to keep his eyes open but tried to rally for Sandborne's sake. "We'd better get moving. I'd like to rest a bit before we have to face them again."

They rode among the pine trees at a slant on their way to the main road when Sandborne pointed at something in the distance. "We've got a rider coming."

Halstead slowed Col's pace and watched the rider approach. He did not look like a trapper or a gunman. Despite his heavy coat, he had the look of a city man. "I don't think he's one of Riker's boys. Doesn't look like one of Langham's deputies, either."

Sandborne squinted at the stranger. "That's Hy Vandenberg. He's a reporter. I met him the morning I rode out here with Langham. He's writing a story about the search for you. I wonder what he's doing all the way out here."

Halstead got Col moving in that direction. "Let's go find out."

Sandborne followed him as he rode out to meet the reporter in the middle of the road.

Halstead cut the man off, causing Vandenberg's horse to stop short as Sandborne came up next to him.

"Deputy Sandborne," the reporter said as he managed to remain in the saddle. "I thought you'd still be in Barren Pines."

"Had a change of plans," Sandborne told him. "What are you doing here, Vandenberg?"

The reporter gaped at Halstead. "God. You're Jeremiah Halstead, aren't you?"

"God doesn't have anything to do with it, but I'm Halstead. Answer Sandborne's question."

"I came to tell Sheriff Langham and Mr. Riker the news. About your warrant, I mean. The judge has rescinded it. Quashed it. Whatever they call it. You're a free man as of a couple of hours ago."

Vandenberg began to reach inside his coat, but Halstead drew his belly gun and held it on him. "Don't do anything stupid."

The reporter's hand shook as he slowly pulled his coat open. Halstead saw an envelope sticking up out of his inside pocket. "It's just the telegram I was talking about."

Halstead kept the gun on him. "Take it out slow."

Vandenberg handed the telegram to Sandborne, but since the deputy was only just getting the knack of reading, Halstead holstered his Colt and took it instead. The words blended into a jumble at first. He had to read it half a dozen times before they made sense.

Sandborne looked on. "Well? Is it true?"

Halstead was wondering the same thing. He

asked the reporter, "Is this really from Aaron? You're sure it's real."

"I wouldn't have ridden all the way out here if it wasn't," Vandenberg said. "You've read it for yourself. No one has a claim on you anymore, deputy. Not a legal one, anyway."

Sandborne looked ready to throw his hat up into the air. "So, it's over. Truly and finally over."

"It sure seems that way." Halstead handed the telegram back to Vandenberg. The moment he had not allowed himself to even dream about during all those weeks in the mountains was finally here. He was free.

And yet, he felt nothing. No joy. No sadness. No relief. Words on a paper had ruined his life. More words on a paper had returned that life to him.

Halstead said, "I don't think Riker or his men will pay it any mind. They've still got a score to settle with me. With the both of us."

Vandenberg tucked the telegram back in his coat pocket. "Is that why you two are out here? Did Fremont and Langham run you out of Barren Pines? I sure wish I could've been there to see you face down Jason Fremont. I'm sure it must have been quite the scene."

"There wasn't much to see," Halstead told him. "Fremont's dead. He tried to kill Sandborne and failed."

"So did a fella named Keane," Sandborne added. "He's dead, too."

Vandenberg's mouth dropped open. "Fremont and Keane are both dead?"

Sandborne ignored the question and asked Halstead, "What do you want to do now?"

Halstead did not want to talk in front of the reporter. "On your way, Vandenberg. You shouldn't have any trouble finding Riker and Langham back there. Just follow the smoke. They're probably still tending to their wounded and dead. Get going."

"Dead and wounded? Who? How many? What happened?" The reporter began to pat his pockets. "I need to write all of this down while it's fresh. Tell me, Jeremiah, how you feel now that you're a free man?"

"Elated. Can't you tell?"

Sandborne slapped Vandenberg's horse on the rump, causing it to bolt down the road as the reporter barely managed to hang on.

Halstead brought Col around, and the two men began riding toward Missoula. "That telegram changes things. Let's get to Missoula and make sure that telegram is real. I'll stay out of sight while you send a wire to Aaron. I don't want to risk any trouble until we know this is genuine."

Sandborne brought his horse into a canter as he rode beside his friend. "I knew Aaron would come through for you eventually. I just knew it."

Halstead kept riding. "Nothing's over yet. We still have Riker gunning for us."

"You work awfully hard on being sullen, don't

you? Can't you just be happy that something has finally broken our way?"

Halstead tried to ignore his aching ribs. "I'll only be happy when all of this is finally over."

While Hy Vandenberg spent time interviewing Glenda, Langham read the telegram to Riker. "It looks official enough to me. Jeremiah Halstead is now a free man."

Riker had refused to even look at the telegram. "Free from the law, maybe, but he's not free from me. My brother is still dead, and I'm still a cripple. Helena doesn't change much out here."

Langham had always had a soft spot in his heart for the sick and the crippled. His father had lost part of his leg at Shiloh, so he knew how difficult life could be for such people.

But in the short time he had known Emil Riker, the man had neither elicited nor sought sympathy for his condition. He knew now that Riker and Glenda had used his grief over the loss of Fremont to get him to join them against Halstead. The showgirl had succeeded in twisting him to her will, just as he had heard she had done to countless other men.

Which was why Langham enjoyed painting a dire picture for Riker now. "You've lost your mercenaries and you've lost Halstead. Sandborne, too. And if this telegram is genuine, which I believe it is, then you've lost my cooperation as well."

Riker laughed. "I wouldn't call that much of a loss."

Langham ignored the insult. "Not just my cooperation, but my authority in what you're trying to do. You have no legal reason to go against Halstead now, and I'll expect you to conduct yourself accordingly when we reach Missoula. If Halstead and Sandborne are there, I won't tolerate any actions against them."

Riker drew his pistol from his hip and pressed the barrel under Langham's jaw.

The sheriff did not try to get away. He knew his career was over, at least in Montana. Once word spread about what had happened in Barren Pines, and it would, no one would vote for him in the next election. He doubted he would even be able to get on the ballot. For all intents and purposes, Riker and Glenda had already killed him. The bullet was little more than a formality.

"Squeeze that trigger if you want," Langham said. "You'd be doing me a favor. You might even be able to blame it on Halstead. But you'll have to kill Glenda, Gains, and the others, too, or it'll be your name on a wanted poster. How fast can a one-armed man reload a pistol anyway."

Riker thumbed back the hammer. "You're about to find out."

Langham heard the metallic sound of rifles and pistols being raised as Gains said, "You're not killing anyone, Riker. Put it away. You don't want to die like this."

"You think I need you? Any of you?" Riker eased the hammer down and holstered his pistol. "I'll run him down alone if I have to. Run him down my own way. This changes nothing. It doesn't change what I set out to do. I'll see Halstead dead if it's the last thing I do."

Langham saw how Riker's face changed at the prospect of revenge. His eyes burned with a dark fire and his face tightened with unbridled hate. This was more than just vengeance for a dead brother, a dead father, and a missing arm. It had become much more than that for Riker. Something sinister and grotesque that he did not dare try to name.

Langham slowly began to back away from him. "Whatever you do, you'll have to do it without me. And you'd better not do it in Missoula. Not while I'm sheriff."

Riker turned his back to him. "Don't worry, Langham. You'll be the first man I kill."

Langham saw Vandenberg and Glenda had stopped their interview. The sheriff offered his hand to the showgirl. "I'll be riding back to Missoula now, and I'd welcome the pleasure of your company."

Glenda regarded his hand but did not take it. "Even now? After all that's happened? All I did to you?"

"There's no fool quite like an old fool. And

while I'm not old yet, but I'm certainly not young anymore, either. There's nothing for you back in Barren Pines, but at least there's a chance of something better in Missoula. It doesn't have to be with me, but I'd be happy if it was. I'll still be sheriff for the next year or so. After that, who knows?"

"Don't shed any tears for yourself just yet, Henry." She took his hand and allowed him to help her climb into the saddle of one of the horses. "In case you haven't noticed, I can be quite convincing when I put my mind to it."

Langham saw Vandenberg had remained where he was. He had an odd look on his face as he kept looking at Riker. "Get on your horse, Hy. We're going back to town right now."

"No," the reporter said quietly. "I'm going to stay here. Someone must write about this. Write about the fury that's to come. That's why I'm here. That's why I was part of this. Nothing is over yet. It's only just beginning. I can see that now. You two had better go on without me. Tell my editor I'm following a great story, and I'll be along when I can."

Langham had no idea what Vandenberg was babbling about, and he was past the point of caring. He got on his horse and, together with Glenda, left the men to whatever fate awaited them.

He would have a reckoning of his own as soon as they reached Missoula.

Chapter 26

Halstead had managed to enjoy one cup of coffee after his meal in the Missoula Hotel's dining room before people and reporters discovered he was in town. Red and Buster were doing a good job of keeping most of them out in the lobby, but no could stop them from craning their necks and shouting questions at him.

Halstead poured Sandborne and himself another cup from the silver pot the waiter had left at their table following their meal. "How many newspapers does this town have, anyway? Helena's only got about three, and it's the state capital."

"There's more than just locals out there," Sandborne said. "Word got out that you might be in the area. The clerk at the front desk told me the town's been filling up with reporters from all over who are looking to write about your capture. It got so bad that he made a couple of guests bunk up double so he could give us a room. You're a mighty famous man now, Jeremiah. People want to shake your hand."

"Or put a rope around my neck." The questions shouted by reporters and citizens made Halstead's dull headache worse. He knew they should have eaten up in their room, but he had been feeling dizzy and winded as he waited for Sandborne to confirm Vandenberg's telegram was from Mackey. He had not been sure he could have made the trip upstairs.

He also had not wanted to hide. It had been a long time since he had last sat in a comfortable chair or ate decent food. He had spent weeks among a barren white landscape with nothing but cold grayness everywhere he looked. He had enjoyed the warmth of the dining room's fire and the soothing varnished wood on the walls. He had also enjoyed the steak with all the trimmings, but the attention he was getting had ruined it. He supposed every comfort in life came with a price. "They act like they've never seen an innocent man before."

Sandborne drank his coffee. "It's time you enjoy some positive attention for a change, Jeremiah. Lord knows you've had enough of the other kind to last you a lifetime."

Halstead's idea of enjoyment was a warm bed and the benefit of Abby's company. "Considering I'm supposed to be a dangerous man, you'd think they'd want to keep their distance."

Sandborne said, "Seems to me that the best way to get rid of them is to talk to them."

Halstead was considering it when he saw a man lugging a camera on a tripod walk into the dining room from the kitchen. "Best flatten down your hair, Joshua. Looks like a man is about to take our picture."

The man opened the legs of the tripod near their table before either Halstead or Sandborne could object. The photographer said, "I was hoping you gentlemen might not mind having your picture taken. Our readers sure would enjoy seeing it."

"As long as you take it from there and as we are," Halstead said. "We won't be posing for you. Be quick about it."

The man took the picture as the powder ignited. The sudden bright flash of light brought Halstead's headache back with a vengeance.

"That was fine," the photographer said as he pulled a pencil and pad from his pocket. "I'll be sure to send a copy to you both back in Helena. How do you gentleman like Missoula?"

"We like it just fine," Halstead told him. "We like it so much, we're on the first train back to Helena in the morning."

The reporter did not write that down. "Tell me how it feels to be a free man, deputy."

Each time Halstead blinked, purple ghosts of the man and his camera danced before his eyes. "All of you boys ask the same question. Go talk to Vandenberg. I told him about it earlier."

The reporter lowered his pad and pencil. "That's why they sent me. Hy left this afternoon hot on a story and hasn't returned yet."

"He's not?" Halstead checked the clock on the

mantel above the dining room's fireplace. It was half-past-five. "We left him out on the road hours ago. He had plenty of time to get back here by now."

"He's in for quite a rough time of it from my editor when he does. He was expecting him to write an exclusive about your freedom. He got word of it before any other reporter in town."

The reporter asked another question, but Sandborne spoke over him to Halstead. "You think Riker might've done something to him?"

Halstead was about to tell him he could not have cared less when he saw Langham enter the dining room from the same back door the photographer had used. The sheriff quickly came to usher him out.

Halstead asked the reporter to repeat his question. "What was that you asked me?"

"About Sheriff Langham," the reporter asked. "Everyone knows he rode out to find you and I'd like to know what happened."

Langham placed his hand over the camera lens. "That's enough for now, Bradley. These men have had quite an ordeal. The least you can do is let them enjoy their meal in peace."

"I'll answer that question," Halstead said.

Langham grew still. Sandborne pushed his chair away from the table, ready to grab Langham if necessary.

Halstead said, "The sheriff was put in a tough

position and handled himself well. He and his deputies treated me fairly. And when a group of bounty hunters came to lynch me, he took control of the situation and made sure no one broke the law. Neither I nor Deputy Sandborne would be sitting here tonight if it hadn't been for him and the bravery of his deputies."

He saw some of the tension drain from Langham as the reporter finished writing in his notebook, picked up his camera, and left through the kitchen.

"That was awfully generous of you, Jeremiah," Langham said. "I wasn't expecting that."

Halstead wiped his mouth with a napkin and put it on the table. "It was the truth. We would've been in that livery when Riker's men rode in if your men hadn't fired those warning shots. No one broke the law, not even you. As for the rest of it, well, we know what happened, don't we?" Halstead picked up his coffee cup. "Now, get out of my sight."

Langham took his leave and strode over to the reporters and townspeople crowding around the entrance of the dining room. He raised his voice and asked them to be quiet as they peppered him with questions about his role in all that had happened.

Sandborne drank his coffee. "You sure are full of surprises. I didn't think you'd let him off that easy."

But Halstead did not see it that way. "He knows what he did. No sense in rubbing his face in it. Besides, we might need him and his men to keep an eye out for Riker until we get on that train tomorrow."

"I'd almost forgotten all about him." Sandborne set his cup back on the saucer. "Any man with common sense ought to know when he's been beat."

But Halstead knew better. "Riker men aren't known for being sensible."

Riker rode through the darkness toward the distant lights of Missoula. Vandenberg followed close behind him.

Gains and the others had ridden ahead to Missoula, intent on finding a doctor to look at Beetner's leg. Riker thought it was a lot of bother for what amounted to little more than a flesh wound. The bullet had gone through his calf and had not hit bone.

But Riker was in no position to make them stay. He would no longer ask anyone to join his quest against Halstead. Now that he had been freed by the law, there was no reward money to pay them. He would see to it that Gains and his men paid for their treachery. As soon as he got back home, he would make sure Valhalla and Battle Brook were closed to them. Gains and the others had picked a side and had lined up against him. There was a price to be paid for that.

Which was why he had been puzzled by Vandenberg's decision to stay when Langham and the others had left.

"Why are you still here, Vandenberg?" Riker asked the reporter. "It won't win you any points with Hubbard or Mannes. They didn't think much of my idea about going after Halstead anyway. They probably half hoped he'd kill me so they could take my share of the town's profits. You'd be better off riding ahead and going back to your life in Missoula. I'll do what needs to be done on my own."

"I stayed with you because I still have a job to do," the reporter told him. "I'm following a story. Maybe the biggest story of my life."

Riker had figured as much. Vandenberg was a mercenary, no better than Gains and his men. But instead of selling his services with a gun, he was peddling his skills with a pen. "I never thought of myself as being so interesting."

"Any fool can write about heroic deeds," Vandenberg explained. "Most of the other newspaper men will write about Halstead's dramatic delivery from justice. My readers are more discerning than that. They'll want to know about you and why you're hell-bent to get Halstead at any cost. That's news, Mr. Riker, and someone's going to write about it. Someone needs to write about it. That's why I intend on seeing how this ends with my own two eyes."

Riker put a finer point on it. "People root for success but they love to watch a man fail."

"If that's part of the story, sure. But you haven't failed yet, Mr. Riker. You're still alive and so is Halstead. I don't know what you're planning on doing next, but I'm going to be there to write it down when you do it. I want the world to know what you're doing and why, especially considering all the odds are against you."

Riker knew exactly what he was up against, but hearing Vandenberg state it so plainly was sobering. Vandenberg's commitment to telling a story might benefit him yet.

"Are you just looking to write down what you see or are you willing to take a part in it?"

The reporter hesitated. "You mean help you go up against Halstead and Sandborne? I'm not much of a gunman, Mr. Riker."

"No one's asking you to be. I asked if you'd be willing to help me. There are other ways you can help bring this story to an end without even touching a pistol."

"If I'm to remain true to my code, impartiality would be best. I don't want to become part of the story."

Riker laughed. A real laugh. The first he had enjoyed since losing his arm. "You made yourself part of the story when you bribed that clerk and rode out here to tell me about the judge withdrawing Halstead's warrant. I was hoping you'd be willing to do a bit more to help speed along the conclusion."

Vandenberg did not answer right away, but Riker could tell he was curious.

"I guess that would depend on what you had in mind?"

Riker had been thinking about that since Gains and the others had ridden back to Missoula. "I'll need you to be my eyes and ears when we get to town. I'll want you to find out what Halstead and Sandborne are up to next. I can't do it because Langham and his deputies will keep a close eye on me as soon as they find out I'm there. They'll be afraid I might do something foolish like go after Halstead while he's sleeping."

"Well? Wouldn't you?"

Riker shook his head. "Not this time. He and Sandborne will be expecting something like that. They'll probably take turns on watch. I'm done doing things Halstead's way. I'm tired of getting beaten by him at every turn. I went after him in Battle Brook and he fought his way out of it. I went after him in open country and he managed to get around me. But this time I'm going to stop him in the one place neither of us can run from."

"How?" Vandenberg asked. "Where?"

Riker had already worked out that part, too. "The train bound for Helena is due in town tomorrow morning, isn't it?"

Vandenberg thought for a moment. "I believe you're right. It's due to leave just a bit after seven and is usually on time."

"And I'd bet my last dollar that Halstead and Sandborne are planning on being on that train. With your help, I'll be on it, too."

He sensed a change in the reporter's demeanor as they continued riding. "You know how much those railroad boys like to talk. Halstead and Sandborne will have you arrested before they even leave their hotel. You'll never be able to sneak on there in time."

"Not alone," Riker admitted. "Everyone will remember a one-armed man buying a ticket. But if you do it, no one will bat an eye."

"You mean you aim to go after him after the train leaves the station?"

Riker knew it was dangerous for a man to have too much faith in his own plans, but this time was an exception. "Cramped confines, lots of innocent people crammed into one place. A train rocking along the rails in the middle of nowhere. I'll finally have Halstead on equal footing for once. Sandborne, too. That might be all the edge I need to do what needs doing."

"But you'll be just as trapped as they are," Vandenberg said. "You wouldn't be able to escape, even if you weren't a . . . well, even if you weren't in your current condition."

Riker said the word for him. "A cripple. A

344

lame, one-armed menace. You don't need to be afraid to say it. I'm not afraid to hear it, just like I'm not afraid of what will happen after. I know I won't be getting out of this alive, but that's not as important as it used to be."

Riker looked back at Vandenberg as the clouds slid by to reveal a full moon. The reporter was as confused as he was interested. "You're a bit younger than me, but one day you'll see that some things are bigger than a man's life. Bigger than his freedom. Halstead has taken my father and brother from me. He took my arm, too. What good is freedom if you can't live freely? And I'll never live freely if I know Halstead's out there somewhere. I'll be content with whatever happens to me if I know Halstead is dead. Even if I fail, it'll make a great ending for that story you're chasing, won't it?"

Riker could almost feel the conflict in Vandenberg's mind. Keane had been the same way when he had first proposed the idea of chasing Halstead back in Valhalla. The notion of going against a legend was daunting at first, but Riker had laid out a plan that had merit. Promise of the reward money had been enough to make him take the risk.

But Vandenberg was a different sort. He was not with Riker for money or glory. He was after a story that would cement his reputation as a journalist. He sensed something wonderful ahead and wanted to be the man who witnessed it. Riker would get his revenge, and Hy Vandenberg would get his story. Yes, there was danger, but there was also something greater waiting for him at the end of this if it worked.

He knew he had the reporter hooked when Vandenberg said, "I have a room at a rooming house at the edge of town. You can wait for me there while I find out what's going on. If Halstead and Sandborne plan to be on that train tomorrow, so will we."

Riker was hopeful for the first time since he had gotten off the train in Missoula. His long journey was quickly coming to an end and so was Jeremiah Halstead's. He could feel it as surely as he could feel the pain in his missing arm.

Chapter 27

Sandborne's sulking was beginning to annoy Halstead as they finished the last of their coffee at The Whistle Stop Café at the station. "What are you so sullen about? We're going home."

"I'm not sullen." Sandborne frowned at his coffee as if there was mud in it. "It's just that I was looking forward to a fine breakfast back at the hotel. Hot biscuits and pancakes and bacon. I didn't think I'd be sipping half-cold coffee in a train station."

Halstead had never known Sandborne to be taken with the comforts of home. He supposed his friend had changed some since spending so much time in Helena. "You can have your fill of all that once we're on the train. You saw all those reporters sleeping in the hotel lobby when we left. We were lucky to have snuck out the back when we did. Besides, I wanted to get the horses settled. Col has had a particularly rough time of it. I wanted her seen to properly before the rush started."

"What about us?" Sandborne said. "Horses don't eat bacon, but I do. Would've liked a plate of it before we left is all."

Halstead looked out the window at the waiting train. When they had first arrived at the station, the conductors had told him it was too early to let them board, so they had to settle for the café instead. Porters and conductors were already busy loading carts full of luggage and getting people settled in their cabins onboard.

Their own cabin was only just outside the café, courtesy of Mr. Rice. The railroad man had insisted on making the gesture as a way to show there were no hard feelings following their conversation the previous evening.

"Glad to see you're among the living, deputy," Mr. Rice had said as he handed Halstead a snifter of brandy. "To your freedom, sir."

Halstead had joined him in the toast but had not wanted the brandy. He and Sandborne had a long day of traveling ahead and he had been looking forward to sleeping in a proper, warm bed for the first time in months. "Sandborne told me you were working to stop my warrant. I guess I have you to thank for that."

Mr. Rice lowered his drink. "As much as I'd like you to be in my debt, there's nothing to thank me for. I doubt my letter on your behalf has even reached the governor's desk yet. You have someone else to thank for that, Jeremiah, and it isn't me. But I take it Deputy Sandborne has already told you about my offer."

"He did. Mighty generous of you, sir."

"Mighty selfish of me would be closer to the mark," Mr. Rice corrected him. "I don't waste my time on fruitless charity, deputy. I only give to museums and civic groups because it's expected of me. I had offered to help you with your troubles because I thought it could benefit me and my railroad. And although you might not need my help any longer, my offer still stands. Your name might be cleared as far as the law is concerned, but the damage to your reputation has been done. Your time as a law man has come to an end whether you wish to admit that or not. That's why I want you to come work for me."

Halstead swirled the brandy in the snifter. He did not know good liquor from bad, but it smelled rich and expensive. "I'm flattered you still want me, sir."

"I don't want you to be flattered, my boy. I want you to agree to my terms. I need men like you. Deliberate, tough men who can help my empire grow. I'll put you in charge of all my detectives, and I'll expect you to handle problems for me before they become problems. You'll make sure things are done my way. I believe we can learn from each other and benefit from the association."

"It's a generous offer, and I'm sorry to have to turn it down."

But Mr. Rice was not prepared to accept defeat. "I imagine the idea of having me for a boss may be daunting, deputy, but everyone works for someone. Even me. You'll be working for me, and I work for my shareholders. I can promise you'll have far more latitude with me than I have with them. You'll be able to run things as you see fit with minimal interference from me. I didn't get this wealthy by looking over the shoulders of the men I hire to run things."

Halstead imagined that was true. "I've been working for people my whole life, Mr. Rice, but being a law man is the only thing I've ever been good at. I know I'd be doing something along those lines if I came to work for you, but I'm only happy doing the real thing. I had a lot of time to think about it while I was on the run up in the mountains." He tapped the star on his lapel. "This might be just a hunk of brass for some but it means everything to me."

Mr. Rice leaned forward in his chair. "I hear you've got a lady friend waiting for you back in Helena. Quite a beauty from what I understand. She'll enjoy living in New York. The railroad detective bureau is headquartered in Chicago, but you can work from Manhattan if you'd like. I can assure you that your lady friend will never be bored. My wife will introduce her to all the right people, and you'll be able to take her to the finest parties. The Van Dorns. The Vanderbilts. Even the Astors will welcome you with open arms. New York can be a wonderful place to live if you know the right people."

Halstead knew Abby was a headstrong woman

capable of speaking for herself but was confident how she would answer. "She's got her heart set on making a life for us in Helena, Mr. Rice, and so do I. But I've got another man for you if you'd like to hear it."

Mr. Rice sat back and opened his hands. "I'm listening."

"Hire Joshua Sandborne instead of me."

Mr. Rice considered it. "He's a good man and I'm fond of him, but he's just a boy."

"We're the same age," Halstead reminded him. "He's a bit rough around the edges, but he's tough and smart. I've seen a change in him since that mess back in Battle Brook. Good changes that would make him a fine addition to your company. You'd be lucky to have him, sir."

Rice had promised to give it some thought and had insisted on giving Halstead and Sandborne a private car for the ride back to Helena.

Halstead left some money on the table to pay for the coffee when he noticed Langham, Red, and Buster out on the platform.

"Looks like they're here to say goodbye," Sandborne said as he got up to leave.

Halstead hoped that was the only reason for their visit.

When they got outside, Langham said, "You boys were smart to come to the station early. There's a whole passel of reporters looking to pepper you with questions back at the hotel.

If you get on board now, you might be able to dodge them."

But Halstead had other concerns besides a few curious newspaper men. "Any sign of Riker or the others?"

"Gains and his men got to town around the same time I was with you in the dining room," Langham said. "They're all staying over near the doctor's office where one of their men is having his leg looked after. Fella by the name of Beetner."

Buster added, "They say they're out of the fight, Jeremiah. They said they'll be heading back to Valhalla as soon as the doctor says their man is fit to travel. They wanted me to tell you that it's over as far as they're concerned and hope you feel the same way. Guess they learned their lesson."

Sandborne asked, "What about Riker and Vandenberg? Are they back yet?"

"Vandenberg is," Red said, "but no one's seen hide nor hair of Riker. When I asked Hy about it, he said Riker stormed off alone. He has no idea where he went."

"That's a lie." Halstead knew Emil Riker. "He wouldn't be foolish enough to just ride off in that kind of weather without provisions." He looked around the platform that was already beginning to get crowded, even though the train was not due to leave for another hour yet. "He's out here somewhere."

"That's my guess, too," Langham agreed,

"which is why I have the rest of my deputies keeping an eye out for him. You'll be able to ask Vandenberg about it yourselves on the train. I hear he's bought a ticket to Helena."

Halstead did not see that as good news. "As long as he stays out of our way, there'll be no trouble."

Langham said, "I'll be glad to send one of my boys with you if it'll make you feel any better."

Despite what he had told the photographer the previous evening, Halstead did not trust Sheriff Langham any more than he trusted Hy Vandenberg. Too much had happened at Barren Pines for him to think otherwise. "Mr. Rice told me he'll have some extra men on the train. We'll be fine."

The sheriff did not push the issue. "All the more reason why you two had better get on board while it's quiet. Even if Riker doesn't show, you'll still have plenty of reporters looking to ask you two all sorts of silly questions."

"The sheriff's right," Sandborne said. "And we've got that private car all to ourselves. No sense in letting it go to waste and tempt fate while standing around out here."

Halstead continued to look through the growing number of passengers gathering on the platform. There was not much difference between standing there or sitting inside with Riker on the loose. They were an inviting target either way.

Langham said, "Don't trouble yourself over Riker. I've spread the rest of my men all over the station. They have Riker's description and know what to look for. A one-armed man will stick out, even in this crowd. If he shows his face, we'll grab him."

Langham offered his hand to Halstead. "No hard feelings about what happened back there, I hope."

Halstead ignored the hand, nodded goodbye to Red and Buster, and climbed the stairs up to the train.

Langham lowered his hand and said to Sandborne, "I guess he's not in a friendly mood, is he?"

"I reckon he's friendly enough," Sandborne said as he followed Halstead onto the train. "At least he didn't shoot you."

In the next car down, in a private compartment of their own, Riker pulled down the window shade. He had seen enough to suit him.

"Halstead and Sandborne just got on board," he told Vandenberg. "You sure you paid that conductor enough to keep his mouth shut?"

"More than enough," Vandenberg assured him as he continued to write in his notebook. He had been working on his column until late the previous night and had not slept. "No one will bother us for the rest of the trip. We'll be left in peace until you're ready to make your move. Don't worry."

Riker gripped the barrel of his Winchester tightly. He had not expected things to go so smoothly. He had written off Vandenberg as something of a fop at first, but he had proven himself to be useful.

The reporter continued to write in his book. "You still going to wait until the train's underway before you go after Halstead?"

It was the third time Vandenberg had asked him that question since they had boarded the train almost an hour before. "I already told you I would. It's the only hope I have of drawing out Halstead on my terms."

"There's no need to growl at me, Riker. I'm in this with you, remember?" He closed the notebook and set it on the bench beside him. "I'm going to see if the dining car is open yet. Maybe find out what car they're in while I get us some coffee. You want anything?"

"Yeah. For you to stay right where I can see you."

Vandenberg said, "Don't worry. The dining car's just one back from us. I'll be back here before you know it."

Riker pulled the pistol from his hip and held it on Vandenberg's middle. "You're not going anywhere. Maybe you're really going to the dining car. Maybe you run into one of your reporter friends and start talking. Maybe Halstead or Sandborne will see you and decide to check this cabin just to make sure you're traveling alone. None of that will happen if you don't leave, which is why you're not getting off that bench until we're already away from the station."

Vandenberg looked down at the pistol aimed at his belly. "You're serious, aren't you?"

Riker thumbed back the hammer. "I'm not laughing."

Vandenberg picked up his notebook and opened it again. "Good thing I didn't have any coffee before I left. I don't have to use the privy."

Riker eased back the hammer and tucked the pistol away. He had made his point. "Good thing for both our sake."

Chapter 28

Halstead had never enjoyed long train rides.

Some found the constant rocking of a train soothing, but it only served to upset his stomach. He preferred the steadiness of the open land on a good horse. The predictability of travel. Of plotting a course and heading out with plenty of supplies for the journey.

But now that he had experienced how harsh a Montana winter could be, he was glad to be moving at a high rate of speed through the elements. He was sure Col was glad of it, too. The mustang had been born for the wide, flat plains of Texas, not the cruel blizzards of the north. He hoped the attendant in the livestock car was taking good care of her as he had promised.

They were just over an hour out of Missoula by the time Halstead decided to stand and stretch his legs. Someone on the train must have told the reporters where they were because the door to their compartment had not stopped rattling since they had pulled out. He might have thought woodpeckers were fast at work if he had not known it was just newshounds looking for a quote for their stories. The conductors did a good job of clearing them out as they made their rounds through the train, but like most pests, they came back after only a while.

Not every train ride was bad, though. He remembered his first conversation with Abby had been on a train like this one. Maybe the exact same train for all he knew. The thought of seeing her again soon as a free man was enough to bring a smile to his face.

"There's a rare sight," Sandborne said without looking up from his dictionary. He had scribbled a list of words on a scrap of paper and had spent the time since Missoula looking them up and writing their definitions beside them. "You're smiling for once. Guess your head's not troubling you anymore."

"Just a dull ache is all." Halstead gestured toward the dictionary in Sandborne's lap. "Where'd you get that? It looks new."

"Miss Katherine gave it to me for Christmas." Sandborne inhaled deeply as he flipped the pages. "I sure do love the way a good book smells, don't you?"

Halstead took his word for it. "Never had much use for books, not even back in the mission."

"You didn't? Then how'd you learn to read so good?"

"I picked it up along the way. I got most of my learning done out in the yard. Just about the only thing the Apache and Comanche boys could agree on was that I deserved a beating. Every day was a new adventure."

Sandborne looked up from his words. "That's just about the saddest thing I've ever heard you say."

Halstead looked out the window at the passing scenery. "I taught them a thing or two in the bargain." He was anxious to change the subject. "I need some coffee. You want any?"

Sandborne closed his dictionary. "It's better if I go. They'll just pester you with questions as soon as you step out that door."

Halstead motioned for him to remain where he was. "You're every bit as famous as I'm supposed to be. I'll go. Besides, you came all this way to bring me back. The least I can do to thank you is to get you some of that coffee you've been griping about."

"Let's split the difference," Sandborne said. "If you find a porter, ask him to bring it to us in here."

Halstead had not thought of that and was surprised Sandborne had. "Listen to you. You've acquired fancy tastes since Battle Brook, haven't you?"

Sandborne returned to his books. "We've got this place all to ourselves. Might as well make the most of it while we can."

Halstead slid open the door of their compartment and looked up and down the narrow aisle for a porter. The train car gently rocked back and forth on its springs. He heard a young boy in the next compartment reading aloud from a book. Someone in another compartment was snoring loudly.

He looked to his right and caught some movement around the corner at the opposite end. Like someone was trying to duck out of sight.

Halstead drew his belly gun and stepped outside.

Sandborne got up behind him. "What's wrong?"

Halstead held up a finger for him to be quiet as he began to creep down the hall, watching for any further movement.

He dropped back when he saw a rifle slide up along the wall and fire. The bullet passed high over him and struck the wall at the back of the car.

Halstead remained flat, keeping his Colt aimed down the car as the shooter flicked the rifle down, working the lever to eject the spent cartridge.

A one-handed move for a one-armed man.

Riker.

Sandborne drew his pistol and crouched by the compartment entrance. The woman next door screamed and hushed the boy as Halstead kept his pistol steady, waiting for the shooter to show himself.

He held his shot until Riker's pinched face peered around the corner. Halstead fired just as

Riker ducked backward. His bullet struck the wall where his head had been only a split second before.

"Drop it, Riker!" Halstead yelled as he dug his heels into the carpet, pushing himself backward. "You've got nowhere to go."

Riker flicked the rifle down again and fired blindly. The bullet struck the floor before he dropped the rifle, opened the door to the next car, and slipped outside.

Halstead fired again. His bullet punched through the glass in the window, shattering it as Riker dashed into the next car.

Sandborne helped Halstead get to his feet before the two men ran down the narrow passageway. A compartment door opened and a man stepped in front of him. "I thought I heard shots."

Halstead hit the door with his shoulder, knocking the man back inside as he continued to chase Riker. He could see the man had already reached the middle of the next car, leaning against the wall as the cars continued to rock from side to side.

He and Sandborne ducked below the broken glass as Riker turned to fire his pistol as he ran. The shot caused the woman to scream again.

Halstead threw open the door, hopped onto the next car, and continued to give chase. Sandborne was right behind him.

As he reached the door at the far end of the car, Riker turned and snapped off another shot. The bullet struck a window as Halstead and Sandborne pressed on.

"He's headed for the dining car," Sandborne called out.

The car rocked again as the train entered a curve, sending Halstead flat against the broken window. He cried out when a jagged shard of glass dug into the meat of his left arm, but he kept going.

The two deputies stopped when they reached the door Riker had just used to escape. They saw the large bulk of the head conductor blocking their entrance to the dining car. His fleshy face was pressed against the glass. His wire spectacles were askew.

"Hold it right there, Halstead!" Riker yelled over the shouts and screams from the other side of the door. "One false move and this fat man dies!"

Halstead stood up, as did Sandborne.

"There's no way off this train," Halstead yelled back. "If you kill him, you die next."

"If I kill him," Riker shouted back, "I've still got a dining car full of hostages back here to keep me company."

Halstead flinched when he heard another shot from behind the conductor.

That was three, Halstead counted. *He's only got three left.*

Riker yelled at his hostages. "The next one who

gets up gets shot in the belly. Stay where you are."

Sandborne whispered, "He's only got three shots left."

Halstead focused on the conductor's face pressed against the glass. "That's three too many for what he's got in mind."

"Nobody has to die today," Halstead shouted to Riker. "You and I can settle this man to man."

"Sure." Riker laughed from the other side of the door. "Toss your pistols and rifles off the train. You and Sandborne. When the good conductor here tells me you've done that, we'll talk. But do it fast before I make an example of one of these nice folks I've got back here with me. And don't try to fool me. If you do, I'll know it and someone will pay the price. But I guess you're used to someone else always paying for the things you do, aren't you, Halstead?"

Sandborne whispered again. "We can't get rid of our guns. We've got our rifles, but—"

"They're useless at this range." Halstead was trying to think. He had thought Riker was a fool for trying to kill him on a moving train, but now he saw the brilliance of his plan. There was nowhere for Riker to run, but nowhere for Halstead to go, either. And there were plenty of innocent passengers between them, including the conductor who now found himself pressed against the door of his own railcar.

He still had three bullets to keep the frightened passengers at bay. They might rush him when he was empty, but not before three innocent people died.

Sandborne said, "I'll double back and make my way to him along the roof. Drop down behind him and get him from the back."

But Halstead knew that would not work. "That roof's caked in ice and snow. So is the ladder you'd need to climb up there. You'd fall off before you got three feet."

Sandborne cursed to himself. "Then how are we going to get him out of there?"

Halstead knew there was only one thing they could do. Something Riker would never expect him to do. "We walk away."

"Walk away?" Sandborne repeated. "You mean we just leave him in there with all those people?"

Halstead began to slowly back away from the door, forcing Sandborne to do likewise. They managed to keep their footing as the car swayed along the tracks.

"He's got nowhere to go," Halstead said, "and he has good cover. He won't risk coming after us. I'll stay at the far end of the car and keep an eye on things here while you go find a conductor. Get word to the engineer driving this train and tell him to hit the brakes as soon as he can. We'll have more options if we're stopped. It's the only chance these people have. Riker's counting on this train to keep moving. The dining car is the last car on this train. Stopping will give him two doors to watch and all the windows, not just this one here."

When they reached the door at the opposite end of the car, Sandborne went ahead while Halstead hid in the small nook at the corner. He was careful to remain flat while keeping an eye on the dining car. The conductor was still pressed against the door.

Halstead had no idea what would happen if Sandborne managed to get the train to stop, but he would worry about that once it happened. For as much as it pained him to admit it, Riker was in charge.

Chapter 29

Sandborne resisted the temptation to smack the assistant conductor out of his shock as they huddled at the front of the first passenger car.

"Mr. Donohue was back in the dining car," the conductor said. "He won't be able to handle so much excitement." His thin build was perfect for navigating the narrow aisles of train cars. "He's not a well man, you see."

"He's well enough to block the door to the dining car," Sandborne whispered, "and he's liable to get much worse with a bullet in him, which is why we need to get this train stopped as soon as we can."

"Stopping the train now isn't possible," the conductor told him. "Not for the next hour at least."

"If you're worried about climbing out there, I'll do it."

"It's not that simple," the conductor told him. "Steam engines aren't like stagecoaches. They don't just stop because someone pulls on the reins. Those rails are slippery and we're going up an incline right now. Hitting the breaks like you want would cause us to slide, maybe even derail. It could be a mile or more before we came to a stop, and that gunman back there would know it. Stopping is out of the question. Mr. Donahue would never allow it and, as head conductor, he's still in charge here. Even the engineer follows his orders."

Sandborne was growing frustrated. "Your Mr. Donahue is five cars back with a gun in his back, so he's not giving the orders anymore. You are and I'm telling you we need to stop this train before Riker starts shooting people."

"And by doing what you want, everyone on this train, including both of us, will certainly get killed. I'm not arguing with you, deputy. I'm telling you it simply can't be done. Not in weather like this and certainly not on an incline. And we'll be going up an incline for the next hour or more."

Sandborne could feel the other passengers in the car begin to take notice of him. They lowered their newspapers and began to talk in hushed tones among themselves. Some appeared to have recognized him and knew his conversation with the conductor could not mean good news for them.

He thought about what Aaron or Billy might do in this situation. He remembered something the marshal had said to him once. *Use what you have, not what you want.*

"If we can't stop now, when can we stop? You said in an hour. What changes in an hour?"

The assistant conductor smiled for the benefit of his passengers as he spoke out of the side of his mouth. "Since you're not a railroad man, I'll tell it in a way you can understand it. We'll hit a flat piece of ground at the top of this gradual hill. There's a tunnel we have to go through, which is why we always slow down when we roll through there this time of year. Ice forms on the walls of the tunnel. Did you see those thick hoops screwed onto the boiler when you boarded the train?"

"No."

"They knock off the ice that forms on the tunnel walls as we pass," the conductor explained. "It keeps ice on the rocky passages from scraping the cars. They're as hot as the boiler and do a good job of cutting through the stuff if we move slow enough. It's a good long tunnel, too. A little more than a mile. It should give you enough time to do whatever you plan on doing about the man in the dining car."

Sandborne knew it was far from perfect, but it would have to do. "Get up there and tell the driver what's happening. Tell him I want this train to stop in that tunnel."

The conductor maintained his smile. "I will but not right now. We don't want these people to panic, do we? Just calmly walk back through the cars and do your best to not look angry. I'll make my way up to the boiler when they've calmed down a bit."

Sandborne tried to hide the anger from his face as he went back to tell Halstead about what he had learned. The conductor might not want the people to panic, but they probably would eventually.

Riker kept his eyes on the nervous passengers in the dining car as the conductor continued to complain. "Please let me sit down."

Riker watched two black waiters standing at the kitchen in the middle of the car. He imagined they were probably planning to make a run at him. He was glad he had thought to order people away from the first two tables in the car. It gave him plenty of room to stop anyone who might try to rush him. He had the men move to the back while keeping the women up front with him. He had a mother and her young daughter sit at the front to discourage anyone who might think about being brave. The girl had buried her face in her mother's skirts as she quietly wept.

He enjoyed the look of panic on the faces of the diners. He imagined they must have thought highly of themselves, eating in such luxury before he had barged in and ruined their meals. He saw the plates of half-eaten food on the white tablecloths as something of a victory.

Mr. Donahue, the conductor, continued to whimper against the train door. "I tell you I can't feel my legs, mister. This always happens if I stand still for too long."

"You picked the wrong line of work for a man with bad knees," Riker said.

"They don't bother me if I keep moving, but standing like this is killing me."

"And I'll kill you if you don't." Some of the women gasped at the idea while the men assured them all would be well. Riker had always found enjoyment in disturbing the gentle.

Riker told the fat man, "You're the only thing keeping Halstead on the other side of that door. If you don't do it, I'll have to pick one of these pretty ladies to take your place. What would your bosses at the railroad think of you then?"

"I'm not asking to leave," Donahue persisted. "I'm just asking for a chair so I can rest my legs a while."

Riker reached for a chair but was quickly reminded that he only had one arm. It was so easy to forget that, especially when he was being annoyed. He held his pistol in his left hand as he hooked his boot under the leg of a chair and kicked it toward Donahue. "Sit down but if you don't keep your knees and head pressed against that glass, I'll shoot you. Your bulk will still be enough to keep Halstead from opening that door."

Without turning around, Donahue pulled the chair to him and sat down, keeping his knees and face against the glass according to Riker's orders.

One of the men at the back of the car spoke up. "What do you plan on doing with us, mister? Do you want money?" He produced a billfold from his jacket and held it up. "You can have everything we have. My watch, too. I'll even help you carry it with you when you leave. Just take it and go. No one will try to stop you."

Riker smiled at the well-groomed man with a sturdy Southern accent. He looked like the noble type. Strong featured and seemed accustomed to getting what he wanted. "You'd be from Virginia, wouldn't you?"

The man stood a little straighter. "I was born there. I call Helena my home now. I have a great many friends there. Friends who could help a man like you get out of this mess if you'd let me help you now."

"I'm from El Paso and my daddy raised us to hate Virginians." Riker enjoyed seeing the proud man sag. "He always said it was your kind who cost us the war. You'd best sit down before I see fit to put you down."

The man slipped his billfold back in his pocket and resumed his seat behind a woman who appeared to be his wife.

A stout old woman dressed in black with white lace around the collar popped up from her chair two tables back from the front. "I've had just about enough of this treatment." The loose skin under her chin wagged while she spoke. "How dare you come in here and terrorize all these good and decent people. You ought to be ashamed of yourself."

Riker did not care for her mouth but admired

her spirit. "I could be forgiven for taking you for a suffragette. Or is it the temperance movement? You're the type. If you can't enjoy a pull on a jug, no one else should either. Ain't that right, Ma?"

"I am not your mother." The woman steadied herself on her table. "I've been fighting men like you my entire life. Weak, small men who are only as brave as the size of their fist or the gun in their hand. I've lived a long time, you craven monster, and I'll not have you trouble these people any longer."

The woman began to come around from the table, and Riker lowered his pistol in the direction of the girl weeping into her mother's skirt. "You might've lived, Ma, but she won't unless you get back in your chair where you belong."

Riker looked up as one of the black waiters began to slowly move up the aisle. He had a towel over his arm. A teapot was in one hand and a cup in the other. He could see the steam rising out of the spout.

"Don't let this man trouble you, ma'am," the waiter said. "Here. Have a cup of tea to help steady your nerves."

Riker ducked his shoulder as the waiter flung the scalding water in his direction. The water sizzled against the wall as Riker shot the man twice in the chest.

The waiter crumpled to his knees as two passengers began to rush toward him.

Riker remained in a crouch, knowing he only had one or two bullets left in the pistol and shifted his aim at the mother and daughter. "One more step and the woman gets killed."

The mother cried out and threw herself across her child. "Don't hurt her! Don't hurt my baby."

The men stopped cold and Riker knew he had held them off. For now.

He spoke to the two men who had moved first. "One of you take this brave man by the shoulders, the other by his legs and carry him back to the kitchen. See if the cook can do something to save him. Be sure and thank him before he passes. He died trying to save you."

He watched the two men carry the waiter back to the kitchen, where the cook and another waiter began to tend to his wounds.

Riker put his elbow back into the chair the conductor was sitting in. "Get on your feet and block that door. Those shots will bring Halstead back around."

The conductor slowly obeyed. Riker stood up and felt a burning across the back of his left shoulder. Some of the scalding water must have hit him after all.

The mother continued to cradle her crying daughter, holding her close against her. He might have found it a touching scene if he'd had the time.

But he had a pistol that needed reloading and only had one arm to do it with.

"You two had better move up front here with me."

The people gasped as the mother clutched her child tighter. "Please don't hurt us. Please."

He kept his voice level. "I won't ask you again. Move."

The mother began to cry, too, as she pulled her daughter with her and moved to the chairs in front of Riker. He looked the woman over closer than he had before. Her coat was not expensive and her dress looked homemade. So did her daughter's. The skin on her hands was rough and calloused.

Riker asked her, "You know how to load a pistol?"

She nodded as she wiped away her tears with her sleeve. "Anything, just please don't hurt her."

He handed her his pistol, then quickly drew a knife from his belt. The mother flinched as he held the blade above her daughter's head.

"Dump out the bullets, pluck new rounds from my belt and feed them in nice and slow. Don't do anything stupid, or someone you care about might get hurt." He looked at the passengers as he said, "And nobody else wants to get hurt, now do they?"

The woman's hands shook as she began to do what she had been told to do.

Chapter 30

Halstead kept his back foot in front of the door as Sandborne tried to barge in.

"Don't rush," he told his friend. "It's over for now."

"I came running when I heard the shots," Sandborne said. "What happened?"

"I saw a waiter throw a teapot at Riker but missed. Riker shot him twice in the chest."

"Then he's down to his last bullets," Sandborne said. "Let's rush him."

Halstead knew that was not a good idea. "He's got the conductor blocking the door again, so I can't see inside. I saw a gun belt on him earlier, so he's probably got someone reloading for him. I don't know for sure, but that's what I'd do if I was him." He remembered why he had sent Sandborne away. "What did the conductor say about stopping the train?"

"Said it can't be done for another hour at least because we're on a hill. But we'll be slowing down when we reach a tunnel in an hour or so. We'll be able to jump Riker then if you want."

Halstead wanted to move now that Riker was busy but could not see what was going on inside the dining car. Riker would have his bearings again by the time they reached the tunnel, but they had no choice but to remain where they were and wait.

Sandborne handed Halstead his Winchester. "I stopped by our compartment and brought these. Figured it would give us some options from here."

Halstead gladly took the Winchester. "You figured right. Too bad that whale is blocking the way or I'd have something to shoot at. He was sitting down for a while, but Riker got him up again when the shooting started."

Sandborne stole another glance down the car. "Maybe Riker's doing us a favor and doesn't even know it."

Before Halstead could ask his partner what he meant, Sandborne had already dashed out of the car and ran back to their compartment. He came back holding his pad and a pencil and gave them to Halstead.

"We can't see in there while he's standing there, but Riker can't see out, either."

Halstead already knew that. "So?"

"So, we use the conductor's size for us. Write down that you want him to fall back when we slow down as we reach the tunnel. I'll run down there right now while he's blocking Riker's view and show it to him. I'd write it myself, but my handwriting is horrible."

Halstead thought it was crazy enough to work. He holstered his belly gun and began to quickly write the brief instructions as the car swayed back and forth on its springs. "There's no way of knowing if he'll do it even if he's not too scared to read it."

"It's still worth a try, Jeremiah. We're just asking a fat man to fall back on a moving train. We're not asking him to go for the pistol or anything."

Halstead finished writing the brief note, tore off the sheet, and gave it to Sandborne. He took hold of his Winchester as he watched his friend run at a crouch down the length of the car.

He watched the conductor shut his eyes and appear to pray as he watched Sandborne draw nearer.

"Come on, fat man," Halstead muttered under his breath. "Open your eyes for two seconds. Just two lousy seconds."

Sandborne reached the door and held the note against the glass as Halstead watched the conductor open his eyes. He was still looking down at the paper when a hand appeared on his right shoulder and forced him to sit back down.

Sandborne dropped, too, and pulled the note with him. Halstead watched his partner pull his pistol from his hip as he remained flat against the door.

Halstead brought his rifle to his shoulder, hoping to see Riker standing above the conductor, but there was no sign of him.

Instead, he heard Riker yell, "You still lurking out there, Jeremiah?"

Halstead cursed under his breath. Riker might have lost an arm, but not his edge. "I'm still here. I'm waiting for the dining car to open. I kind of had my heart set on a cup of coffee."

"You're not missing anything," Riker shouted back. "Someone offered me tea just now, but I didn't care for it none. Had a chance to rest a bit, though. Got myself reloaded and everything in case you're wondering."

"Too bad you didn't ask me to help. I've got about fifteen bullets out here and every one of them has your name on it."

"I'm sure they do. Sorry for not standing in the door when the fat man sat down, but I didn't want to make it too easy for you. I know how much you enjoy a challenge."

"Don't worry about me. You'll make a mistake, and I'll put you down when you do. Just be sure you save that last bullet for yourself. You're going to need it."

"You were always a thoughtful man, Jeremiah, but don't trouble yourself about me. You'll be long dead before it comes to that. Neither of us are getting off this train alive."

Halstead could not see Riker but had a rough idea of where he was. To sound this clear through two closed doors, he must be right behind the conductor. There were two panes of glass between him and Riker. Even with his Winchester, Halstead knew his first bullet would probably go wide, especially on a rocking train car.

He knew his instinct would make him adjust the second shot, which would come closer to Riker. He might be lucky enough to get off a third before Riker got to cover. Maybe then, some of the men in the dining car would seize the opportunity and stomp him like the bug he was. And if they did not, Sandborne was close by and would take him if he could.

Halstead did not like relying on others, especially civilians, to do his job for him, but he did not see any other way around it.

Riker mocked him again. "Why so quiet, Jeremiah? Don't tell me you're getting scared."

No one had ever been able to get under his skin quite like Emil Riker. "Not scared. Just daydreaming is all. The thought of standing over your dead body is enough to bring a smile to my face."

"You won't have the chance, old son. You'll already be heading down to the other place before my time comes. I ought to know because I'll be right behind you."

Halstead lowered his rifle and sat on the floor. At the far end of the car, Sandborne rested his pistol across his stomach. They both had a long wait ahead of them before they reached that tunnel.

Chapter 31

Riker fought to stay awake as the gentle rocking of the train threatened to lull him to sleep. That was how he realized the train was beginning to slow down. A quick glance out the nearest window confirmed it.

He kicked around the corner at the legs of the conductor's chair, causing the fat man to jump out of his seat.

"Why are we slowing down?" Riker shouted.

The conductor twisted to look out the windows. "I think we're approaching Weaver Pass. It's a narrow tunnel the railroad cut through the mountain a couple of years ago. Thick chunks of ice always form on the walls this time of year. If we enter the tunnel too fast, the ice will shear off the sides of the railcars, so we always go through it at a crawl."

Riker had not considered they might have to go through a tunnel at some point, much less slow down. "How slow will we go?"

"Five or ten miles an hour," the conductor told him. "We'll have to stop entirely if any ice is fouling the tracks. It's been warmer than normal the past couple of days, and it's not unheard of for a large chunk of it to drop and block the way."

Riker cursed himself for not having thought of

that earlier. "We can't have that. Tell the driver to speed this thing up. Just blast through anything in our way. I've seen these things turn cows into jelly."

"And I've seen ice fall in chunks thicker than ten cows, mister. Hitting something that dense and that big at speed would wreck us and kill every man, woman, and child on this train. The engineer wouldn't do that even if I could get word to him, but I can't. Not from all the way back here."

Riker knew speed was his only salvation. Speed was his only advantage keeping Halstead and Sandborne at bay. If the train stopped, it would give them time to move against him. Both men were excellent shots and would find a way to pick him off eventually.

"How long before we reach the tunnel?" Riker asked Donahue.

"I don't know. I haven't been watching." He took the pocket watch from his vest and checked it. "I'd say within five minutes, more or less."

Riker thought fast. He had fifty people trapped with him in the dining car. There was a door at both ends and too many windows to watch at once. But he was not done yet.

He made Donahue stand up and block the door with his bulk as he stepped into the aisle. "I want everyone to start pulling down those window shades right now. Get them closed and keep them closed."

The captives in his half of the dining car took their time complying. He did not dare walk down the aisle to make sure the windows in the back were shut. He would not give the passengers or the waiters a chance to jump him as he walked by.

He said to Donahue, "I want you to get up front and tell the engineer to keep going. I don't care if it means you have to climb over the coal in the tender car to do it. If this train stops, people back here will die."

"And I've already told you he won't keep going at present speed. Everyone will die if he does."

Riker pressed the barrel of the pistol against the back of Donahue's head. "You'll die if you don't get it done. Just don't think about doing anything stupid, Donahue. The girl and her mother die first if anyone comes barging in here after me. Get moving."

Riker stepped back to give Donahue enough room to pull open the door. He watched him step outside and try to push open the door to the next car, but it would not open. He watched the conductor work the handle, but it would not budge. He put a shoulder against it, but it only caused the glass to rattle.

Donahue stepped back into the car. "The door is frozen shut. I can't make it through to the next car. You're welcomed to try if you don't believe me."

Riker began to feel panic creep into his belly as the train begin to slow even further. "Then put your elbow through the glass and open it."

"Then what?" Donahue asked. "The door is frozen stiff. Even if I broke the glass, I can't fit through there. It's too narrow, and I'm too big."

Riker went off balance as the train dropped into a lower gear and Donahue fell forward into the aisle. The fat man was flat on his face.

Riker realized he was exposed as glass broke and a white-hot fired burned down the middle of his scalp.

Riker looked up in time to see the muzzle flash of a rifle.

Halstead had been proud of Sandborne when he had reached up from the base of the door and grabbed the handle, preventing Donahue from turning it. He was glad the conductor had remembered the note and made a half-hearted attempt at opening it before going back into the dining car.

Halstead had brought the Winchester to his shoulder and took careful aim at the center of the fat man's back. He raised it higher and to the right, ready to compensate for the rocking motion of the slowing train if he had a chance at Riker.

And as the train jerked to a crawl, Donahue fell forward as he had been instructed to do.

Riker looked down at the fallen conductor.

Now.

Halstead fired. The bullet punched through both panes of glass and tore through the top of Riker's hat, sending it flying.

Halstead levered in the next round and fired again. That shot arced lower and struck Riker in the chest just below the throat.

His next shot caught Riker in the right shoulder, causing him to twist in that direction as he fell.

Halstead lowered his rifle and yelled to Sandborne, "He's down. Move!"

He was running now as one of the waiters and another black man in a chef's hat rushed up the aisle with knives and descended on the fallen Riker.

Sandborne got to his feet and moved into the dining car as Halstead closed in.

But Halstead took his time as he walked down the narrow aisle of the coach.

He remembered the warrant Riker and his friends had issued for his arrest. He remembered having to run from Helena. From his friends and the woman he loved.

He remembered the bitter cold and the long nights he had spent in caves in the wilderness. The hunger and fear that had stalked him constantly.

He remembered the trappers who had tried to kill him or throw him in jail all because of Riker's blind quest for vengeance.

He remembered the beating he had received at the hands of a giant and how he had barely escaped with his life.

He remembered the nightmares that rose from the dark to claim him each night and the man who had cost him three years of his life. The same man who had passed his same evil to his sons in their blood.

No, Jeremiah Halstead was in no hurry to rush his moment of victory over the last member of the family who had plagued his life for as long as he could remember. He had earned the right to savor this moment.

He knew the time for rifles and pistols had passed and drew his father's knife from the scabbard at the back of his vest. Some scores could only be settled by the personal touch of the blade.

He ignored the icy wind that struck him as he moved into the dining car and found Sandborne in the middle of a crowd now huddled over Riker. He knew his enemy was down. He knew his bullets had struck him at least twice.

Halstead gripped his Bowie knife tightly. He had to make sure Riker was dead. He had to know it was finally over.

"Get away from him," Halstead ordered the civilians. "I've still got a job to do."

A stout old woman pushed her way into the aisle, blocking his path with her cane. "No, deputy. What's done is done. Anything more would be murder."

Halstead was about to push her aside so he could finish what he had started, but her stern gaze gave him pause.

"Remember yourself, deputy." She jabbed at the star on his vest. "Remember what that means. Put the knife away."

The storm of his rage began to part and he slid the knife back into its scabbard.

He looked over the top of the old woman's head and asked Sandborne, "Is he dead?"

"No."

Sandborne told the people to back away, revealing a glaring Riker bleeding on the carpet of the dining car. The cook had a meat cleaver at his throat. The waiter was aiming Riker's pistol down at his tormentor's head.

Sandborne pointed to Riker's head wound. "One bullet creased his skull, which is where most of the blood is coming from." He moved to the hole in the upper part of his chest. "Your next two shots caught him here in the right shoulder. I checked him and they went right through. They didn't hit anything vital."

Halstead grew dizzy as the train began to slow even further and Riker's bitter voice echoed in his ears.

"You've won, Halstead. Finish it, damn you! Finish me just like you know I'd finish you."

But Halstead knew the old woman had been right to stop him. She made him remember what the star he wore meant to him. Riker and his kind had almost taken it from him once. He would never let anyone take it from him again.

He told Sandborne, "You and Donahue had better see if there's a doctor on board. We need to patch him up, or at least try."

The round-faced chef kept the blade at Riker's throat. "This man shot Reggie, mister. There's no way he gets to live after that."

Halstead wished the man knew how much he understood. "Is Reggie alive?"

"Barely," the waiter with Riker's gun said. "And no thanks to this man, either."

"No. It's thanks to you. Bring me some towels from the kitchen so we can stop the bleeding. And if it makes you feel any better about it, it's not a request. Go check on your friend. He needs you more than Riker does."

The chef reluctantly withdrew his cleaver and the waiter handed Halstead the pistol before they went back to the kitchen in the middle of the car.

Sandborne and Donahue left to look for a doctor as Halstead ignored the gratitude he received from the passengers as he took a knee beside his fallen foe.

"I've got some bad news for you, Emil." He opened the pistol's cylinder and dumped the bullets on his chest. "You're going to live long enough to hang."

Riker drew in a ragged breath. His eyes were bright with fury and hate. "I'll live long enough to make you regret this, Halstead. By God, I'll see you pay for what you've done to me and my family. I'll drag you down to Hell with me."

Halstead tucked the gun in the back of his pants. "Wouldn't it be nice to think so."

The waiter returned with cloth napkins and a length of rope before he dumped them on Riker's chest. Halstead took one of the napkins and stuffed it in Riker's mouth. "Best bite on this while I pack those holes. This is going to hurt."

Chapter 32

Upon arriving in Helena, Halstead and Sandborne watched as two porters boarded the baggage car with a stretcher to carry Riker to the cart that would take him to jail.

The rope the waiter had given them still bound Riker's left arm flat against his body. Two nurses who had been on the train had tended to his shoulder wounds and stopped the bleeding.

The gash on the top of Riker's skull had been bandaged. The passengers had cheered as Halstead and Sandborne moved Riker to the baggage car. They remained with him for the duration of the trip.

The porters lifted Riker onto the canvas stretcher and were about to carry him out when Abby Newman ran up the ramp and leapt into Halstead's arms.

Sandborne stepped away as Halstead embraced her. His sore ribs ached as she squeezed him with all her might, but he did not complain.

"I thought I lost you," she whispered.

"Maybe you did for a while, but I'm back now. And I'm not going anywhere. That's a promise."

She withdrew enough to look up at him as he thumbed away tears from her cheeks. She had always been beautiful to him, even when she was crying.

"You're so thin," she said. "And your face is swollen. What happened to you? Were you in a fight?"

"A few," he said. "But that's not important now. I'll be fine. Better than before."

She wrapped her arms around his waist and together, they walked down the ramp from the baggage cart. "I know I'm not supposed to tell you this, but I know how much you hate surprises. Katherine and Aaron are throwing a big party at the hotel to welcome you home."

Halstead wished they had not done that. He was happy to be back, but after all that had happened, he did not feel much like celebrating.

"The whole city will be there," Abby went on. "Everyone's awfully excited that you're back home where you belong."

He did not doubt they were. "Too bad they weren't as excited to defend me when I needed it."

"You know how people are, Jeremiah. You can't expect everyone to run at trouble like you do."

No, he supposed he could not. "That's because they're smart."

She nudged him with her hip. "You're smart, too. And tough. And mine."

He kissed the top of her head. "You've got that right."

They found Sandborne standing with Aaron and Billy beneath the awning of the station building. It was a blue-sky morning without a cloud in the sky, and the sun had begun to melt some of the top layers of snow.

Mackey looked him over from head to toe as he approached. Halstead could not remember the last time he had seen such a broad smile on the marshal's face.

"Good to see you, Jeremiah. You look better than when you left."

Abby continued to hold on to him as the two men shook hands.

"You're getting soft in your old age, Aaron. You never used to be one for compliments."

Billy stepped forward and hugged both him and Abby. "Welcome home, boy. We all missed you."

"Don't worry about your horses," Mackey said. "I've got someone to bring them back to the livery for you."

"Make sure someone gives Col an extra bale of hay and all the carrots she can eat. She's earned it."

Sandborne stayed out front as they began to walk back into town together.

Mackey said, "I was sorry to see Riker survived the trip. I was hoping he'd be decent enough to die on the way."

"I hate the man," Halstead admitted, "but he's tough. You can't take that away from him. Did you get that telegram I sent from Avery Station?"

"I did," Mackey said, "but we'll talk about that later. Abby will skin me alive if I talk about business so soon. Besides, we got you a present."

Billy handed him a small box wrapped in tissue paper. "Since you were thoughtful enough to bring us a souvenir from your travels, Aaron and me chipped in. Bought you something special."

Halstead felt himself begin to blush. "You boys didn't have to do that. Breathing free air and keeping my star is enough of a present for me."

"Nonsense," Mackey said. "We think you'll find it'll come in handy in the future."

Halstead gave the box a shake. He thought it might be a pocket watch but did not hear a rattle.

"Open it," Abby encouraged. "It's not polite to just put a gift in your pocket."

She released him long enough for him to undo the paper and open the box.

Inside, he found a paper eye mask.

Billy said, "We figured you could use it when you join that circus that's coming to town in the spring. Since you were thinking about becoming an entertainer and all."

Abby examined the mask. "I don't understand."

But Halstead did. "You couldn't wait to tell them, could you, Joshua?"

Sandborne kept leading them toward town. "Sent the wire as soon as we got back to Missoula. Sent it with my own money, too."

Halstead normally did not like teasing, but he was in too good a mood to mind it. "I'm never going to hear the end of this, am I?"

"Can't see any reason why you would," Billy said.

They stopped when they reached the hotel where two men were busy hanging a long canvas banner across the large front porch that read "Welcome Home Jeremiah Halstead."

After all that had happened, the sign made him feel awkward. "I was hoping for something a bit quieter."

Abby pulled him toward the hotel. "Come see what we've fixed up for you. I hope you'll like it."

He loved her for hoping he would. "I'm sure it's perfect, but I can't go in there right now. I've got to talk to Aaron and Billy for a bit. I promise I'll be in to see it as soon as I can."

Abby pouted. "I was kind of hoping I'd have you all to myself. Aaron promised."

"And you will," Halstead assured her. He gave her the box with the paper mask. "The quicker I talk to them, the quicker I'll be back."

Abby gave him a final embrace and a kiss on the cheek before heading back to the hotel alone.

The four law men continued to walk on in the direction of the jail.

"You don't need to talk to us now," Billy said. "It's nothing that can't wait until the morning. Or the next day. Abby missed you something awful. You ought to spend time with her."

Halstead imagined she had missed him almost as much as he had missed her. But he still had something he needed to do. "Guess it all hasn't settled in yet. Doesn't feel like anything's changed."

Mackey said, "I was the same way when I came back to Dover Station from the cavalry. My father insisted on throwing a big party for me, and I wanted nothing to do with it. But I went because he said the celebration wasn't just for me. It was for all the people who'd missed me while I was gone. It's the same for Abby and your friends. Folks weren't quiet about calling for your head when they thought you were guilty, so there's no reason why you shouldn't celebrate now that you're free. Besides, Katherine and Abby have gone to a lot of trouble to welcome you back."

"I'm sure they have, and I'm grateful." Halstead meant it, too. "But Riker's still my prisoner, and I won't be able to enjoy anything until I know he's locked away for good." He knew the next part would be touchy. "You said you got my telegram. Were you able to talk to the judge?"

Mackey squinted against the glare of the sun coming off the snow as they got closer to the jail. "I talked with him. He was against Owen's warrant from the beginning and, because of all you've gone through, he's agreed to your request. But I can't understand why you made it."

"It doesn't seem right," Sandborne added. "After all he put you through. All he put us through."

"I asked for it *because* of what he put me through." Halstead knew there may come a time when he could explain himself to his friends, but today was not that day. "Now that it's settled, I'd like to see him. Riker, I mean."

Mackey grew quiet like he always did when he heard something he did not like.

And, as was his custom, Billy filled the silence for him, "You sure that's a good idea, Jeremiah? You just got back to town. Riker can wait for a couple of days. It's not like he's going anywhere."

"He can wait," Halstead said, "but I can't. I'd like to see him. Alone."

"I had the men bring him straight to the infirmary," Mackey said. "If you need to talk to him, you can talk to him there. With a guard close by."

"And no pistols," Billy added.

"Or the knife," Sandborne said.

Halstead should have known they would not have forgotten ten about the knife. "You boys act like you don't trust me."

Mackey said, "I trust you with my life, but not Riker's. You can see him if you hand over your rig, but not before."

He handed his pistols butt first to Sandborne. He handed his knife to Billy. He had always appreciated a good blade.

"Thank you, Aaron. Thank you both for everything."

Mackey led them to the jailhouse door and unlocked it. "You can thank us by not killing Riker."

Halstead walked past the guard as he entered the prison infirmary. A man in a white coat spoke to a nurse at the foot of a bed at the far end of the room. Halstead had never been in this part of the prison before and did not know their names. Bars on the windows cast jagged shadows across everything.

"I'm Deputy Halstead," he told them when he reached the bed. "I'm here to see Emil Riker."

The doctor was a thin man with fallow cheeks and a ruddy complexion. "Riker's been talking about you." He pointed to the bed at the end of the row. "He's right over there, but he's mighty restless. He may be your prisoner, but he's my patient now. He needs quiet to recuperate from his injuries."

Halstead walked past them. "I won't be long."

He stopped at the foot of an iron bed and saw Riker's left arm shackled to the headpost. His legs were strapped to the thin mattress and his bandaged head was propped up on a pillow.

His right shoulder was wrapped in bandages, including the stump of his missing arm.

Riker looked at him with the same hatred he'd had on the train. "You come here to boast?"

"No. Just to tell you that it's over. For you. For me."

Riker sneered. "My daddy always said you were a stubborn boy. I already told you nothing's over between us as long as I'm breathing, and I'm still breathing as clear as any fool can see."

"No. You're dead. Dead to me and dead as far as anyone else is concerned. I had Marshal Mackey talk to the judge on your behalf. A real judge this time, not the one Mannes talked into signing a warrant against me."

"Isn't that rich? Guess I should expect to swing in the morning."

"You taught me how the law really works, so I managed to do you a favor."

"I don't want any favors from the likes of you," Riker spat.

"I told him that even after all the trouble you caused in Barren Pines, you didn't kill anyone. Even that waiter you shot on the train lived. I had the judge and the state's attorney agree to let your lawyer plead you guilty without the possibility of parole. You won't hang, Emil. Not tomorrow or on any other day. You're going to spend the rest of your life behind bars."

"I'll never agree to that. Mannes won't either."

Halstead was glad to break the news to him. "Mannes went home and he's not coming back. The court has appointed a lawyer for you. A lawyer who didn't think much of your warrant, either. Since it's his duty to get you the best deal possible and seeing how you're in no condition to appear in court, he's going to enter a plea on your behalf."

Riker tried to reach out for him, but the shackle kept his arm in place. "I'd rather hang."

"I know you would, which is why you won't. You're going to die in a place like this, Riker. Die the way you and your daddy hoped I'd die when you framed me. Slow and alone. Forgotten." He gestured at his missing arm. "Prison's no picnic for a whole man. It's even worse for a cripple like you."

"I've got money!" Riker raved. "Friends. They won't turn their back on me. They wouldn't dare."

"They already have. And now, so am I. I just wanted to make sure you heard it from me."

As Halstead walked away, he heard the chain of Riker's shackle rattle and the bed springs creak as he struggled in vain to get free. The doctor and nurse rushed past him as the prisoner continued to scream, consumed by madness at the finality of his incarceration.

"Halstead!" he bellowed as the doctor tried to quiet him. "Nothing's over, Halstead! I'll see you dead for this! Do you hear me? Haaaalsteaaaaad!"

The echo of his name followed him past the guard at the door and up the stairs to Mackey's office. The warmth of the morning sunlight streaming through the windows felt good upon his face. He was looking forward to his party but wanted to retrieve his Colts and knife first.

For he knew no party would last forever. He still had a job to do.

He had a duty to perform and laws to uphold.

Jeremiah Halstead, Deputy United States Marshal, was back.

Terrence P. McCauley is an award-winning writer of crime fiction and thrillers. Terrence has had short stories featured in *Thuglit*, *Spintetingler Magazine*, *Shotgun Honey*, *Big Pulp*, and other publications. He is a member of the New York City chapter of the Mystery Writers of America, the International Thriller Writers, and the International Crime Writers Association. A proud native of the Bronx, NY, he is currently writing his next work of fiction.

Find him on Twitter or Facebook or visit www.terrencepmccauley.com.

Center Point Large Print
600 Brooks Road / PO Box 1
Thorndike, ME 04986-0001 USA

(207) 568-3717

US & Canada:
1 800 929-9108
www.centerpointlargeprint.com